PEN

FOUNDER EDI

Editors: Robert Baldick

Theocritus was born in ab
the scene of his early life
some time at Cos studying
in Alexandria where he won favour at the court of Ptolemy Phila-
delphus. He is thought to have returned to Cos but probably
spent his last days in Syracuse, where he died in about 240 B.C.

The precise dates of Moschus' life are uncertain, though he was
probably writing around 150 B.C. Like Theocritus, he was born
in Syracuse. Nine *Idylls*, some of them suspect, have been attri-
buted to him, including the short epic on *Europa*.

Bion of Smyrna, who was writing about fifty years after Mos-
chus, was born in Phlossa, a small town near Smyrna. His
surviving works comprise a number of *Idylls* and fragments.

Anthony Holden was born in 1947 and educated at Oundle and
Merton College, Oxford, where he read English. While at
Oxford he was editor of *Isis*, the university magazine, and
president of the O.U. Poetry Society. His verse translation of
Aeschylus' *Agamemnon* was performed in Oxford and at the
international drama festival at Delphi in 1967, and was pub-
lished in 1968. He has also translated Euripides' *The Bacchae*,
performed in Washington in 1970 and as an off-Broadway rock
musical in 1971, and *Medea*. He works as a journalist, won the
1972 Pfizer Award for Young Journalists, and has contributed
to the *Sunday Times*, the *New Statesman*, the *Sunday Telegraph*
and the *Financial Times*. He is co-author of a forthcoming book,
The St Albans Poisoner, a study of the Graham Young case.

Greek Pastoral Poetry

THEOCRITUS
BION
MOSCHUS
THE PATTERN
POEMS

*Translated with an
introduction and notes by*
ANTHONY HOLDEN

PENGUIN BOOKS

Penguin Books Ltd, Harmondsworth, Middlesex, England
Penguin Books Inc., 7110 Ambassador Road, Baltimore, Maryland 21207, U.S.A.
Penguin Books Australia Ltd, Ringwood, Victoria, Australia
Penguin Books Canada Ltd, 41 Steelcase Road West, Markham, Ontario, Canada

—

This translation first published 1974

—

Copyright © Anthony Holden, 1973

—

Made and printed in Great Britain
by Hazell Watson & Viney Ltd
Aylesbury, Bucks
Set in Monotype Ehrhardt

For
JOHN HARRISON
sine quo non

Βουκολικαὶ Μοῖσαι σποράδες ποκά, νῦν δ'ἅμα πᾶσαι
ἐντὶ μιᾶς μάνδρας, ἐντὶ μιᾶς ἀγέλας.

The pastoral Muses once were scattered; now
they are together in one fold, one flock.

CONTENTS

INTRODUCTION

Among the scenes hammered out by Hephaistus on Achilles' shield, we learn in Book XVIII of the *Iliad*, was a vineyard at grape-gathering time. The slopes were wrought in gold, the bunches themselves in black and the vine-rods in silver. Picking their way along the narrow path, past the blue enamel stream and the fence of tin, came a happy band of harvesters carrying off the vintage in their baskets. They danced to the music of a shrill young treble, who 'matched the pure notes of his tuneful lyre to the beautiful song of Linus'.

Homer's choice of scene is significant, its detail revealing. The picture is replete with all kinds of literary motifs, as yet undeveloped and so unfragmented. But, semi-consciously perhaps, he is already drawing a distinction between the physical labours of country life and its spiritual nourishment. The native toil, albeit welcome, of cultivation and harvesting is implicit in its aftermath of seasonal merrymaking and religious celebration; this, as much here as in Hardy's barn dances, is a quality of rural life quite distinct from its timeless use in literature. But the implications of Homer's treatment of the scene go far beyond the straightforward narrative of its nearest contemporary, Hesiod's *Works and Days*; there is the same gulf between them as between Vergil's *Eclogues* and his *Georgics*.

Homer's pastoral scene, in other words, is already making instinctive use of that way of life to moral ends: its spiritual qualities, he implies, are worthy of depiction by an immortal on a hero's armour. Already, therefore, in the pre-literary era of the oral tradition, what we may call the pastoral ethic is at work, though not yet codified. A range of values is appreciated, and openly recommended in the set terms of the oral tradition – in this case, of the epic. The meaning of pastoral in literary terms had been realized; other singers and writers

would keep the primitive flame alive, but it was to be Theo-
critus – early in the third century B.C. – who would endow the
genre with a more than rudimentary form.

The origins of the tradition taken up by Theocritus remain
obscure. Pastoral has its natural place, of course, in any folk
tradition, but the founding father of the oral pastoral has
generally been named as Linus, here specified by Homer.
Pausanias quotes the two commonly held versions of Linus'
brief life: one, as the son of a princess of Argos by Apollo,
who plagued the city after she had exposed their child; and
two, as the son of Amphimarus and Urania, killed by Apollo
for daring to challenge his skill in music. A third tradition,
recorded by Apollodorus, makes him Heracles' music teacher,
killed by a blow from his ungrateful pupil's lyre. He appears
in Theocritus XXIV, *The Infant Heracles*, in a garbled
version of the first and third of these – as Heracles' tutor in
literature and language, the son of Apollo, but perhaps sur-
prisingly described as 'old'.

Linus it undisputably was, however, who lent his name
to a type of dirge, later broadened into contemplative
pastoral song. From there the oral tradition inevitably frag-
mented; but among its recorded practitioners are Stesichorus
and Diomus, the latter probably mythical, followed by
Sophron and Epicharmus, both influences on Theocritus. In
Epigram XVIII the poet immortalizes the memory of Epi-
charmus as 'pioneer of comedy' – either a categoric rejection
of the view that pastoral can have its oblique forms, or a
diversionary tactic to disavow his influence.

Theocritus himself, it is clear from internal evidence, first
came under pastoral's spell when visiting the poetry school of
Philitas on the island of Cos. From his friends and colleagues
there, recreated in Idyll VII, *The Harvest Feast* (see n. 14),
he assimilated a version of pastoral not yet entirely liberated
from the style of romance. In his purest idylls – such as I,
Thyrsis' Lament for Daphnis, III, *The Serenade*, and VII
itself – he was giving both form and substance, quite apart
from the hexameter, to a loosely defined species of poem. In
more idiosyncratic idylls – IV, *The Herdsmen*, V, *The Goat-*

herd versus the Shepherd, and X, *The Reapers*, for instance – he blends this with a greater worldliness which was to become the genre's lasting rationale. A device common to all his pastoral invention was the use of Doric dialect, a literary Doric, which in its turn was to influence the adoption of pastoral to the respectively esoteric ends of subsequent literary schools.

Theocritus appears to have been a Sicilian, the son of Praxagoras and Philinna, born in Syracuse between 320 and 300 B.C., most probably in 308. Of even these bald facts we cannot be sure, for the external evidence of the poet's life – to support what we may glean from the Idylls and Epigrams – is very scant. Most of our evidence derives ultimately from *Suidas*, the tenth-century lexicon, a unique source of evidence but notoriously unreliable; beyond it there are merely a few fragments from what must have been scholars' introductions. *Suidas* itself directly gives us little more than Epigram XXVII, most likely to constitute one such introduction by another hand. Its purpose is to clear up the confusion with the other Theocritus, a rhetorician of Chios, with whom the poet has been variously identified. We may, I believe, accept the distinction,[1] and perhaps even share Fawkes' amazement 'that the old grammarians will not rest satisfied, but endeavour to rob him of both his parents and his country'.[2]

There is no convincing need to doubt the specified Sicilian parentage. Simichus, the alternative suggestion for his father's name, is clearly a misguided derivation from the self-applied pseudonym of Idyll VII, the bucolic masquerade. It is surely not too unacademic to assume from within the poems that Theocritus was of Sicilian birth.

There is a lofty precedent. Vergil made just such an assumption, identifying his avowed master with the Sicilian landscape as a precondition of ancient pastoral, as he implies in the dedication of his Fourth Eclogue:

1. This is disputed. See the note on Epigram XXVII.
2. Francis Fawkes, *Theocritus, The Idylliums*, London, 1767, Introduction.

Sicelides Musae, paulo majora canamus
Sicilian Muses, let us sing of rather weightier things

Even more specific, perhaps, is the opening of the Sixth:

Prima Syracosio dignata est ludere versu
Nostra nec erubuit silvas habitare Thalia.
My first muse, Thalia, saw fit to toy with Sicilian verse;
she made the woods her home, and did not blush for that.

Theocritus is referred to as Sicilian in an epistle of the Emperor Julian (332–63 A.D.), in the *De Litteris Syllabis et Metris Horatii* of Terentianus Maurus (late second century A.D.) and in Manilius' *Astronomica* (first century B.C. – first century A.D.).

The fragments tell us that the poet spent much of his youth around the Aegean, including those formative years on the island of Cos. It is suggested that, with his friend Nicias, he was initially a medical student under Erasistratus of Samos. He certainly became a pupil of the Samian poet Asclepiades, probably before studying in Cos under Philitas, mentioned in XVII as the tutor of Ptolemy. Theocritus' indulgence in occasional topical reference has all too frequently been held against him; but the Coan idyll, the only pastoral poem *à clef*, makes exquisitely pastoral use of the bonhomie of those bohemian days.

He must have returned, fully fledged, to Syracuse in about 275 B.C., and appealed for the patronage of Hiero, newly elevated to command of the army, in the poem we have as Idyll XVI, *The Graces*. It seems that this may have been the title-poem of a collection, now lost as such and probably in substance; this, presumably, would have substantiated his claim for subsidy. But the plea, despite its withering criticism of withholders of patronage, fell on very stony ground; and our poet turned for support to the East and to Ptolemy Philadelphus,[3] ruler of Egypt, and patron of the renowned school of Alexandria.

Around the time of Theocritus' birth, Alexandria's unique library and museum had caused the most able

3. See Appendix, pp. 228–9.

writers at work to gravitate there and almost instinctively form a school of writing, whose principles were already formed at the island schools of the Aegean. As Philitas held literary court on Cos, so did Simias on Rhodes and Asclepiades on Samos; on the near-by mainland, Menecrates and Zenodotus were teaching in Ephesus, Hermesianax and Phoenix in Colophon. Theirs was in spirit an elitist movement, which sought to raise the dwindling quality of Greek literature by treating the best-known local folklore and legends in the most refined and intellectual literary terms.

At Alexandria this deliberately ambitious artistry found expression in precise distinctions of form: all the established poetic methods and devices were adopted by the scholars with more than a mere personal modification or idiosyncratic intrusion. The movement's very intellectualism was its new direction; they were bent on reproducing their country's indigenous art in their own terms, so the reworkings had a required novelty, but a novelty of purely studied, calculated qualities.

The technique, however little its palpable design may appeal to modern sentiments, succeeded, not least in terms of Theocritus himself, whose contribution to the pastoral tradition rests precisely on an Alexandrian rationalization of loosely established forms. He was there mainly in the first ten years of Alexandria's four golden decades, 280 to 240 B.C., after which the movement suffered a predictable decline as the savant and the dilettante took over from the scholar-poet. A great morass of undigested epic and flimsy epyllion follows over the next century and more. There was to be a brief revival at the beginning of the first century B.C., thanks to the new air breathed into Alexandrian stolidness by Meleager and his contemporaries; but Alexandria's reputation as the literary capital of the Greek world became an increasingly hollow one, finally disposed of in 145 by Ptolemy Physcon, who saw fit to expel all the city's accumulated community of scholars.

The panegyric in Theocritus' Idyll XVII, *In Praise of Ptolemy*, may have been spontaneous, in search of hire and

salary after his rebuff from Hiero; or it may have been in
response to a welcome invitation to come to Alexandria. It is
likely the ruler would have kept in touch with the avant-
garde developments in Cos, under his old mentor, and that
the name of Theocritus may have reached his ears without
motions from the poet. Idyll VII, 91 ff., implies as much, and
may suggest a summons:

> The Nymphs have taught me too to sing
> many such songs . . .
> fine songs, which fame perhaps has carried as far
> even as the throne of Zeus.

No monarch of Ptolemy's vanity could resist such flattery,
which may well be seen as a calculated gambit on the poet's
part, secure in the knowledge that such collections as *The
Graces* would reach the Alexandrian court. The elusiveness of
the poem's date permits, indeed encourages, such speculation.

The voyage to the east was eventful and may have been a
fruitful period. It included a stop-over at Cos to revisit his
old friends and colleagues, and perhaps to gather more
material about Ptolemy's birthplace for inclusion in court
poetry. He also travelled via Miletus, carrying with him Idyll
XXVIII and its eponymous distaff for Nicias' new bride.

XV, *The Adonia*, shows the poet to be a seasoned resident
of Alexandria, placing his sojourn there at least partly be-
tween 278 and 270 B.C. XIV, *Aeschinas and Thyonichus*, is
also clearly of the Egyptian period. His work as one of
Ptolemy's laureates must have demanded many of the lines
in praise of famous children, as Arsinoë bore and brought up
the royal offspring; thus XXII, *The Dioscuri*, and XXIV, *The
Infant Heracles*, join the presumably earlier XVIII, *Helen's
Bridal Hymn*, among the domestic court work. It is on such
scanty speculation that the dating, and so the chronological
order, of the poems has come to rest; but it seems likely that
during this period Theocritus grew away from the bucolic
work which occupied his early Alexandrian heyday to the
more grandiose public poetry which forms the tail-end bulk
of this collection.

Theocritus the Alexandrian not only became one of the movement's luminaries, but inevitably was constrained to take a stand in the central dispute between Callimachus and Apollonius Rhodius on the changing nature of epic poetry. The Alexandrians' appetite for didacticism led to the exaltation of epic as the major poetic form, so a dispute such as this over epic style was one which struck at the root of all the work being done on elegy, hymn, narrative poetry, epigram, iambus and paignion. Callimachus of Cyrene, the elder statesman of the Alexandrian school, had laid it down that the epic's qualities were best realized by an abandonment of the grand manner and a reversion to the epyllion style more accessible to a less exalted audience. His pupil, Apollonius of Rhodes, dared to dispute this judgement and speak out in favour of the traditionally grand epic in the Homeric style – of which his own early, later revised, poem, *The Argonautica*, was put forward as a stereotype. Callimachus won the hour, but it was an indecisive victory, as successive generations under Alexandrian influence adopted both styles with equal respect – Rhianus being the prime exponent of the long, lofty epic, Euphorion and Eratosthenes of the epyllion. We have no evidence that Theocritus' friendship with Callimachus was more than a respectful acquaintanceship, but he clearly takes his – the more revolutionary – position in the debate, giving the lines to Lycidas in Idyll VII:

> I hate the builder who tries to raise
> his roof as high as Oromedon's peak
> no less than I hate those cocks who strut
> in the Muses' yard, wretchedly trying
> to match Chios' nightingale with their crows.

If my suggestion that this poem is pre-Alexandrian is to be accepted, these lines are, of course, a neophyte's distant contribution to the debate, which may indeed again constitute an application for membership of the literary circle. But it is an attitude which we may assume the poet maintained as his stature grew; the nature of his own innovations points to an allegiance to Callimachus. The early date is further reinforced by the references to Ptolemy's treatment of Sotades implied by the Comatas section (see nn. 17 and 54). Suggestions have been made that this criticism of the monarch forced Theocritus to beat a hasty retreat from Alexandria, and have thus argued the poem's later date. But they may be dismissed, I believe, as the kind of fiction which readily blossoms from so frustrating a dearth of historical evidence. One cannot believe that a poet with so calculated a sense of priorities about his work and its patronage would throw his position away with this bold a gesture; nowhere else in the idylls do we see evidence of the rebel with the courage of his political convictions.

For the same reasons we may also dismiss, I believe, the legend prompted by Ovid's *Ibis*,[4] 549–50, that Theocritus died an ignominious death at the hands of Hiero. Edmonds[5] quotes a scholiast's interpretation of Ovid's

> *Utve Syracosio praestricta fauce poetae,*
> *Sic animae laqueo sit via clausa tuae,*
> Just as the poet of Syracuse was strangled,
> so your life too may be ended with a noose.

to the effect that 'the Syracusan poet Theocritus ... was arrested by King Hiero for making an attack upon his son, the king's object being merely to make him think that he was going to be put to death. But when Hiero asked him if he would avoid abusing his son in future, he began to abuse him all the more, and not only the son but the father too. Whereat the king in indignation ordered him to be put to death in real earnest, and according to some authorities he was strangled and according to others beheaded.'

4. The ibis, according to Lewis and Short, was 'a bird held sacred by the Egyptians ... which lived on water animals'. In Alexandria the bird had a reputation for dirty habits, and so its name was attached to Apollonius Rhodius by Callimachus in a verse attack which has not survived (but is mentioned in Strabo's *Historical Sketches*). Callimachus' poem served as a model for Ovid's *Ibis*, a comprehensive catalogue of disasters and deaths called down as a curse on the poet's enemy.

5. J. M. Edmonds, *The Greek Bucolic Poets*, The Loeb Classical Library, London/Harvard, 1928, Introduction.

The evidence for accepting this is apparently that 'when Theocritus was sixty-five Hiero's son Gelo would be nineteen; we know of no other Syracusan poet who met such a fate; and ... Ptolemy's [treatment] of Sotades shows how the most enlightened rulers of the day could deal with adverse criticism'.

The story does seem, however, to confirm that Theocritus spent his last days at Syracuse, and probably died there. We know of no convincing reason or date for his departure from Alexandria; but it has been generally agreed that he died around 240 B.C., in his mid seventies. Statius refers to him as '*Siculus senex*'.

Although it is certain that we have lost much of Theocritus' work in other, related genres, it is arguable that what we have represents a high percentage of his output. The nature and style of his work are not those of a prolific, though versatile, writer; and what guidance on dating we have places all his work within the four major decades of Hellenistic poetry, 280 to 240 B.C. My own view is that much of the work which recommended him from a distance to Ptolemy has been lost, and that the poems we have were written largely in the Alexandrian climate, that of the city poet writing calculated pastoral – an attitude which, as we shall see, was to constitute a rationale for later, more sophisticated practitioners. Certainly Theocritus' regrettable transition from pure pastoral to sub-epic and public verse took place there. And it may be that the tranquil, more lyrical love poems – such as XII, *The Beloved Boy*, XXVII, *The Seduction*, XXIX, *For A Boy* (i), and XXX, *For Another Boy* – were the product of a mellow, nostalgic retirement. The autobiographical implications of XIV, however, seem to suggest that the poet's hair was turning grey while he was still in Alexandria.

The list recorded in *Suidas* attests that Theocritus produced the full Alexandrian gamut of different verse-forms: bucolics and epigrams, which constitute most of what we have; hymns, such as XVII; lyrics, such as XXVIII, XXIX and XXX; plus elegies, iambics, funeral laments and large heroic works, which all seem to have vanished without trace.

There is also specific mention of two supposedly large works or collections, *The Heroines* and *The Daughters of Proteus*, of which we know no more than their names.

But it is also significant that some of the poems we do have – such as II, XIV and XV – do not fall readily into *Suidas'* categories. We can perceive their natural affinity to aspects of the Theocritus canon, but the departures of form are puzzling. The latter two smack particularly of the society poet, and nestle uneasily amid the body of the Idylls.

It is therefore obvious that the Idylls as we have them were not intended by the poet to stand as any kind of unified collection, let alone in any kind of order. They are rather the victims of historical convenience and the tidy minds of the old grammarians. It is equally doubtful that the poet himself applied the word 'idyll' to his poems; this was almost certainly added by editors of the first century B.C., again as a matter of convenience. Not too much, therefore, is to be read into the word, which is a diminutive form of εἶδος, shape or appearance. It may be translated, I think, 'little poems', perhaps to distinguish Theocritus' work from that of his contemporaries. The suggestion that it conveys a sense of 'little pictures', and that Theocritus' perception is thus of a visual nature, is an unfortunately popular critical misconception. The lyric odes of Pindar were so called because the εἶδος ἁρμονίας in which they were meant to be sung was appended to each.

All the poems in the collection, with the exception of XV, despite its celebration of Adonis, are either purely pastoral, or the product of a pastoral-orientated consciousness. By that I mean to suggest that such poems as the homosexual love lyrics – XII, XXIII, XXIX and XXX – are finely in tune with what I have called the pastoral ethic, though not of course set in a pastoral landscape. Their observations on the nature of love, and the behaviour required of those involved as their pastoral duty, their code of values, illustrate the more direct and less stylish love poems of the specifically pastoral terrain, such as III, XI, XX and so on.

Similarly, the epic qualities of XXII and XXV are closely

related to Theocritus' pastoral code, but provide it with a third dimension – the entry of the great man, the archetype, a familiar poetic figure, into a world peopled by definition by remote and unknown individuals in a purer state of being. This extra dimension makes possible the pastoral qualities of XIII, *Hylas*, where the worldly and the unworldly are juxtaposed to just this effect.

Theocritus, I believe, made very calculated use of his versatility to expand a world into which he was just feeling his way. For he did not, as did his inheritors, write consciously manipulated pastoral; he was in no position to do so. To him the pastoral setting was sufficiently new and thus unorthodox among formal poetry to make its own points; there is no heavy-handed allegory, no overt moralizing, no schematic linking of pastoral figures to present-day shadows, none of the artful formality which is an inevitable symptom of the poem's coming-of-age as a literary form. He was using the idea, not the genre, and it was thus sufficiently original to require no exegesis from within.

It is in such a setting that the pastoral at times appears to be at its most absurd, when it is in fact at its most native, its most refined. The conclusion to XXVII is a case in point. The instinctive inevitability with which Daphnis and his girl return to their respective herds after their rather coy love-making seems laughable to a modern audience, and would be a misjudgement in any post-medieval pastoral. But here we have what may – not, I hope, facetiously – be called pastoral pastoral: that is, pastoral still itself in a state of innocence, not yet institutionalized into a literary form. The behaviour is natural because it is directly and honestly, not artificially, exploited. On whose shoulders would Theocritus' shepherds more naturally cry than on those of their cattle? It would have been dishonest of him to have written otherwise.

The point is made clearer by those instances where Theocritus himself falls into the kind of trap he laid for his successors. In XXII he loses control of the opening within ten lines, and is carried off into an absurd attempt at an epic simile, quite out of place and quite disastrous. This is

because of his Alexandrian brainwashing, which at times
such as this forced the incidentals of erudition on innocent,
undeserving and totally unsuited verse forms. Theocritus is
attempting to work within the rubrics of an acknowledged
literary framework, and has misjudged his attempt, which
anyway amounts to little more than a gesture. One feels that
Callimachus could have played Pound to his Eliot here, and
shown him how to temper intellect with decorum.

This is what many of his successors were to misjudge about
the pastoral. They did not realize that the artificiality of the
form requires it to be adapted to its age, not just employed as
a formula. Milton, for instance, created the environment in
which *Lycidas* could succeed, despite the dissenting criticisms
of Johnson; Shelley wrote *Adonais* in a vacuum, and so pro-
duced nothing more than an elegant artefact.

One important area of concern here is the use of dialect as
a staple ingredient of pastoral. Theocritus makes much of the
traditional use of literary Doric, which became a required
facet of Greek pastoral. The qualities of his characters, and
so their role in the poem's exposition, are often defined from
the mouth in this way – as, for instance, are many of Dickens'
comic characters. But to attempt to recreate this in a different
age clearly requires radical adaptation; moreover, it requires
rethinking of the role of arcane or current habits of speech in
any given society. In these translations, for instance, I have
been content to render Theocritus' use of dialect and literary
Doric in terms of current colloquialism, as I believe dialect
has little serious place in all but specialist modern literature,
or in the more esoteric regional writing. To have consigned
Theocritus' 'rude rustics' to a Scottish peat-bog or a Somer-
set orchard would have been to distort his intentions, as that
particular literary device has not survived 2,000 years of
literary change. The same principle would have applied had
I been attempting to write original twentieth-century
pastoral.

This point is true of Theocritus as of any pioneer. He
could afford to make use of obvious devices – the refrain, the
singing match, dialect, the formula poem – because he made

them his and pastoral's own. And so his quality is not merely the accidental advantage unique to the pathfinder, but an awareness of this and a deliberate control of it. Theocritus' achievement lies in the variety of pastoral he creates, proving that he was aware even at that early stage of the dangers of formulaic poetry, and was himself of sufficient Alexandrian discrimination to sidestep them. It was not enough to establish a new style; it had to be established in such a way as to allow for variation, adaptation, and, ultimately, a tradition. This perception must be in the literary metabolism of any founding father; without it, the genre would be stillborn.

As it was, Theocritus' new ground in fact lay fallow for a century or more. His only two successors and inheritors as Alexandrian pastoral poets were Moschus and Bion, of whose lives we know little, and whose work is the subject of doubt and confusion. Both worked in the second century B.C., but there has been considerable argument over who was the senior. Speculation finally comes to suggest that Moschus was at work *circa* 150 B.C. and Bion *circa* 100. *Suidas*, the earliest source of reference, is the most categoric that the pastoral poets' chronological order was Theocritus, Moschus, Bion.

Suidas tells us that Moschus was a Syracusan, who studied with Aristarchus at Alexandria somewhere between 180 and 144 B.C. He was a grammarian, mentioned by Athenaeus as the author of a standard text on the dialect of Rhodes. The seven poems in this collection are those generally collated by the main manuscripts, though some are definitely not by Moschus and all are from different sources. IV, V and VI are preserved in the fifth-century A.D. anthology of Stobaeus, all of them complete and well-rounded, short enough to earn the name if not the style of epigrams. VII, similar in shape and effect, comes to us from the *Anthologia Planudea* (4.200), and has been incorrectly ascribed to Moschus because of its mention of Europa and the bull, dealt with in Moschus II. That poem itself, a strictly Alexandrian epyllion in 166 hexameters, has no more than an ascription; but the prolonged 25-line description of Europa's basket conforms to the terms of the Callimachus-Apollonius dispute, and so must be of the School. (Compare Theocritus' longer description of the golden cup proposed as a prize in the song-contest of Idyll I.) The introductory dream of Moschus II is another epic device. The finest sustained poem in the Moschus collection, III, *The Lament for Bion*, cannot of course be his if *Suidas'* chronology is to be accepted. It is generally ascribed to a disciple of Bion, but may remain for convenience in the Moschus canon, and may by no means be excluded from any pastoral collection because of its central place in the mainstream of the tradition, alongside the lament for Daphnis in Theocritus I and Bion's *Lament for Adonis*. Some editors also attribute the apocryphal pastoral, *Megara*, to Moschus, for reasons less than substantial; I have excluded the poem, an antiphonal lament in hexameters between the wife and mother of Heracles, from any place in this collection because of its altogether inferior quality, quite apart from its dubious credentials. It is most probably the work of an unknown Hellenistic poet, of this or a later period.

We again rely on *Suidas* for biographical details of Bion, who was born at Phlossa, a small town near Smyrna, and seems to have founded or at least prompted a thriving school of lyric poetry. Lyric, as may be seen in the eighteen poems and fragments collected here, was more his forte than orthodox pastoral; he is referred to in the third-century compendium of Diogenes Laertius as 'a lyric poet'. Less sickly-sweet, more simple and direct than Moschus, Bion is at times flippant, at others sententious, and is the most openly erotic of the three poets in this collection. Some of the pieces collected here are clearly fragments, again preserved by Stobaeus; E. A. Barber[6] has suggested they may include a *Hyacinthus* and a *Galatea*. Bion strikes the most modern note of the three, the most free-thinking, at times almost humanist, though XVIII – clearly a fragment – is a concise summary of much theistic Greek moralizing:

6. E. A. Barber, *The Oxford Classical Dictionary*, Oxford, 1949, Bion (2).

Everything blessed by heaven is possible.
There's nothing a man may not do,
may not easily do, with the will of the gods.

Set beside the implications of Bion's fragments, this appears
mere appeasement. More characteristic of his peculiar origin-
ality is the two-line extract, XV, which survives in strangely
perfect, almost *haiku* form:

Enough little drops of water, they say,
can dig a channel in a stone.

The *Lament for Adonis* was initially ascribed to Theocritus,
but has since the Renaissance been made over to Bion, largely
on the strength of apparent references to it in the *Lament for
Bion*. It is the most extravagant of pastoral's three central
laments, and as a result the most astringent. It appears to
conform with the stylistic dictates of Callimachus, echoing
some of his more lyrical work, though allowing greater
emotional abandon than he would have approved. Similarly,
Moschus I, *The Fugitive Love*, is strictly in line with Calli-
machus' metrical teaching, as are many of the fragments, but
II, *Europa*, is looser and more eccentric, which has led some
to doubt Moschus' authorship. It may rather show how the
authoritarian influence of Callimachus was less timidly ad-
hered to by later Alexandrians who had come to appreciate
the specialist legacy of Theocritus.

The reader will of course be struck by the very limited
pastoral content of Moschus and Bion in these collections.
The fact is that for better or worse they are a traditional ad-
junct to Theocritus, included with him in the manuscripts'
pastoral anthologies because of their evident debt to him.
The common factor of the other poems gathered here and in
the tradition is the dependence on the myths habitually
worked by pastoral, plus the close relation of epigram and
epigrammatic fragment to the genre. Already we can dis-
tinguish the form and content of pastoral, the one rational-
ized by Theocritus, the other adopted and interpreted by his
successors. As pastoral was variously adapted to the style and
mood of all subsequent schools of poetry and drama, the one

was also – spasmodically but systematically – to give way to the other.

The distinction between pastoral as form, as convention, and pastoral as subject, as content, is a vital one to any study of the Greeks' influence on European literature. It goes hand in hand with an analogous distinction between pastoral and romance, two often confused, rarely intertwining genres, which are brought together by the similar attitudes they propound. The seductive conclusion of overlooking these distinctions is to subvert to pastoral ends any work which treats of nature or the natural life, of the humble and remote, of the simple as opposed to the lofty or the complex, of states of innocence, of the processes of corruption.

The countryside has always been with us, preaching no overt sermons, a ready prey to the aestheticists of all disciplines, and only later to the polemicists. Its characters and inhabitants are self-sufficient, and may be so as artefacts; it is for the critical reader to metamorphose them into archetypes and allegories. Their lives and loves are peculiar to themselves, and not the property of any single genre. Pastoral was to be used, however, as a political device by a number of schools; my contention is that it is so by its very nature, its *ratio operandi*. The error of those who dispute this principle is to adopt many a non-pastoral work into the canon.

We may take as a starting point Professor Gilbert Highet's rather ingenuous portrait of the pastoral landscape:

Pastoral poetry and drama evoke the happy life of shepherds, cowboys, and goatherds on farms in the country. Ploughmen and field-workers are not introduced, because their life is too laborious and sordid. Nymphs, satyrs, and other flora and fauna also appear, to express the intense and beautiful aliveness of wild nature. Pastoral life is characterized by: simple love-making, folk-music (especially singing and piping), purity of morals, simplicity of manners, healthy diet, plain clothing, and an unspoilt way of living.[7]

This is all very well; but the implication that this is an end-in-itself world is vitiated by his closing caveat: '. . . in strong

7. Gilbert Highet, *The Classical Tradition*, Oxford, 1949.

contrast to the anxiety and corruption of existence in great
cities and royal courts'. Where in Theocritus, about whom
Professor Highet is talking, is the internal evidence for this?
And is there not a considerable degree of the 'laborious and
sordid' life of ploughmen and field-workers? One need only
go to the laborious work of the bully-reaper in Idyll X, the
sordid dirty jokes of Lacon and Comatas in V. Nevertheless,
Professor Highet's view of Theocritus' music is that, 'like the
sound of a brook or the glow of sunlight through leaves, [it]
transfigures even ordinary thought and commonplace figures
with an unforgettable, inimitable loveliness'.

There is here the tangled confusion which has so often led
to misconceptions of pastoral. The most heinous is the sug-
gestion that Theocritus was a political writer, deliberately
contrasting country and city life; this is a confusion of func-
tion and condition. It is certainly no coincidence that Theo-
critus, the first conscious writer of pastoral, wrote from an
urban context, namely the courts and libraries of Alexandria.
And it is true that his inheritors turned this fact to political
ends, and converted pastoral into a didactic genre. But Theo-
critus himself was by nature a Sicilian, not a cosmopolitan
academic, and any loaded interpretation of his work comes
purely from outside. Moralizing lies in the mind of the
reader, and Theocritus is the critics' unhappy victim.

Formal pastoral has always been the product of an urban
society, but only after the Hellenistic age was this deliberately
and essentially so. Its function for many subsequent ages was
to assume a degeneracy, a decline in standards, between the
age described and the age describing; its purpose became to
point the difference, even the reasons. But pre-Hellenistic
and Alexandrian pastoral also fathered a school outside the
mainstream of socio-literary life which clung to the un-
motivated recommendation of simple, native virtues; it was
so used by Middle English and medieval European writers,
mostly of a religious bent, and was so mimicked by later
stylists such as Pope, whose youthful pastorals unfortunately
do no more than mummify the convention. Operating, there-
fore, on one or the other plane, pastoral can become both the

least and the most escapist of literary forms. It is a confusion of the two planes which led to such abuses of the genre as that of Samuel Johnson,[8] whose wilful misunderstanding of Milton's intentions in *Lycidas* made him the natural father of the contemporary instinct that pastoral is both fey and irrelevant. It has tended more than any other genre to be fawned on and patronized; critical talk of rustic charms and sensual delights simply drag the misconception further down. Its quality on either plane, conscious or unconscious, is to illustrate in the pastoral way of life the deficiencies of all others, either specifically or by inference. Pastoral is unavoidably a yardstick for other kinds of society; this is what distinguishes it from simple nature poetry. It may be used as a spur, a means of cleansing or redemption, never as a retreat. Thus in the twentieth century, although the conventional pastoral is dead, the concept survives in other disciplines, and has worked its way into the fabric of a literature dominated by the individual under stress. Notions of alternative societies, refuge in fantasy, the innocence of childhood or insanity, the creeping paralysis of moral corruption amid materialist gamesmanship and physical pollution – all have the same rationale. Apt material for pastoral may even be found in the lunar landscape.

The earliest example of the pastoral spirit in literature may be the poem from the Sumerian civilization of Mesopotamia quoted by Professor Frank Kermode,[9] in which 'a girl prefers a farmer (socially superior because economically more highly organized) to a shepherd'. Material on which Theocritus must surely, however, have drawn is the myth of the golden age in Hesiod's poem to the *Works and Days*, a landscape which Vergil was to recreate in his Arcadia. Theocritus invented no such specific terrain, but characterized its inhabitants in lasting roles – notably, of course, the shepherd, who is adopted as the hero of innocence. No idealized, unflawed innocence this, but a realistic, earthy honesty com-

8. Samuel Johnson, *Lives of the Poets*, 1781, Life of Milton.
9. Frank Kermode, edr, *English Pastoral Poetry*, London, 1952, Introduction.

∴ vergil concentrates as much on the setting – builds it up.

pletely free from design or worldly aspiration; in this shape he comes to stand for child, lover, poet, and unconscious mystic. The dual meaning of the Latin word 'pastor' is no coincidence; the rare virtues accorded the shepherd, the at times pre-lapsarian status he takes on, naturally prefigure the religious qualities he represents in the Christian era. Shepherds throughout the Bible, notably those who were the first on earth to be privy to the birth of Christ, are performing a specifically pastoral function.

Theocritus established and codified the landscape. He was content simply to present the pastoral ethic in its raw state and leave the reader or listener to his own conclusions, never intruding himself into the scene in the manner favoured by his legatees. It must thus be naturally accepted that his country characters are endowed with the wisdom of the city, that they live – as it has been aptly put – beyond their intellectual means. This is an easily palatable convention to which all genres cling at one time or another. I have already argued that Theocritus' deliberate versatility of technique allowed the pastoral room for development; I would say the same of his stance as poet. Though the first to write pastoral as such, he was in the pastoral poet's classic and necessary position, the difference being that he was a city poet writing of a life of which he did have significant personal experience. This attitude was reversed as the genre was politicized, and the enumeration of pastoral virtues performed by the poet who had had no personal access to them. This became a most effective device, as those virtues naturally became a conscious antidote to the occupational hazards of civilized life. To censure such a writer, as Johnson did Milton, for never having himself battened flocks or driven a field is thus entirely to miss the point. We do not require contemporary theologians to be transported to heaven in chariots of fire.

Vergil is generally depicted as the elevator of the pastoral to true philosophic status, fusing it with personal wisdom into a kind of pre-Christian gospel. His promoters tend, while frankly acknowledging his debt to the Idylls, to illustrate Vergil the philosopher-poet in terms of Theocritus the facile bard. But it is quite wrong to make qualitative distinctions between the two, to weigh them up as rivals. Vergil simply developed the form, and used it differently, as indeed did his own inheritors – partly because he was a more studious poet, more of a freelance philosopher, and partly because his age gave him more to be polemic about. The famous Fourth Eclogue can be directly interpreted in either lyric, political or Messianic, even Christian, terms; indeed, it has led to suggestions that the poet may have read the prophecies of Isaiah. But he is in this, whatever conclusions one may unravel from the poem (one of the most discussed ever written), a product of his times; no such lofty optimism was required from Theocritus, whose toils in the libraries of Alexandria were simply in praise of the quiet virtues he saw as the stuff of a good life. Thus Heracles, whom we may think of as the Theocritean superman, certainly embodied rare qualities of violence; but they were tempered with pastoral man's sense of the noble, of the pure and the natural – and, highly important, the need for some bard to immortalize the tale for posterity.

The achievement of Vergilian pastoral was to clarify the relationship between the country life extolled and the mind of man. His rustic heroes, his lovers and his swains, are more readily identifiable with the youth of his own society than are those of Theocritus, a token of the way in which he made the pastoral life-style closer to, and more compatible with, that of the city. It derived less authority from its remoteness, its sheer historical authenticity, becoming a more natural mould for his audience to cast themselves in. Vergil adopted the rudiments of allegory from Theocritus, and sophisticated them almost to the level of symbolism; in smoothing out the crudeness, the awkwardness of the way of life which emerged from the Idylls, he ennobled the form into a more obviously instructive source of wisdom.

Vergil, by the same token, disposed more efficiently of that view of nature which subverts the pastoral ethic – country life as a boorish and rather dirty occupation carried on by simple-minded people who think of sheep, goats and cows as rare and noble creatures rather than the submissive and frankly smelly animals they in fact are. Greg [10] quotes the remarks of two critics bringing this charge against Theocritus; to Fontenelle, the shepherds of the Idylls '*sentent trop la campagne*', and to Symonds 'his cowherds and goatherds savour too strongly of their stables'. These are crude dismissals; in truth, Theocritus manages to achieve an effect of inverted purity from the less seemly mechanics of country work; Vergil sidesteps the problem altogether by manipulating his reader into assuming any such basics to be part of the natural life's lofty, unstinted ideal. Those critics who lose patience with a surfeit of farmhands, earth and dung are taking the same cul-de-sac as Johnson.

Vergil, then, ironed out and refined Theocritus' acknowledged achievement: there were now textbook models from pastoral poet and disciple alike. As it was, Vergil's more advanced, more complex pastoral was to be the more influential. He had many immediate minor imitators, but the form hereafter begins to fragment. Its kinship with romance is acknowledged in Longus' Greek novel, *Daphnis and Chloe* (third century A.D.), but we must here observe that romance is only a cousin of pastoral. The morality implied rests on similar values, and there had been pastoral elements in the work of Longus' two fellows, Heliodorus of Syria (the *Aethiopica*, *c.* 220 A.D.) and Achilles Tatius (*Clitophon and Leucippe*, *c.* 300 A.D.); their choice of a different genre, however, with its own established tradition, was quite deliberate.

But the content of conventional pastoral made a direct appeal to the medieval imagination, and there was much activity before the great Renaissance revival. Highet points to thirteenth- and fourteenth-century France, with Adam de la Halle's shepherd play, *Robin et Marion* (*c.* 1250) and Philippe de Vitri's poem *Le Dit de Franc Gontier*; with this last, however, one is already well enough into the fourteenth century to be acknowledging Petrarch's influence. In England

10. W. W. Greg, *Pastoral Poetry and Pastoral Drama*, London, 1905.

there had already been the delicate *Sir Orfeo*, owing as much to romance as to pastoral, and a number of short lyrics by unknown writers which recall some of Bion's less ambitious work. Gower wrote of Actaeon and of Ceix and Alcyone, but here again it is more the pastoral spirit than the convention which is being invoked. Closer, yet on very different ground, is the journey of Piers Plowman, whose duties to Holy Church as the pledged object of his love anticipate the kinship of courtly love with pastoral devotions.

It is in this period that romance and pastoral are most closely combined, and the tradition is dominated by the *Roman de la Rose*, composed in two parts *circa* 1240 and 1280. The first 4,058 lines, by Guillaume de Lorris, paint the ideal, enclosed world of *courtoisie*; the remaining 18,000 lines, by Jean de Meung, detail the outside world of cynicism and corruption to point the contrast between the two views of love. From it grew Chaucer's own *Romaunt of the Rose* – only part of whose 7,700 lines he may actually have written. But there is enough in the same vein in the rest of his work – mostly that outside *The Canterbury Tales* – to show his assimilation of the medieval reworkings. It must be said, however, that though these 200 years of pastourelle and ballad, of the genteel English lyric and the stylish Provençal troubadour, kept alive the flame of pastoral–romance, there was no return to either Greek or Roman convention, and the work seems largely to be independent of their direct influence.

The real link between Hellenistic–Roman pastoral and the Renaissance revival comes in 1504 with Jacopo Sannazzaro's *Arcadia*, a series of eclogues connected by a prose narrative, which spread quickly throughout Europe and was immensely influential. Sannazzaro, the son of Spanish immigrants into Italy, had one vernacular pastoral from the early fourteenth century to guide his adoption of the classical models, Boccaccio's *Admetus*, which made the same use of a verse–prose blend. Boccaccio had set an important precedent by insisting on vigorous allegory; the seven nymphs who convert his shepherd's love from the physical to the spiritual have a glorious revelation as the seven cardinal virtues. Sannazzaro, in true classical style, saw that such heavy-handedness was alien to purist pastoral, and defeated its own ends. His tale is a romance in strict pastoral terms, in which a lover is purified by Arcadian adventures before returning to his original urban society. The moral is there, implicit and unequivocal, but there is none of the blunt medieval underlining. The poem, in twelve sections of eclogue and prose, circulated from 1481 until its publication in 1504; it was translated into French in 1544 and into Spanish in 1549. As Vergil made direct transliterations from Theocritus, so Sannazzaro makes them from Homer, Theocritus, Vergil, Ovid and later classical authors; and the rich, elaborate, stylish result is, in Genouy's words, 'the most complete manual of pastoral it is possible to imagine'.[11]

Sannazzaro was slavishly copied all over Europe. The second coming of pastoral owed its vigour to the Renaissance delight in pre-cast forms into which allegory and other instruments of imitative poetry could be poured. While harmonizing with the hard-wrought principles of artificial poetry, it still allowed scope for virtuoso individuality. Sannazzaro's most successful disciple was Jorge de Montemayor, whose *Diana* (1560), though less academic, was even more studied and aped than the *Arcadia*. Montemayor, an Italian courtier, chose to emphasize pastoral love, and while lifting many of Sannazzaro's incidents dwelt less on authentic classical models. Again, the *Diana* is more precisely a romance, but a romance with so distinctly pastoral a rationale as to draw its imitators away from romantic psychology. Reverting more to Boccaccio's loftiness, its busy scenes and many-sided characters were used by Shakespeare in *Two Gentlemen of Verona*, and – as Highet discerns – by Cervantes in his *Galatea*, and in the ideals of *Don Quixote*:

I will buy a flock of sheep, and everything that is fit for the pastoral life; and so, calling myself the shepherd Quixotis, and you the shepherd Pansino, we will range the woods, the hills and the meadows, singing and versifying.

11. H. Genouy, *L'Arcadia de Sidney dans ses rapports avec l'Arcadia de Sannazzaro et la Diana de Montemayor*, Montpellier, 1928.

There is even a distinct echo of Theocritus XII, *The Beloved Boy*, and one directly plagiarized line, in Quixote's reasoning:

> Love will inspire us with a theme and wit, and Apollo with harmonious lays. So shall we become famous, not only while we live, but make our loves as eternal as our songs.

The activity in southern Europe continued apace, with Tasso's *Aminta* (1581) and Guarini's *Il Pastor Fido* (1590). In France, the movement had been taken up by Clément Marot (1496–1544) whose eclogues and sonnets were set in his native landscape; his successor, Pierre de Ronsard (1524–85) made direct translations of Theocritus and Vergil. All were eagerly translated into English and adopted as models – most directly, Montemayor's *Diana* for Sidney's *Arcadia*, and Guarini's *Il Pastor Fido* for Fletcher's *The Faithful Shepherdess*. These major English works also had a strong English lyric tradition to draw on; the spread of the pastourelle had been taken up by Henryson, notably with his *Tale of Orpheus* (1508) and the better known *Testament of Cresseid* (1593), under Chaucer's influence but with significant novelettish innovation. His work led to the lyric strength in England in the late sixteenth and early seventeenth centuries, with much pastoral detail in Drayton, Marlowe, Lodge and countless minor poets down to Sir Walter Raleigh.

But the pastoral was most fully explored in the English Renaissance by Spenser and Sidney. Sidney was of the two the more influenced by the European revival, Spenser by the classical sources; and Sidney is the lesser for it. Neither lived long, but both achieved a prolific body of work, Sidney's all published posthumously. His lovers' dialogue, *Astrophel and Stella*, displays more a stylist's interest in the devices and trappings of pastoral than a poet's assimilation of its spirit. His heavily influenced *Arcadia*, which owes a huge debt to Sannazaro, is equally concerned with technique at the expense of inventiveness.

Spenser it was who, of all English writers, fledged the form most fully, adapting it to various styles, and understanding its versatility – a true inheritor of Theocritus. The sequence of eclogues which makes up *The Shepheardes Calender* is based on Vergil's pattern, but reproduces the uncluttered landscape and temperate *Zeitgeist* of Greek pastoral like no other work in the language. All the traditional themes are treated anew – love shared, love unrequited, praise of a patron, laments on tragic deaths, a singing match, moral allegories and a defence of poetry itself. Based also on the recent work of Mantuan and Marot, one of Spenser's successful innovations was the use of Colin Cloute as a persona for the author. Spenser's is the implicit, unspoken resolution of the art-nature conflict which is the perpetual leveller of pastoral priorities; and it is achieved by a return to the less lofty pastoral of the Greek landscape. For Spenser's version of Arcadia is peopled by characters in the Hellenistic mould, who cannot from their own mouths promote truths above their station; instead, they guide the reader through the months of the year, and so through the calendar of a man's life, in such a way that the values are formed in his own mind, with reference to his own preconceptions. The cancerous influence of Boccaccio's obtrusive allegories had finally been discarded.

The critical reception accorded the *Calender* shows that pastoral was already being underestimated by all but its practitioners, and is characteristic of an age when the form can be totally ignored by some major writers while their peers are obsessed by it. Sidney betrays his misreading of Theocritus when he says of the work, which was dedicated to him, 'Spenser has much poetry in his eclogues, indeed worthy the reading if I be not deceived. That same framing of his style to an old rustic language I dare not allow, since neither Theocritus in Greek, Vergil in Latin, nor Sannazzarro in Italian did affect it.'[12] That same framing of his style is the one authentic recreation of Theocritus' use of dialect by any of his imitators; Sidney will not acknowledge the entire Dorian tradition, let alone Theocritus' distinctive accents, and Spenser's remarkable adroitness in adapting them to an only distantly related tongue.

E.K., writing of the same work, anticipates Johnson's

12. Philip Sidney, *The Defence of Poesie*, 1595.

careless judgement that pastoral is a lightweight form worthy only of a poet's apprenticeship. In a sentence which requires some unravelling, he says:

... which moved him rather in aeglogues than otherwise to write, doubting perhaps his ability, which he little needed, or minding to furnish our tongue with this kind, wherein it faulteth, or following the example of the best and most ancient poets, which devised this kind of writing, being both so base for the matter and homely for the manner, at the first to try their abilities and, as young birds that be new crept out of the nest, by little first to prove their tender wings before they make a greater flight. So flew Theocritus, as you may perceive he was already fledged. So flew Vergil, as not yet well feeling his wings. So flew Mantuan, as being not full summed.[13]

The list continues. So much, yet again, for Theocritus, judged worthy only of short shrift by this Renaissance critic who is dubbing him – I take it – a sort of literary Peter Pan, still playing with toys in his literary maturity.

Spenser, beyond this first substantial work, was the earliest Englishman to appreciate the variety of pastoral, in form as well as technique. His *Astrophel*, on the death of Sidney, is directly derived from the three classical laments; his *Epithalamion* and *Prothalamion* have their origins in Theocritus' Idyll XVIII, *Helen's Bridal Hymn*. Both ethic and landscape are woven into the fabric of all his work, notably the *Amoretti* sonnet sequence and the *Faerie Queene* itself.

His only successor in this close sympathy with the classical source is Milton, who in one corner of his poetic output is forty years later smoothing out Spenser much as Vergil did Theocritus. *Lycidas* is a scholarly reworking of the lament, more urbane, more highly polished and thus more complacent than the native art of Spenser; and it was this more obviously bookish quality which provoked Johnson's attack, and his charge of insincerity. He was too doctrinaire a critic to allow that a grief is often best controlled by formalization, and that this is a central function of any poetic lament or obituary. Johnson's accusations of lack of true feeling were levelled

13. E. K., Dedicatory Epistle to *The Shepheardes Calender*, 1579.

not only against *Lycidas*, but against the whole pastoral rationale. He accepted formality but barred its more artificial variants; and in denying the susceptibility of emotion to this kind of detachment, he was denying part of the very nature of poetry.

Again, Milton the scholar threaded pastoral into *L'Allegro* and *Il Penseroso*, and more openly into his masque, *Comus*. But *Lycidas* remains the last major reworking of a classical model in an age which had steeped itself in traditional sources. Milton's other use of the genre had that coldness with which Keats upbraided the Grecian urn. Only Marvell, and to a lesser extent Herrick, Carew and their minor contemporaries, were again to write purely pastoral verse before its stylized re-emergence among the Romantics and Victorians. The early seventeenth century saw the final reworkings of the pastourelle, in its most elegant form, a basis for suave love lyrics which nevertheless could recall the glazed eyes and general mindlessness of Theocritus' lovers, for all the beauty of their sentiments. In *The Mower Against Gardens*, and the great *Garden* itself, Marvell distils the point at which pastoral loses its own nature and is absorbed into the vastly more substantial world of the metaphysical poets.

The increasing use of pastoral in drama has its finest, if most oblique, expression in several of Shakespeare's plays, most importantly in *As You Like It*. The Forest of Arden, where Duke Senior and his men 'fleet the time carelessly, as they did in the golden world', becomes the focus for various sides of the conflict between court and country (especially the superb dialectic between Touchstone and Corin) and love is seen on four ascending pastoral planes. Implicit in the Duke's residence in the forest is an eventual return to court, for which he and his men are re-equipped by the appreciation of pastoral values they acquire. Many of his speeches (of the winter wind: 'This is no flattery: these are counsellors / That feelingly persuade me what I am')[14] amount to an exegesis of pastoral concepts. Only Touchstone and Jacques remain in the forest; the one, despite his early protestations, to satisfy

14. Shakespeare, *As You Like It*, II, i, 10–11.

straightforward country lusts, the other to pursue his eccentric brand of mystical inquiry. The play hinges on the redeeming effect forest life has on Senior and his men, so that the problems of civilized life – here, of court society – are classically resolved by reference to the pastoral code, not by total immersion in it.

Shakespeare's other employment of pastoral, with the important exception of *Venus and Adonis*, has more of his personal stamp upon it, particularly among the ideas he gathers in the final plays. The Bohemia sequence in *The Winter's Tale* performs a purifying process akin to that of *As You Like It*, in that the wooing of Perdita by Florizel constitutes a re-wooing of Hermione by Leontes, with the urban intervention of Polixenes as the test of good faith. But here, as in *Cymbeline* and *The Tempest*, pastoral is finally an incidental element, as the issues at stake are of more moment than it can contain.

The rest of Elizabethan drama's encounter with the pastoral was little more than a regrettable, if elegant, flirtation. In *The Sad Shepherd*, Ben Jonson's masque, the pastoral hero becomes Robin Hood, and the evening is spent among exquisitely turned but unfortunately slight Sherwood frivolities.

We have seen the end of the pastoral tradition, traditionally used. The young Pope dallied with it in the enthusiasm of youth, and Dryden characteristically used Theocritus as the springboard for some daring sexuality (see his translations in nn. 73 and 75). But the 'kind' has become obsolete, to be revived only as a curiosity, and here begins the line of poems which, with the disappearance of conventional form, make more and more effective, while cryptic, use of the subject-matter and guiding concepts. Among the formal revivals are Shelley's *Adonais* and Arnold's *Thyrsis*, both products of the Hellenistic age more than their own. Shelley uses the framework for his own rather limp blend of grace and high emotion, and Arnold for a somewhat arch Miltonian revival. Far more successful are the adaptations of pastoral thought to the style of the age, as Keats manages in *Lamia* and Arnold in *The Scholar Gypsy*. Refreshing also are the works where accepted ideas of pastoral are critically used: take, for instance, Arnold's *Bacchanalia* and *Epilogue to Lessing's Laocoon*, or Wordsworth's reflections in the shadow of Helvellyn:

> But lovelier far than this the Paradise
> Where I was rear'd; in Nature's primitive gifts
> Favor'd no less, and more to every sense
> Delicious, seeing that the sun and sky,
> The elements and seasons in their change
> Do find their dearest Fellow-labourer there,
> The heart of Man, a district on all sides
> The fragrance breathing of humanity,
> Man free, man working for himself, with choice
> Of time, and place, and object; by his wants,
> His comforts, native occupations, cares,
> Conducted on to individual ends
> Or social, and still followed by a train
> Unwoo'd, unthought-of even, simplicity,
> And beauty, and inevitable grace.[15]

Soon after this follows the climax of the passage:

> So that we love, not knowing that we love,
> And feel, not knowing whence our feeling comes.

And thereafter begins the famous exegesis of the poet's 'two principles of joy' which amounts to a *locus classicus* for any student of pastoral, with its catalogue of characters and qualities, rejected and preferred, springing from the simple

> Shepherds were the men who pleased me first.

But both periods also have examples of deliberate rejection of pastoral opportunities. Tennyson, for instance, despite a long line of precedents, rejects the pastoral elegy in favour of *In Memoriam*, and no one can regret the decision. The very broadness of the themes made familiar in pastoral poetry leads to a tendency to co-opt poems which really have a very distinct life and purpose, even ethic of their own – Tennyson's *Lotus Eaters*, for instance, or lyrics as distinct as Gray's *Elegy*

15. William Wordsworth, *The Prelude* (1805 text), VIII, 144–58.

in a Country Churchyard and Eliot's *Marina*. This blurring of margins arises from pastoral's pre-emption of rural themes, which for centuries left the poetry of nature and natural objects an obligation to make a conscious break. There are pastoral elements in Blake's juxtaposition of innocence and experience, in the Romantics' correlation of art and nature, in the aestheticism of the pre-Raphaelites, in Yeats' Irish lore, in the poetry of war. But the pastoral presence is of two incomplete kinds: first, the examination of the complex in terms of the simple without the appropriate trappings of the convention; and secondly, the qualitative presence of the kind pastoral supplies to Beethoven's Sixth Symphony or Manet's *Déjeuner sur l'herbe*.

The form has survived in other disciplines – for instance, Picasso's continued use of nymphs, fauns and satyrs, music such as Stravinsky's *Rite of Spring*. Occasionally a literary work will appear which makes modernistic but direct use of a timeless pastoral; but they always appear – as does, for instance, Laurie Lee's *Cider with Rosie* – to be well outside the mainstream of current work, and little to do with the development of any particular genre or school. At its lowest ebb, the pastoral has simply been employed as a familiarly evocative base to which the practitioner adds his own transparent art; the effect, as in Gide's *La Symphonie pastorale*, is one of predictable dilution. In marked contrast are the novels of E. M. Forster, where the pastoral of youth and age, of innocence and corruption, of class-conscious disputes between the thoroughbred countryman and the urban squire, all provide a quite characteristic dimension, most notably in *Maurice*, the 1914 homosexual novel published posthumously in 1971.

It is left to the dilettante poet, the stylist Oscar Wilde, to sound the death-knell of classic pastoral form amid the attitudes of his age. Wilde, with characteristic *suaveté*, bestows a polished villanelle on Theocritus:

> Slim Lacon keeps a goat for thee,
>   For thee the jocund shepherds wait,

> O Singer of Persephone!
> Dost thou remember Sicily?

and discerns the twentieth century's forthcoming rejection of all pastoral values:

> O goat-foot God of Arcady!
> Ah, what remains to us of thee?
>
> Ah, leave the hills of Arcady,
> Thy satyrs and their wanton play,
> This modern world hath need of thee.[16]

If the conventional pastoral is dead in form, it is because its qualities of soul survive, as a necessary adjunct to an art more and more conditioned by the split in society from which pastoral was born. We need more than ever to sing of Galatea now that her beach is being tarmacked over as an international airport. And as the modern artist-critic applies contemporary techniques of analysis to works of every age, and veins of pastoral are struck like gold in the most unlikely quarries, we have conclusive proof that the pastoral ethic is a constituent of the air by which poetry breathes. The distance between pastoral's founding father and the position in which his tradition now finds itself is aptly witnessed in the work of Mr William Empson[17] on the subject, in which he argues the case of pastoral as proletarian literature; for in collating such disparate titles as *Troilus and Cressida*, *The Beggar's Opera* and *Alice in Wonderland* under the heading of pastoral, amid Marxist and Freudian convolutions, he manages to complete an analysis of unique insight without once mentioning the name of Theocritus.

The Translation

The translation is based on the text of A. S. F. Gow (Cambridge University Press, 1950, revised edn 1952) adopting minor variations here and there, mostly recorded in the notes.

16. Oscar Wilde, *Pan*, 18–22.
17. William Empson, *Some Versions of Pastoral*, London, 1935.

Gow's edition is a massive work of scholarship, which has thrown invaluable light on a large number of problems, and made these poets much more accessible to the twentieth-century audience. I have also had frequent recourse to R. J. Cholmeley's 1930 edition, and to J. M. Edmonds' 1912 versions, now sadly dated.

To these, especially Gow, I respectfully refer the reader anxious for more scholarly information than I have been able to provide, notably on points of metre, dialect, sources and authenticity, all of which could only be cursorily discussed in this volume.

Some of the versions I have looked over in the course of my work have attempted to reproduce Theocritus' manifold use of dialect, inevitably with disastrous results. Although characterization from the mouth in this way is an important facet of the poet's technique, it is not one which readily lends itself to a modern English version without distortion, as I have argued (p. 20). I have been content therefore to try and control the colloquial force of the English to match the undulations of the Greek style.

No attempt, obviously, has been made to reproduce any of Theocritus' complex and highly skilled metrical schemes; to try and recreate Greek metres in English is clearly pointless. I have employed a free verse technique, which I hope some readers may sometime take the trouble to try reading aloud. Many of the songs within the poems are in regular metres designed specifically for them; some, notably the epigrams, are in stricter form, mostly pentameters.

The superior figures in the text refer the reader to further details in the Notes. Problems prompted by proper names to which no note is attached may generally be solved by reference to the Glossary, but only if the name has some existence outside the poet's imagination.

Acknowledgements

The fifty-odd months of my life which Theocritus has inhabited pale considerably beside the sixteen and more years

A. S. F. Gow has devoted to the poet; and I suspect the ratio between our contributions is in at least direct proportion. Gow's monumental edition deserves my especial thanks here, for I have leaned on it very heavily.

Mrs Betty Radice, editor of the Penguin Classics, has been a source of constant help and encouragement for which I am most grateful. She was particularly understanding when the theft of some early versions from a friend's car led to a rather protracted delay.

My respectful thanks are also due to the late Sir Maurice Bowra, then Warden of Wadham College, Oxford, for his genial comments on some work he looked over with me; to many friends for listening with patience, but especially to John Morley and John Harrison for sharp criticisms which led to many an improvement; and to Mark, Jane and Amanda for the gift of a first edition of Francis Fawkes's 1767 version of the Idylls, an unfailing *placebo* in darker moments.

Merton College, Oxford,   A. I. H.
1968–
Old Bricket Wood, Hertfordshire,
1972.

THEOCRITUS

The Idylls

1. *Thyrsis' Lament for Daphnis*

THYRSIS
There's subtle music in the whispers of that pine
down by the spring; yet your piping, goatherd,
rivals it. You shall have second prize
to Pan. Should he select as his reward
the he-goat's horns, the she-goat shall be yours;
if he take her, then you shall have her kid.
Kidflesh is good until they come to milking.

GOATHERD
Sweeter, shepherd, and more subtle is your song
than the tuneful splashing of that waterfall
among the rocks. If the Muses pick the ewe
as their reward, you'll win the hand-reared lamb;
if they prefer the lamb, the ewe is yours.

THYRSIS
Come, goatherd, by the Nymphs: please, come sit down
here on this hill, among the tamarisks,
and play for me. I'll watch your goats.

GOATHERD
No, shepherd, no, not I. Not at midday;
I'm afraid of Pan. It's the time he rests,
weary from the hunt. His temper is quick;
fierce anger is always on his breath.
But you, Thyrsis, you used to sing of Daphnis
and his death. In the art of country song
you have no equal. Come then: you sit with me,
here beneath this elm, facing Priapus' stream,
where the shepherds have their seat among the oaks.
And if you sing as you sang that day,

in your contest with Chromis of Libya,
I shall give you a goat to milk three times,
which though it has twins will yield three pails.
And I shall give you a cup, deep, two-handled,
new made, highly polished with perfumed wax,
yet smelling still of the engraver's knife.
Along the lip wind shoots of ivy, rich ivy
with golden leaves, spiralling around itself,
exulting in its yellow fruit. Inside a woman,
a woman worthy of a god, is carved:
she wears a cloak and headdress. On each side
stand two young men who both have fine long hair,
each quarrelling with the other, turn by turn.
But these things do not touch her heart.
For now she turns to him and smiles, and now
to him, while they, both hollow-eyed with love,
still waste themselves away in vain.
Beside them an old fisherman is carved
standing on a jagged rock, gathering his net
for a mighty cast: he struggles hard.
That old man, you'd say, puts all his strength
into his fishing. His hair is grey,
his sinews heave and swell around his neck;
yet his is the strength of a youth in his prime.
Close by that old and weather-beaten man
there is a vineyard, rich, well-stocked
with ripening, reddening bunches: a young boy,
lolling on the wall, keeps watch. On either side
a fox: one ranges up and down among the vines,
rifling the ripest; the other eyes the boy's wallet,
setting his villainous heart upon it,
determined not to let the child alone
until it has deprived him of his breakfast.
This guard, meanwhile, is busy weaving,
threading reeds and rushes, fashioning a trap
for insects. His mind is on his work;
he has no thought of vineyards or of wallets.
And, last, around the cup at every turn

46

supple acanthus winds. It is a sight to see,
to wonder at, to dazzle country eyes.
I paid Calydna's ferryman a goat for it,
and I gave him a giant milk-white cheese,
but never has it come near my lips, never yet:
it lies untouched, immaculate. My friend,
if you will sing that song, it's yours:
and gladly, too. Such beauty would deserve it.
No, no mockery. I mean it. Come, man
surely you don't mean to take your song
to Hades? All is forgotten there.

THYRSIS
Sing, beloved Muses, sing my country song.

I am Thyrsis of Etna, blessed with a tuneful voice.

Where were you, Nymphs, where were you,
where when Daphnis died?
In the valleys of Peneius?
In Pindus' pretty glades?
You were nowhere near Anapus,
nowhere near that mighty tide,
you were not on Etna's summit
nor by Acis' spring.

Sing, beloved Muses, sing my country song.

For him the wolves were howling,
for him the jackals bayed.
When Daphnis died, the lions
of the forest wept.

Sing, beloved Muses, sing my country song.

Great herds of bulls and cattle
were gathered round his feet
with crowds of lowing heifers
and their moaning calves.

Sing, beloved Muses, sing my country song.

47

The first to come was Hermes,   *messenger of the gods,*
Hermes from the hills,   *patron of herdsmen.*
saying, 'Daphnis, who torments you?
Who is it you love?'

Sing, beloved Muses, sing my country song.

Then neatherds, shepherds, goatherds,
came to ask him what was wrong.
And Priapus said, 'Poor Daphnis,   *Son of*
why waste yourself away   *Aphrodite*
when by every glade and fountain
that girl looks for you?'

Sing, beloved Muses, sing my country song.

'Your love is cursed, you're helpless.
You're no herdsman now.
More like a common goatherd   *a jilt?*
who looks with jealous eyes
and who weeps that he is human
when his goats make love.'

Sing, beloved Muses, sing my country song.

'You see the young girls laughing
and you weep more tears
that you can't join their dances . . .'
But answer came there none.
Though the herdsman's love was cruel   *i.e. Daphnis's*
it was bravely borne.   *love.*

Sing, Muses, sing again my country song.

Then Cypris came and smiled   *Aphrodite (so called*
though she raged within.   *because she shines on*
'So mastering love is easy?'   *Cyprus).*
she said. 'Not so it seems.
Have you not yourself been mastered
by that same cruel love?'

Sing, Muses, sing again my country song.

'*Jealous Cypris,*' *Daphnis answered,*
'*hated by mankind,*
so you think my sun is setting,
that my light is nearly spent?
Daphnis even down in Hades
will make war on love.'

i.e. he won't love Br.

Sing, Muses, sing again my country song.

'*Do men not talk of Cypris*
and the herdsman still?[1]
Go, take yourself to Ida,
go see Anchises there.
You'll find oaks, and sedge, and honey-bees
buzzing round their hives.'

Cypris glories and this
(a translation note
only).
another of Aphrodite's
mortal lovers.

Sing, Muses, sing again my country song.

'*Is not Adonis in his heyday?*
Does not he too tend sheep?
He shoots, kills hares, goes hunting
for all kinds of beast.'

lover of Aphrodite
i.e. Summer.

Sing, Muses, sing again my country song.

'*Go, look for Diomedes;*
tell him, "I have won.
I've outdone Daphnis the herdsman.
Now come, fight with me."'

Refers to episode in Bk. 5 of
Iliad — Diomedes attacks
Aphrodite, wounding
her, even though a God.

le Diomedes

Sing, Muses, sing again my country song.

'*Farewell now, wolves and jackals,*
now farewell, mountain bears.
You'll see no more of Daphnis
in your forests or your groves.
Farewell to Arethusa,
and fair Thybris' streams.'

Daphnis.

Sing, Muses, sing again my country song.

'*I am Daphnis, I'm the herdsman,*
I drove cattle here;

here I brought my bulls and heifers
and I watered them.'

Sing, Muses, sing again my country song.

'O Pan, O Pan, where are you?
On Lycaeus' slopes?
On Maenalus? On Helice?
O come to Sicily!
Leave the sacred tomb of Arcas[2]
to the gods' great love.'

Cease, Muses, come cease my country song.

'Come, Pan, my pipe awaits you,
its breath still honey-sweet;
its wax is firm, its binding
still tight around the lip.
Now I am bound for Hades:
Eros calls me there.'

Cease, Muses, come cease my country song.

'May violets grow on thistles,
may they grow on thorns!
May narcissus grow on juniper!
The world must change.
Daphnis dies! Pears grow on pine trees!
Now the deer must chase the hounds,
and the screech-owl's song sound sweeter
than the nightingale's!'

Cease, Muses, come cease my country song.

And with these words, he finished.
He would rise again
if Aphrodite's wish were granted.
But his thread was spun.
Fate took Daphnis to the river;
the waters closed above his head,
took the man the Nymphs had cherished
and the Muses loved.

Cease, Muses, come cease my country song.

Let me have the goat, the pail;
I would milk her now,
make my libation to the Muses,
bid them many times farewell.
In time, I trust, I'll sing you
a less mournful song.

GOATHERD
Sweeten your sweet mouth with honey,
Thyrsis, and with honeycomb. Eat your fill
of Aegilus' finest figs, for your voice
outsings the cricket's. Here is the cup:
smell, friend, its sharp freshness –
you would think it had been dipped
and bathed in the holy well of Hours.
Here, Dusky; she is yours to milk.
You others, stop that frisking,
or you'll get the ram worked up.

Little fond of realism.

II. *The Sorceress*

Where are my bay-leaves? Bring them, Thestylis.
And where are my love-charms? Come,
crown the bowl with purest purple wool
that I may cast a spell on my cruel love
and bind him to me:[3] my harsh love,
who for twelve days now, the wretch,
has not been near me, nor even knows
if I'm alive or dead. Such cruelty!
He hasn't even knocked at my door.
His heart is easily allured; I'm sure
Eros and Aphrodite have made off with it.
Tomorrow I'll go to Timagetus' wrestling school.

Definitely has an amitat.

I'll see him there, and ask him what he means
by treating me like this. I'll tick him off.
But for now I'll bind him with spells of fire.

Moon, shine bright. For I sing to you, goddess,
my soft chants, and to Hecate below,
in whose path even the dogs tremble
as she comes and goes across the graves
of the dead, over their dark blood.
Hail, dread Hecate! Be with me to the end.
Give my drugs the power of Circe's,
or Medea's, or those of golden-haired Perimede.

Draw, magic wheel, draw my man to my home.

First barley glows on the fire. More, Thestylis,
throw more on. Where are you, idiot? Head in the clouds?
Am I to be laughed at by you as well, you wretch?
Scatter them, and chant, 'These are Delphis' bones.'

Draw, magic wheel, draw my man to my home.

Delphis has wounded me. For him I burn these leaves.
As their crackling grows, as they suddenly catch fire
and burn away to nothing, not even an ash left,
so may the flames consume the flesh of Delphis.

Draw, magic wheel, draw my man to my home.

Now for the bran. Artemis, you can move
Hades' adamant, so move all else unmoveable.
The dogs howl, Thestylis, howl around the town;
the goddess is at the crossroads.
Quick, beat the gong.

Draw, magic wheel, draw my man to my home.

The sea is still, still are the winds,
yet the fire in my heart is never stilled.
My whole being is aflame for the man,
the man who has made me a slave,
not a wife, and – to my shame – no virgin now.

II. THE SORCERESS

Draw, magic wheel, draw my man to my home.

As I melt this wax, with the goddess' help,
so may Delphis of Myndus soon melt with love,
and as Aphrodite turns this bronze wheel round
so may Delphis turn and turn at my door.

Draw, magic wheel, draw my man to my home.

I pour three libations, goddess, cry three times:
Whether with woman or man he now share his bed,
may he as utterly forget them as men say
Theseus in Dia forgot fair Ariadne.[4]

Draw, magic wheel, draw my man to my home.

Coltsfoot is an Arcadian herb; all the foals
run mad for it, all the mares around the hills.
So too may Delphis run mad to this house
from the oily sweat of the wrestling school.

Draw, magic wheel, draw my man to my home.

Delphis once lost this fringe from his cloak;
I tear and tear it now in shreds, and throw it
in the flames. Why do you cling to me so,
heartless love, like a leech from the marsh,
sucking me dry of my dark lifeblood?

Draw, magic wheel, draw my man to my home.

I'll boil up a lizard and take him some poison
tomorrow. You, Thestylis, take these herbs
and smear them while it's still dark
round his door; and as you do it, whisper,
'These are the bones of Delphis I smear.'

Draw, magic wheel, draw my man to my home.

How to weep for my love, now I'm alone?
Where to begin? Who has cursed me so?
One day Eubulus' daughter, our own Anaxo,
was taking a basket to Artemis' grove,

53

and in the procession, marching beside her,
were many wild beasts, among them a lioness.

Hear, Holy Moon, how love came to me.

And our next-door neighbour, long since dead,
Theumaridas' Thracian nurse, implored me
to watch them go past. So I went along
in my fine silk dress, with Clearista's shawl
on my shoulders. I should never have gone.

Hear, Holy Moon, how love came to me.

When already halfway along the road,
near Lycon's house, I saw them coming:
Delphis and Eudamippus together.
Their beards shone out more golden than gold,
their breasts brighter, Moon, than even you;
they were fresh from the noble arts of their school.

Hear, Holy Moon, how love came to me.

One look, and I totally lost my mind.
My heart was on fire; great pain already;
the colour quickly drained from my cheeks.
I thought no more about any processions,
nor do I know how I came to get home.
But a fever parched me, my whole frame shivered,
and I lay on my bed ten days and nights.

Hear, Holy Moon, how love came to me.

My skin had turned a deathly yellow,
the hair was all dropping out of my scalp;
there was nothing left of me but skin and bone.
What witch's house did I not then visit,
what hovel, in search of some magic cure?
But it was no slight sickness. And time ran on.

Hear, Holy Moon, how love came to me.

So I told my maid, I told her the truth.
'Come, Thestylis, find me some magic cure

54

for this foul disease. I am utterly his,
and I suffer for it. Go, look for him;
stand guard by Timagetus' wrestling school.
He goes there often to sit and relax.'

Hear, Holy Moon, how love came to me.

'And when you're sure that he's quite alone,
beckon him secretly, tell him I call
and bring him here.' That's what I said.
So she went, and she led him to my house,
his skin still oiled. The moment I sensed
his light foot stepping through my door . . .

Hear, Holy Moon, how love came to me.

. . . I turned colder than snow from head to foot;
I began to sweat, my brow damp as dew;
I could speak not a word, not even the sob
of a sleeping child as it calls on its mother.
My whole fair frame went as stiff as a doll's.

Hear, Holy Moon, how love came to me.

When he saw me, the faithless man,
he looked away, turned his eyes to the ground,
and sat on my bed, saying, 'Simaetha,
I was coming, believe me, when you called.
Your message beat my arrival by no more
than I outran young Philinus the other day.'

Hear, Holy Moon, how love came to me.

'I would have come; by sweet Love, I would,
as soon as night fell, with two or three friends,
bringing Dionysus' apples in my robe for you,
with Heracles' sacred shoots whitening my brow,
wreathed all around with purple bands.'

Hear, Holy Moon, how love came to me.

'Had you taken me in, we would surely have shared
a mutual joy, for my good looks, my grace,

55

are both well known around this town.
Had I kissed your pretty lips, I'd have slept in bliss.
But if you'd barred your doors, if driven me away,
I'd have been back with lights and axes against you.'

Hear, Holy Moon, how love came to me.

'But I'm here. And first my thanks are due
to Cypris; then, lady, to you, who snatched me –
all but consumed – from the furnace. For often love
can burn a flame fiercer than fire itself.'

Hear, Holy Moon, how love came to me.

'His fits of madness are known to drive virgins
from their inner rooms, to frighten brides
out of their husband's still warm bed.'

He stopped speaking and I, I as always
too gullible, took hold of his hand,
and pulled him down on my soft, soft bed.
Flesh quickly warmed to flesh; our cheeks
grew flushed; we whispered sweet nothings.
Good Moon, I shan't labour it: soon we made love;
it was good; our every desire was fulfilled.
He found no fault in me, nor I in him:
till yesterday. But now, today, as rosy Dawn
was carried by her horses from the sea,
the mother of Melixo and of Philista,
our flute-player, came and told me –
with many other things – that Delphis was in love.
Whether with woman or man she wasn't sure;
she only knew of his desire. And that he drank,
day and night, to Love, in unmixed wine,
and then at length would rush out, run off
shouting, to smother his beloved's house in flowers.
Her tongue wagged, that gossip, but I'm sure
it's true. For he used to come and see me
three, four times a day, and he'd often leave
his Dorian flask with me. But now it's been

twelve days since I so much as glimpsed him.
He's in love with another, it is clear. I am forgotten.

So now I will bind him with my love charms.
But if he goes on making me suffer,
by the Fates, he'll knock at the doors of hell for it.
Such, Lady Moon, is the power for evil
of the many drugs I keep in this chest;
an Assyrian stranger taught me the art.
But now farewell, turn your horses to the sea;
I'll endure my desire as I have till now.
Farewell, holy Moon, on your shining throne;
and farewell, all you other stars, clustered around
the chariot of tranquil night, fare you well.

III. *The Serenade*

I'm off to serenade Amaryllis.
Tityrus grazes my goats on the hill.
Feed them, good Tityrus, lead them to water.
And watch that ram, the yellow Libyan,
or he'll be butting you.

My Amaryllis, my beauty, why can it be
you no longer seek me out from your cave
and call me in? Me, your lover?
Do you hate me? Or is it, perhaps,
at closer range, I seem snub-nosed?
My chin's too long? I'll hang myself,
for you one day. I will, I know.
I've brought you, see, ten apples,
picked just where you asked me;
tomorrow I promise I'll fetch you some more.
But look, I'm in pain. My heart's in a turmoil.
How I wish I were that buzzing bee
that I might so easily fly into your cave

57

through the ivy and fern you hide behind.
Now I know Love. He's a formidable god.
A lioness suckled him, brought him up
deep in the woods. And now I'm tortured
to the very bones by his slow fires.
Your bewitching glances are solid stone,
my Nymph, my love, my dark-browed beauty;
come to my arms, your goatherd's arms,
for he longs, he longs to give you his kiss.
Even in empty kisses there is fond delight.
You will make me tear this garland to pieces,
Amaryllis, my love, this crown I made you
of ivy, of rosebuds and sweet celery.
What lies ahead for me? What but pain?
You are deaf to my every complaint.
At the cliff where Olpis the fisherman
watches for tunny, I shall bare my back
and throw myself off into the waves:
if I die, you at least will be satisfied.

   It was not long ago I learnt the truth.
You were on my mind; I was wondering
if you loved me, so I slapped the leaf
of love-in-absence firmly on my arm[5] –
but no, it didn't stick; uselessly
it shrivelled up on my smooth skin.
Agroeo, too, the prophet of the sieve,
told me a truth the other day
as we were harvesting side by side:
I loved you, she said, with all my heart,
but you took not a moment's notice of me.
Look, I've kept you a snow-white goat,
with two kids, which Memnon's dusky girl
keeps asking for. And she shall have them
since you persist in showing me such disdain.

   My right eye twitched.[6] Can she be coming?
I'll lean here, beneath this pine, awhile,
and sing for her. Perhaps she'll notice me;
she cannot be made all of adamant.

58

Hippomenes, to win his bride,
dropped apples as he ran.
Atalanta saw, was overcome,
fell deep in love with him.

From Othrys down to Pylus
wise Melampus drove his herd.
Alphesiboa's mother thus
fell into Bias' arms.

Adonis, as he grazed his sheep,
drove Cytherea mad
with love, and even as he died
she held him to her breast.

I would I were Endymion
who sleeps unending sleep,
or Iasion, whose luck, my love,
you profane may never know.

My head aches, but that's nothing to you.
I will sing no more. I'll just lie here,
here where I've fallen, till the wolves devour me.
Let's hope you'll find that as sweet as honey.

IV. *The Herdsmen*

BATTUS
Tell me, Corydon, whose are these cows? Philonda's?

CORYDON
No, they're Aegeon's. He gave me them to graze.

BATTUS
And at evening, I suppose, you milk them on the quiet?

59

CORYDON
No, the old boy keeps an eye on me.
He puts the calves to their mother's teats himself.

BATTUS
But where has he disappeared, their herdsman?

CORYDON
Didn't you hear? Milon took him off to the Alpheus.

BATTUS
Him? He wouldn't know olive-oil if he smelt it.

CORYDON
They say he's a match for mighty Heracles.

BATTUS
And my old mother would say I could beat Polydeuces.

CORYDON
Well, he took a spade and twenty sheep with him.[7]

BATTUS
Milon might as well have coaxed a pack of wolves to run
    amuck.[8]

CORYDON
And his heifers miss him. Just listen to that row!

BATTUS
Poor brutes! Some herdsman they've got themselves.

CORYDON
Poor brutes is right. They've gone right off their food.

BATTUS
Just look at that calf. All skin and bone.
Perhaps, like a cricket, she lives on dewdrops?

CORYDON
God, no. Sometimes I graze her by the Aesarus,
and give her a great bundle of fresh hay;
sometimes she plays around in Latymnum's shade.

BATTUS
That bull's so thin – the reddish one.
I'd wish it on the sons of Lampriadas[9]
when they sacrifice to Hera for their town.
That place is full of no-goods.

CORYDON
And yet I take it down to the salt lake,
to Physcus' fields, sometimes to the Neaethus
with its buckwheat, its fleabane,
its fragrant balm – a right old cornucopia.

BATTUS
Well, Aegeon, it's all your own fault.
Your cattle will die off, every last one,
as you thirst for victory and its corruption.
The pipe you made yourself is mildewed.

CORYDON
No it's not, by the Nymphs. Not so;
he left it me, a gift, as he set off to Pisa.
I'm a bit of a singer myself, you know.
I can give you Pyrrhus' songs, or Glauce's . . .

*Croton's a fine town,
as fair as Zacynthus;
the Lacinian shrine
faces out to the East;
there Aegon the boxer
devoured eighty loaves,
took the bull by the hoof,
led it down from the hill
for the fair Amaryllis:
the women they screamed
and the herdsman he laughed.*

BATTUS

Ah, the fair Amaryllis. Dead though you are,
I'll never forget you. You're the only one.
I loved you once, as now I love my goats;
then you left us. Cruel, cruel indeed
is the hand which guides my life.

CORYDON

Cheer up, Battus, old friend. There's always tomorrow.
Where there's life there's hope;
only the dead are without it.
All will always be as Zeus decides:
rain one day, blue sky the next.

BATTUS

I'm all right –
quick, get the calves up out of there.
They're chewing the olive shoots, the bastards.

CORYDON

Hey, Daisy! Fatty! Up the hill! Get up!
Are you deaf? If you don't get out of there,
by Pan, you'll come to a sticky end.
Just look at that: sneaking back again.
My god, if I had my knotted club,
I'd fetch you such a . . .

BATTUS

God! Corydon, look at this!
This thorn just got me in the ankle.
How thick these thistles are!
Damn that heifer. It was gawping at that
made this happen. Can you see it?

CORYDON

Yes . . . yes . . . and I've got it
with my nails. Here it is!

BATTUS
Can a wound that small have tamed a man like me?

CORYDON
When you walk around the hills,
don't go barefoot, Battus.
There are thorns and brambles everywhere.

BATTUS
Tell me, Corydon:
does the old boy still lay
that dark-browed little piece he fell for?

CORYDON
He does indeed, my friend.
Just the other day, by chance,
I caught them at it in the stable.

BATTUS
Good for him, the old lecher!
That family's not far behind
the satyrs and the spindly Pans.

v. *The Goatherd versus the Shepherd*

COMATAS (the goatherd)
Beware of that shepherd over there, the Sybarite, my goats:
it's Lacon. He pinched my fleece-coat yesterday.

i.e. slave of Sibyrtas

LACON (the shepherd).
Get out of that stream! Out, my lambs! Can't you see,
it's Comatas, who nicked my pipe last week.

COMATAS

Pipe? What pipe? Can you, Sibyrtas' slave,
possess a pipe? You that, like Corydon, were content
to hoot on an old straw whistle all day?

LACON

My pipe was given me by Lacon, knowall.
And what's this fleece-coat, tell me now,
that I'm supposed to have pinched? When did Eumaras,
your master, ever sleep in one – let alone his slave?

COMATAS

The dappled one, given me by Crocylus,
when he sacrificed that she-goat to the Nymphs.
You were green with envy at the time, you shark,
and now you've gone and left me naked.

LACON

No, never, by Pan of the shore, never did Lacon,
son of Calaethis, pinch any coat of yours.
No, my friend, not I; or may I run amuck
and throw myself from that cliff into the Crathis.

COMATAS

Nor I, my friend, by these Nymphs of the lake,
no, nor I. As I pray for their mercy and help,
never did Comatas make off with any pipe of yours.

LACON

May I die like Daphnis if I take your word for it.
But this is child's play. Come, bet me a goat,
and we'll have a singing match till you call halt.

COMATAS

Well, a pig once challenged Athena, I suppose.
My bet is laid. Your turn. Come,
stake me some fine fat lamb against it.

V. THE GOATHERD VERSUS THE SHEPHERD

LACON

You sly old fox! What kind of match is that?
Who'd shear hair instead of wool?
Who'd milk a dry bitch before a suckling goat?

COMATAS

He that's as sure of victory as you, a wasp
buzzing against a cricket. But since my kid,
it seems, is second best, I'll lay this billy-goat.
Now let battle commence. You first.

LACON

Keep calm. You're not on fire. You'll sing much better
if you relax here among these trees, beneath this olive.
There's that cool waterfall nearby. Here's grass
for us to lie on, and here the locusts chatter.

COMATAS

I'm perfectly calm, thank you. It saddens me,
that's all, that you – my pupil since your childhood –
dare look me in the face like that and challenge me.
But that's how kindness has always been rewarded;
nurse wolf cubs, puppies, and they grow up to bite you.

LACON

When have I heard, when learnt, from you
a single worthwhile word? I don't remember it.
This is plain envy, sheer spite. Typical!

COMATAS

When I bugger you, you'll feel it. Your she-goats
will bleat, and your rams will screw them.

LACON

May you be buried no more deeply than you bugger,
you old hump-back.[10] You just come here now,
and you'll sing in your last country match.

COMATAS

No, I'll not go there. Here are oaks, and sedge,
here bees hum happily round their hives.
Here are two cool springs of water; here birds
chirrup on the trees; and the shadows here, by me,
are far more cool than yours. What's more,
this pine here is dropping cones everywhere.

LACON

Come here, and you'll walk on lambskins,
on sheep's wool softer than sleep.
Your goatskins there reek even worse than you do.
Here I'll set up for the Nymphs a big bowl
of pure milk, and one of fragrant oil.

COMATAS

If you come here, you'll walk on tender ferns,
on flowering pennyroyal. You'll lie back
on goatskins four times as soft as your fleeces.
Here I'll set up for Pan eight pails of milk,
eight pots filled with brimming honeycombs.

LACON

Well, you stay where you are, for all I care.
You sing from there then. Walk your own path.
And you can keep your oaks. But who, tell me,
who shall be our judge? If only Lycopas,
the herdsman, were in sight somewhere.

COMATAS

Who needs Lycopas? I'll tell you what:
we could call that man, that woodcutter,
who's picking heather over there near you.
It's Morson.

        LACON

        Yes, let's call him.

                COMATAS

                Go on then.

66

LACON

Hey, friend, come here and lend us your ears,
just for a while. We two have a match on,
to see who's the better singer of country song.
Now be just, good Morson. Show me no favour;
and don't look too generously on Comatas.

COMATAS

Yes, that's right, Morson, by the Nymphs.
No bias towards Comatas, no overrating Lacon.
This flock here belongs to Sibyrtas of Thurii,
and these goats, friend, to Eumaras of Sybaris.

LACON

My God, who cares? Who's asking, idiot,
if they belong to Sibyrtas? Or me? You do go on.

COMATAS

My dear man, every word I speak is true.
I'm no braggart. It's you that picks the quarrels.

LACON

Right, you've said your piece. Let's leave it at that.
Our friend here wants to get home in one piece.
My God, Comatas, you've got a big mouth.

COMATAS

The Muses love me more
than Daphnis, with his voice.
I killed two goats for them the other day.

LACON

Apollo, too, loves me.
This fattened ram's for him.
His autumn festival will soon come round.

COMATAS

My she-goats, all save two,
have twins. They're full of milk.
The milkmaid said, 'Poor man, you work alone?'

LACON
While Lacon here, alas!
fills twenty kegs of cheese,
And shags his pretty boy among the flowers.

COMATAS
But watch Clearista throw
sweet apples at her man
and blow him kisses as he passes by.

LACON
I'm driven nearly mad
by Cratidas, running
to meet his man, his hair gold on his neck.

COMATAS
Anemones and thorns
may never match the rose,
the dog-rose in the shadow of the wall.

LACON
And acorn-husk falls short
of wild apple's taste;
the one is sour, the other honey-sweet.

COMATAS
Soon I shall catch a dove
and give it to my girl,
the ring-dove nesting in that juniper.

LACON
And when I shear my ewe
I'll take its soft, black fleece
and give it to my sweet boy as a cloak.

COMATAS
Hey, come away, my kids!
That olive's not for you!
Graze on this slope among the tamarisks.

V. THE GOATHERD VERSUS THE SHEPHERD

LACON
Hey, Daisy, over here!
Now, Primrose, leave that oak!
Feed here, towards the east, where Dapple is.

COMATAS
I have a cypress pail
I'm keeping for my girl,
and a bowl – both fashioned by Praxiteles.

LACON
And I've a hunting dog
that slaughters sheep and wolves:
it's for my love, to chase his wild beasts.

COMATAS
Off, locusts, get away,
stop jumping my yard wall;
my vines are dry, so leave the stems alone.

LACON
Look, crickets, do you see
how angry I've made him?
Just so, I'll bet, you drive the reapers mad.

COMATAS
I hate the bush-tailed fox
who sneaks down every night
and plunders Micon's vineyard after dark.

LACON
It's beetles I can't stand:
they scoff Philonda's figs
and make their getaway on wings of wind.

COMATAS
Don't tell me you've forgotten
when I got you on the ground
and you raped me blissfully against the oak?

LACON

I don't remember that.
But I won't forget the day
Eumaras tied you up and flogged you here.

to curl
bite!

COMATAS

Now, Morson, can you see?
Is someone getting wild?
Dig up some witch's grave and get him squills.[11]

This is clearly convincing
too insulting by
Comatas—
reminds
him of his
slave status

Temper

LACON

I, too, have someone riled,
as, Morson, you perceive.
Run to the Haleis, fetch him cyclamen.

COMATAS

Himera, flow with milk,
and you, Crathis, with wine,
grow red, and may your reeds blossom with fruit.

milk
&
Honey

LACON

Grant Sybaris honey streams,
and may my love, at dawn,
draw honeycombs, not water, in her urn.

COMATAS

I feed my goats on clover
and all their favourite herbs.
They walk on moss, sleep deep in strawberries.

Diet
of
animals

LACON

My flock of sheep, meanwhile,
may eat their fill of balm;
for them, the rock rose grows abundantly.

COMATAS

Alcippa did not kiss me
or take me by the ears
when I gave her that dove. I love her not.

Love.

VI. THE SINGING MATCH

LACON
But I love Eumedes.
When I gave him his pipe,
he kissed me very sweetly, tenderly.

COMATAS
Hoopoes can't challenge swans,
nor magpies nightingales,
but you, poor fool, just love to pick a fight.

MORSON
I bid the shepherd cease. To you, Comatas,
Morson awards the lamb. When you offer it
to the Nymphs, be sure to send him a good piece.

COMATAS
I will indeed, by Pan. Now snort away, my goats,
to all your hearts' content. I've got the last laugh,
and what a laugh, over this shepherd here.
In the end it's I that have won the lamb.
I could touch the stars. Things are looking up,
my goats, and tomorrow I'll wash you in the lake.
  Hey you, that ram there, Whitey:
if you so much as touch any of these she-goats
before I've made my offering to the Nymphs,
I'll geld you. Look, he's at it again!
If I don't have your balls, I'll have my own![12]

VI. *The Singing Match*

Damoetas and Daphnis the cowherd, Aratus,
once met with their herds in one place.
One's beard was red, the other's half-grown.
And side by side they sat down near a stream.
The day was hot, the time was noon,

71

and they began to sing. Daphnis was first,
for it was he had issued the challenge.

Polyphemus, Polyphemus, Galatea pelts your sheep
with apples, calls you names, like Goatherd,
says that you are cursed in love.
And you, poor fool, poor fool, just sit there,
piping sweetly, beautifully,
but never looking up at her.
See there, again, she's hit your sheepdog,
he that shadows you, that guards
your flock. Look how he gazes out to sea
and barks at her. See how he's mirrored
in the handsome waves, lapping gently
on the sand where he runs. Beware, beware!
He'll jump at her as she leaves the water,
jump at her and tear her flesh,
her exquisite flesh. Even from there
she flirts with you, beguiles, arouses.
Wanton woman! Wanton as thistledown,
thistle parched dry by the hot summer air,
she runs when you love her, pursues you
when you don't, leaves no move unmade,
keeps you in check. For often in love,
Polyphemus, Polyphemus, often in love,
all that's foul seems most fair.

Then Damoetas took up the song in reply:

I watched her, by Pan, as she pelted the sheep.
Nothing escaped me, not my one sweet eye,
with which I hope to see till my end:
may Telemus the seer inherit the curse
he's predicted for me, he and his children.
And I myself, to tease her back,
never give her a glance, keep assuring her
there are other women to be wed. It works:
she's driven almost mad, by Apollo, jealous of me!
From the sea she watches, her eyes seeking out

72

my caves, my flocks. It was I persuaded the dog
to bark. For when I used to go wooing her,
he would lay his head in her lap, and whine.
If she sees me keeping this up, I reckon
she'll send to me. But I'm shutting my door
till she swears to marry me, to make my bed
on this island herself. I know what they say,
but I'm not bad looking. I glanced in the sea
in a moment of calm, and knew what I saw
was a manly beard, a clear single eye,
and teeth gleaming brighter than Parian marble.
To scotch the envious sea-spirits' curse
I spat three times upon my breast,[13]
as the witch Cotyttaris taught me.

Damoetas' song was finished. He kissed Daphnis,
and gave him a pipe. Daphnis returned a pretty flute.
Damoetas then began to play, Daphnis to pipe,
and the calves at once to dance in the grass.
Neither was the victor; both had proved supreme.

VII. *The Harvest Feast*

Eucritus, once, and I were walking from town
down to the Haleis; Amyntas made us three.
We were going to a harvest feast for Deo
held by Phrasidamus and Antigenes,
sons of Lycopeus, born if ever any were
of an illustrious line, from Clytia and Chalcon:
the very Chalcon who set his knee against the rock
and brought Burina forth, springing at his feet,
watering elms and poplars, spreading their shade
over the holy place, a vaulted leaf-green roof.
Before we were even half-way there,
before Brasilas' tomb had come into view,

we met another traveller, a man of Cydonia,
and by the Muses, the best of companions.
His name was Lycidas; he was a goatherd.
Just one look, and there was no mistaking that:
before all else, he was every inch goatherd.
He wore on his shoulders a heavy goatskin,
shaggy, brownish, and reeking of goatsmilk;
across his chest was an ample belt
holding together his timeworn shirt;
his right hand carried a wild-olive crook.
He smiled at me quietly, a glint in his eye,
and with laughter on his lips he asked:
'Where are you headed this heat of noon?
Even the lizard sleeps in his wall, Simichidas,[14]
and you won't see the crested lark on the wing.
Is it some banquet you're bidden to,
or some citizen's cellar, that you're in such a rush?
The pebbles sing as your shoe sends them flying.'
'Lycidas,' I replied, 'dear friend, it is said
that you outplay all herdsmen, all reapers,
when it comes to the flute. And I'm always pleased
to hear it said; it warms me to the heart.
Yet I flatter myself I could give you a match.
We're on our way to a harvest feast:
some friends of ours are holding a banquet
for well-dressed Demeter, loading her with first-fruits,
for she has filled their threshing-floor high,
the goddess, with rich abundance of barley-grain.
But the day and the journey are ours to share,
so come, let's sing a country song,
and maybe each shall learn from the other.
For the Muse has smiled on my voice, too;
I'm always hailed as the best of singers.
But I'm not so fast, by Zeus, to agree;
I reckon I'm still no musical match
for Sicelidas of Samos, or for Philitas:
I rival them as a frog a cricket.'
I said it to make him accept my challenge.

The goatherd replied, with a friendly laugh,
'I give you my stick. For you are a sapling,
fashioned by Zeus in the shape of truth.
I hate the builder who tries to raise
his roof as high as Oromedon's peak
no less than I hate those cocks who strut
in the Muses' yard, wretchedly trying
to match Chios' nightingale[15] with their crows.
But come, Simichidas, no more delay;
let's begin our country song, and I . . .
see if you like this little tune;
I wrote it the other day in the hills.

'*Though now the Kids stand in the western sky*
and southern winds fan up a heavy sea,
Ageanax shall have an easy passage to Mitylene.
Let Orion brood over the deep, if only Lycidas
be preserved from death in Aphrodite's fires;
for my love of him consumes me in its heat.
The Halcyons[16] shall calm the ocean's waves,
the south wind, and the east stirring its depths —
the Halcyons, before all other birds
the favourites of the sea-green Nereids.
May fortune speed Ageanax' intent
to sail to Mitylene, see him safely there.
When that day comes, I'll crown myself with dill,
with roses and with snowdrops. I'll lay me down
and drink a Ptelean wine beside the fire;
I'll have some chestnuts roasted. On my couch,
quite elbow-deep in fleabane I'll lie back,
amid asphodel and parsley, richly curled.
I'll toast Ageanax in style; with every drop
I'll think of him, and drain it to the lees.
Two shepherds then shall play their pipes for me:
one from Acharnae, one Lycopian.
And Tityrus, beside me, will sing songs
of Daphnis and his love for Xenea;
and of the weeping of the hills around

and of the oaks which sang a dirge for him
beside Himeras' waters, while he lay,
pining, melting away like mountain snow
on high Haemus, on Athos, Rhodope,
on distant Caucasus. And he shall sing
of that malicious tyrant, profane man,
who once locked up a goatherd in a chest,[17]
and how the snub-nosed bees flew from the fields
to the cask of cedarwood, and fed him flowers
because the Muse had blessed his lips with nectar.
Ah, you knew joy that day, my Comatas!
Shut in that chest and fed on honeycomb,
it was a long, laborious year for you!
Oh, that you were living now, in my time!
I could have herded your fine goats with mine
along the hills, and listened to your voice,
as you lay down beneath the oaks or pines
and sang the songs that made you, Comatas, divine!'

His song was ended. 'Lycidas, my friend,' I said,
'the Nymphs have taught me too to sing
many such songs, as I've kept my herd on the hills,
fine songs, which fame perhaps has carried as far
even as the throne of Zeus; but of them all,
this is the best, this with which I honour you.
So listen now, as befits one loved by the Muses.

'*The Loves have sneezed on poor Simichidas.*[18]
The wretch loves Myrto as his goats the spring.
But it's a boy Aratus loves: he pines,
my dearest friend, he aches for him.
Aristis knows – this prince, this best of men,
whom even Phoebus would stand by and hear,
by his own tripods, as he played his lyre –
Aristis knows how deep in love he is,
just how his heart is burning for this boy.
O Pan, ruler of Homole's handsome plain,
Pan, bring this boy, unbidden, to his arms,
to those dear arms, whoever he may be,

whether baby Philinus or any other.
Do this, dear Pan, and may the Arcadian boys
never more chastise you with their squills
when they're underfed ;[19] *may they spare your back,*
your arms. But if you won't, may nettles be your bed,
and may you scratch yourself from head to foot,
be bitten all over. And when winter comes,
may you be high and dry on Hebrus' banks,
close by the Bear, among the Edonian hills ;
in summer, may you have to herd your flock
among the far-flung Ethiopians
beyond the Blemyan rock, past which the Nile
is no more seen. Now come away, sweet Loves,
blushing like rosy apples, come away,
leave Hyetis, leave Byblis' peaceful streams,
leave Oecus, golden-haired Dione's high domain,
and aim your bows at pretty Philinus,
shoot, wound that cruel little child for me,
for he will take no pity on my friend.
Now, truly, he is riper than a pear,
and all the women say, "Ah, Philinus,
you'll lose your lovely bloom. It falls away."
Let's watch no more, Aratus, at his gate,
stop wearing out our feet. Let someone else
be crowed at, shivering, by the morning cock ;
let someone else, let Molon, take the falls.
Heaven grant us peace of mind, and some old witch
to spit on us and keep all harm at bay.'

My song was done. Lycidas, laughing lightly as before,
gave me his stick to pledge our friendship in the
  Muse.
He turned off left, taking the road to Pyxa,
but Eucritus and I, with young Amyntas,
headed on toward Phrasydamus' place;
there we threw ourselves down on deep and fragrant
  rush-beds,

rejoiced among the newly gathered vine-shoots.
Tall elms and poplars murmured in profusion overhead;
near by, the sacred water from the Nymphs' own cave
bubbled up and sparkled; among the shady branches,
inky crickets chattered busily; far away,
the tree-frog's croak was muffled in deep thistledown.
Larks and linnets made their song, the dove his moan,
bees hummed and hovered round the springs.
The harvest's richest smells were everywhere;
the air was filled with fruit-time's fragrance.
Pears lay round our feet, apples by our side,
rolling in abundance; wild plums in bunches
weighed the boughs right down to the ground.
We broke the wine-jars' four-year seals.
Nymphs of Castalia, high on Parnassus' slopes,
was it quite such a vintage as this
old Chiron poured for Heracles in Pholus' rocky cave?
Was it quite such nectar had Polyphemus dancing
around his folds by the Anapus? Polyphemus the shepherd,
the mighty man who heaved mountains at ships?
Say, Nymphs, was either quite such a drink
as you served for us from your spring that day
by the shrine of Demeter of the Threshing-Floor?
I pray that I may one day plant again
the great winnowing fork in her heap of corn
as the goddess smiles her blessing on us,
with wheatsheaves and poppies in either hand.

VIII. *The Second Singing Match*

Menalcas was once herding his flocks, they say,
across the long hills, when he met fair young Daphnis,
who grazed his cattle there. Both were red-haired,
both mere boys; both had fine voices, and played well.

Menalcas saw the other first, and called:
'Daphnis, keeper of those mooing cattle,
will you sing with me? I bet I'd win,
no matter how many songs we decide on.'[20]
'Menalcas, shepherd of those shaggy sheep,'
Daphnis replied, 'you're just a piper.
You'd never beat me even if you strained a muscle
    singing.'

MENALCAS
Shall we see then? Will you make a bet?

DAPHNIS
Yes, we'll see. Let's agree a bet.

MENALCAS
What shall we stake? What's big enough?

DAPHNIS
I'll stake a calf. And you a pedigree lamb.[21]

MENALCAS
No, not a lamb. My father's very strict,
my mother too. They count the flock each night.

DAPHNIS
What then? What shall the victor win?

MENALCAS
I have a pipe I made myself, the very best,
with nine stops, well waxed at top and bottom.
I'll stake that. But nothing of my father's.

DAPHNIS
Why, I too have a nine-stop pipe,
also well waxed above and below.

I made it recently. Look, my finger
is still sore, where a reed split and cut me.

MENALCAS
But who'll be judge? Who'll hear us sing?

DAPHNIS
Look, there's a goatherd – see his spotted dog
barking round his kids. Let's call him.

And the boys shouted. The goatherd looked up,
and came over. They were ready to sing, and he
to judge between them. So they drew lots;
first to sing was lusty-voiced Menalcas; then,
in his turn, Daphnis took up the country song.
This was how Menalcas began:

MENALCAS
Come woods, come rivers, heavenly race,[22]
if you've ever liked Menalcas' songs,
then feed his lambs. If Daphnis comes,
may his heifers, too, be fed.

DAPHNIS
Come streams, come meadows, sweeter ground,
if Daphnis sings like the nightingale,
fatten his herd. If Menalcas comes,
may his sheep find pasture here.

MENALCAS
There sheep, there goats bear twins ; and there
the hives are full, the oaks grow tall:
where Milon walks. If he depart,
both man and earth grow dry.[23]

DAPHNIS
Here's Spring ; there's pasture ; everywhere
teats flow with milk, the young grow strong:

where Naïs walks. If she depart,
both man and beast decay.

MENALCAS
Go, he-goat, husband of the ewe,
to the forest's depths – Snubnose, come here –
go, hornless goat, tell Milon there:
'Proteus the god kept seals.'[24]

DAPHNIS
[*This verse is missing from the text.*]

MENALCAS
Neither Pelop's land, nor Croesus' wealth
do I desire, nor the speed of the wind,
but to sing with you beneath this rock,
watch the ocean and my sheep.

DAPHNIS
As storms to trees, and drought to streams
are death, traps to birds and nets to beasts,
so love of women kills men. Great Zeus,
I love them ; so do you.

When the boys had sung in turn awhile,
Menalcas began the last refrain:

MENALCAS
Spare my kids, wolf, spare my goats ;
and spare me too, though I am small,
and one above so many.

Lampurus, my dog, do you sleep?
And soundly? Guard-dogs shouldn't rest
when the shepherd's just a boy.

Feed, my sheep. Come, don't hold back.
The grass is soft, and it'll grow
again before you're tired.

Feed on, feed, fill your udders full,
that the lambs may drink ; and with the rest
I'll stock the cheese kegs up.

Then Daphnis' clear voice closed their song:

DAPHNIS
A dark-browed girl said yesterday
as I drove my cattle past her cave,
'How fine, how fine he is.'

I didn't answer her, not I,
or tease her back ; I just looked down,
and went upon my way.

I love the heifer's voice, her breath,
both sweet to me. In summer I love
to sleep beside a stream.

As oak needs acorn, king needs crown,
as tree needs fruit, and cow needs calf,
so the herdsman needs his herd.

The boys' song was finished. And the goatherd said:

'Your lips are lovely, Daphnis, and your voice
exquisite. I would rather hear you sing
than taste sweet honey. The pipe is yours.
Take it, for you have won this match.
And if as we go herding together
you'd teach me too to sing,
I'd pay for my lessons – you'd have that goat,
the one which always overflows the pail.'

Daphnis rejoiced in his victory, and clapped
his hands, and jumped for joy, as a fawn
skips round her mother. But Menalcas
was downcast, his heart heavy with grief,
as a virgin when she's wed. And from that day
Daphnis was reckoned the greatest of herdsmen;
while still a boy, he married the nymph Naïs.

IX. *The Third Singing Match*

Daphnis, sing a country song. You first;
and when you've begun, let Menalcas follow.
Put the calves beneath the cows, the bulls
among the barren heifers. Let them graze together,
let them wander at will among the leaves,
never straying away. Sing me country songs
from your side; let Menalcas answer from his.

DAPHNIS
The calf's is a fine voice,
and fine is the cow's,
fine is the tune of the herdsman's pipe,
and my song, too, is fine.

I lie by the cool stream
on white skins piled high,
the skins of my heifers, storm-blown from the cliff,
as they grazed on strawberries.

When high summer scorches,
I'm worried as much
as the lover is by his mother's frown
or his father's warning words.

That was Daphnis' song for me. Menalcas followed:

MENALCAS
Etna, my mother,
I too live in a cave,
a comfortable cave in the hollow rocks:
my dreams furnish all my needs.

I have many she-goats
with me, many ewes;

their fleeces lie at my head, at my feet.
I've a fire of dry oak-logs;
on the flames I roast sweetmeats,
chestnuts when it's cold;
I look on winter as the toothless man
on nuts when cakes are by.

I applauded them both, and gave them fine gifts:
for Daphnis, a crook from my father's farm,
cut as it grew, yet as smooth as a craftsman's;
for Menalcas, a shell, a rare one
I'd spotted myself on the Icarian rocks,
sharing its meat among five of us.
Then Menalcas blew a blast on his shell.

Pastoral Muses, all hail! Now grant me
the song I sang that day for those herdsmen;
and stop these blisters growing on my tongue.[25]

As cricket loves cricket,
as ant loves ant,
as hawk is drawn to hawk, I'm in love
with singing, with the Muse.

For sleep's no more welcome,
or sudden spring sun,
flowers give no more delight to the bees:
may music always fill my house.

So my heart is the Muses'.
And those whom they love
are favoured indeed, for they're safe from the spells
of Circe's magic drugs.

x. *The Reapers*

MILON
Bucaeus, what now? What's the matter, man?
You can't drive straight, as once you could;
you can't keep up; the men leave you behind,
as the flock a sheep who's hurt her foot.
What of you this evening? Or in the heat of day,
if now at the start you can't work your row?

BUCAEUS
You're made of rock, Milon, hard and unyielding.
You can reap till night. But did you never,
perhaps, long for someone far away?

MILON
Never. Good workmen think of nothing but their job.

BUCAEUS
Did you never, perhaps, lie awake for love?

MILON
Not I. It's wrong to let a dog taste leather.[26]

BUCAEUS
But I, Milon, I'm in love. Near ten days now.

MILON
Clearly the cask is yours to draw on;
for me the dregs, sour and soon gone.

BUCAEUS
I haven't hoed the ground before my door
since it was sown; and this is why.

MILON
And which girl is it tortures you?

BUCAEUS
Polybotas'. She that played her pipe
for the reapers at Hippocion's that day.

MILON
God finds out sinners.
You've asked for this of old, and now it's yours:
a grasshopper to cuddle you all night.[27]

BUCAEUS
You laugh at me now. But Wealth is not
the only god who's blind. Remember fickle Eros.
And stop this big talk.

MILON
Big talk be damned.
Come, lay your crop aside,
and sing some love song for your girl.
There was a time you used to sing;
that way you'll make light of your work.

BUCAEUS
Pierian Muses, join my hymn to this maiden's grace,
for all that you touch you make lovely.

My beautiful flute-player, Bombyca,
men call you the Syrian,
the slight, the sunburnt,
yet I, I alone, my honey girl.
The violet is dark,
dark the lettered hyacinth,
yet these of all flowers
are counted the first.
As goat pursues clover, as wolf goat,
as crane chases plough, so I,
I for you, am mad.

Ah, if only I had such wealth
as men say Croesus owned!
Then would we both be carved in gold,
and stand in honour of Aphrodite,
you with your pipe, with rosebud or apple,
and I in new robes, new Amyclean shoes.
My beautiful flute-player, Bombyca,
your knuckle-fine feet, your poppy-sweet voice!
My words cannot speak of the charm of your ways.

MILON

A fine singer, and we never knew!
How well he measured out his tune,
what harmony! And look at me:
what has my old man's beard to show?
Well, listen now.
This is the song of bold Lityerses.

Demeter, rich in fruit, in grain,
may this be an easy, a prosperous harvest.
Binders, bind up your sheaves;
let no one say:
'These men are rotten timber.
Their wages go to waste!'
Be sure the crop you've cut lies facing north,
or to the west; thus it will grow more rich.
When threshing, never sleep at noon,
for ear and stalk then part most easily.
When reaping, start with the waking lark,
stop when he sleeps; rest through the heat.
The frog's is a happy life, lads.
He needs no slave to pour his drink:
enough is always by him.
Steward, you're mean. Boil better lentils,
or else you'll cut your hand with cummin-splitting.

Now that's the song for men to sing
as they're busy working in the sun.
You keep your skimpy love, Bucaeus,

tell it to your mother.
Serenade her in the morning
when she's sitting up in bed.

XI. *The Cyclops*

There's nothing else, Nicias,[28] no other cure
for love; no other antidote, I say, no salve:
only the Muses. Theirs is a gentle remedy,
relieving mortal pain – yet not easy to find.
But you know this, I think, you know it well,
being a doctor, and indeed one they much love.
It's how the Cyclops, my countryman, found comfort
in his love for Galatea. Polyphemus, so the old story goes,
the beard still fresh around his lips and temples,
loved her not with apples, with roses or locks of hair,
but with headlong passion. All else seemed worthless.
Often his sheep would return of their own accord
from their green pastures to the fold, as he sat
on the shore, amid the seaweed, wasting away
with love, singing all day of Galatea.
He nursed deep in his breast an angry wound,
a pain in his heart from great Cypris' bow.
Yet he found this cure; and he'd sit on a rock,
high up, looking out to sea, and would sing:

Pale Galatea, paler than cream,
why cast your love away?
Gentler than lamb, livelier
than calf, ripe as reddening grape,
why come to me only in my sweet sleep?
Why vanish so quickly as soon as I wake,
running as ewe runs from wolf?
I've loved you, lady, since first you came
with your mother to pick hyacinths on my hill.
I showed you the way. And since that hour,

since I saw you, my love has not changed.
But you, by Zeus, you think nothing of me.
Yet I know, pretty one, why you run away.
It's because of my eyebrow, my single eyebrow,
which stretches across the full width of my face,
from ear to ear, one, long and hairy ;
and because of the single eye beneath it,
and the one broad nostril above my lip.
Such I am. Yet still I herd a thousand cattle,
and the milk I drink is theirs, the richest.
Never am I without cheese, summer or autumn,
or deepest winter ; my kegs are always full.
And I can sing as no other Cyclops —
often of you, sweet apple of my love,
and of myself, I sing deep into the night.
For you I am raising eleven fawns, each
with a collar, and four bear cubs.

Come to me ; come, and you'll never lack a thing.
Leave the grey sea to beat on the shore ;
your nights will be better spent in my cave.
There are laurels around, and tall cypresses,
there's ivy, dark ivy, and grape-sweet vines.
There's icy water, which densely wooded Etna
provides from her white snow, an ambrosial drink.
Now who, tell me, who would prefer sea and waves?

But if you think me too rough, too ragged,
I've logs of oak, an undying fire,
beneath those ashes ; I offer you my soul
to burn, and my single eye as well,
than which, believe me, I love nothing more.
Alas, that I was not born with fins,
to swim deep down and kiss your hand,
since you'll never let me kiss your lips.
I would have brought you pure-white lilies
or fragile poppies with scarlet flowers.
But one grows in summer, the other in winter,
so I could never bring you both at once.

Now, lady, now were some sailor to come,
at once I'd learn from him how to swim,
then I'd know why you choose to live in the sea.

Come, Galatea, and as you come forget —
as I do now, sitting here — to return.
Come now, help me shepherd my flock,
help me milk them and set their cheese with bitter rennet.

My mother's to blame ;[29] she it is
who has wronged me. For not one word
has she said to you on my behalf,
as she's watched me grow thinner day by day.
I'll tell her my head aches and both my feet throb,
so she too may suffer, may share in my pain.
O Cyclops, Cyclops, have you lost your mind?
If you'd any sense you'd be weaving baskets
to carry your cheese, and gathering grass
to feed your sheep. Milk her that is here ;
why chase those that run from you?
One day, perhaps, you'll find another Galatea,
another more fair. For many young girls
persuade me to play night games with them,
and laugh knowingly when I do what they ask.
It's clear that on land, at least, I'm someone.

So Polyphemus shepherded his love with song
and found more comfort than money could buy.

XII. *The Beloved Boy*[30]

You are come, dear boy; two nights and days,
and you are come; but they that yearn grow old in one.
As spring is sweeter than winter, apple than sloe,
as the ewe is fleecier than her lamb,

as the virgin more chaste than the thrice-wed woman,[31]
as fawn is swifter than calf, and the sharp voice
of the nightingale is sweetest of all birds,
so has your coming delighted me, and I run to you
as the sun-weary traveller to the shade of an oak.
My prayer is that the Loves may breathe on us,
on both alike; that we may live forever in a song:

How honoured were those two in days long past:
the one breathed out (as Amyclaeans say)
the other in[32] (a Thessalian phrase);
quite equally they shared a mutual love —
an age, with lovers always loved, of gold.

To Father Zeus and the immortal gods I pray
that when two hundred generations have gone by
some man may come to me at Acheron, whence
there is no return, and he may say:
'The famous love which long ago you shared
men sing of still, especially the young.'

Believe, that when I praise you in your beauty,
my face has none of the liar's spots.
For if at times you cause me pain, always
you heal the wound at once, and bring
a double joy, beyond all measure, as we part.

Nisaeans, men of Megara, first among oarsmen,
may you prosper and be blessed for the honour
you have shown to Diocles, the Attic stranger,
lover of young men. Always in the early spring
the boys still gather round his tomb and hold
their contest in the art of love. And he whose kissing,
lip on lip, is judged most sweet, will return home
to his mother, dressed in victory garlands.
It is a lucky man they choose as judge!
He must surely pray to pretty Ganymede
that his lip may share the power of Lydia's touchstone[33]
which money-changers use to try true gold.

XIII. *Hylas*

Love was not born, Nicias, for us alone,
as we have thought, whichever god fathered it.
Nor are we the first to see true beauty
in the beautiful – we who are mortal
and cannot see tomorrow. Even Amphitryon's son,
the steel-hearted, who fought the angry lion,
even he loved a boy – pretty Hylas it was,
with his long wavy hair. Heracles, what's more,
as any fond father teaches his son,
taught the boy all that had won him fame,
all that had made him the fine man he was.
He never left his side; no, not at noon,
not when Dawn's white horses climbed to the sky,
not when chickens clucked and looked to their beds
as their mother flapped her wings on her smoky perch.
This was to fashion the boy after his own mind
and to bring him up a true and worthy man.
So when Jason, son of Aeson, set his sails
in search of the golden fleece, with his band
of heroes, supreme men, from cities all over Greece,
the man of many labours, son of Alcmena,
Queen of Midea, went along with them to Iolcus.
And he took young Hylas down with him
to the good ship Argo – which didn't even touch
the Clashing Rocks, but scurried through them,
swift as an eagle, into deep Phasis' great gulf;
since which day the Rocks have never moved.
It was the time the Pleiads rise, spring
opens into summer, and the young lambs
find pasture in the distant uplands;
it was then the crew of godlike heroes determined
to set sail. They sat deep in the Argo's hull

and with three days of fresh southerly wind
came into the Hellespont, dropping anchor
at Propontis, where the Cianian cattle
plough broad furrows with their sturdy shares.
They disembarked onto the shore, and two by two
cooked their meal that evening; but one sleeping-place
was prepared for all – a meadow they had found,
deep in straw and leaves for them to rest on;
they cut themselves tall sedge and slender rushes.
Golden-haired Hylas had gone with a bronze urn
to fetch water for Heracles and mighty Telamon –
the two companions always shared one table.
Soon, by a hollow, Hylas saw a spring in the rushes,
deep among dark celandine, green maiden-hair, a crop
of bushy parsley, with wild marsh grass all around.
And in midstream there stood some water nymphs
about to dance – the unsleeping nymphs,
goddesses feared by all good country people:
Eunica, and Malis, and Nycheia
with her springtime eyes. The boy reached down,
in eager haste, to dip his great pitcher in the stream:
but they at once all clutched his hand,
for love of the Argive boy had ruffled
all their gentle hearts. And he fell headlong
into the dark waters, as a shooting star
plunges precipitously [34] down into the sea,
and the sailor cries, 'Tighten!' to his shipmates,
'Tighten the sails! The sea wind's getting up!'
And Hylas wept. The nymphs took him on their knees,
and tried to comfort him with soothing words.

Amphitryon's son, meanwhile, was worried about the boy,
and had set out after him, with his Scythian curved bow,
and the club he always grasped in his right hand.
Three times he shouted 'Hylas!' with all the force
his deep voice could muster; and three times
the boy replied, but his voice was sadly faint
beneath the water; though close at hand,

he sounded further and further away.
When some fawn cries out on the hills, the lion
hurries down from his lair, to find a ready meal;
so Heracles, in his longing for the boy, raged
among the untrodden thorns, covering many miles.
Lovers are single-minded; and as Heracles struggled,
fought his way through forests, over hills,
Jason and his quest were quite forgotten.
The ship stood ready, sails set, tackle stowed,
the others all aboard; so through the night
they cleared a slipway, and awaited Heracles.[35]
But he, meantime, was running wild,
wherever his feet would carry him,
for a spiteful god was tearing at his heart within.

And so it was pretty Hylas came to be numbered
among the blessed, and the heroes to mock,
to laugh at Heracles, call him, 'Deserter!'
for leaving the Argo and her thirty oars. In time,
he came on foot to Colchis, and unfriendly Phasis.

XIV. *Aeschinas and Thyonichus*

AESCHINAS
Thyonichus! My friend, how good to see you!

THYONICHUS
And you, Aeschinas. It's been a long time.

AESCHINAS
Long indeed.

THYONICHUS
But what's your trouble?

AESCHINAS
Things aren't too good with me, Thyonichus.

THYONICHUS
That'll be why you're so thin, then,
why you've grown this vast moustache
and all these shaggy kiss-curls. The other day
some Pythagorean turned up, looking just like you –
pale face, bare feet. And he said he was from Athens.

AESCHINAS
And was he too in love?

THYONICHUS
Yes, indeed – with loaves of barley bread, it seemed.[36]

AESCHINAS
Ah, you can joke, my friend. As for me,
pretty Cynisca torments me. I shall go mad
any moment. I'm only a whisker from it now.

THYONICHUS
That's you all right, dear Aeschinas –
always over-hasty, wanting things your own way.
Come on now, tell me all about it.

AESCHINAS
Well – there was the Argive, and I,
and Agis, the Thessalian jockey,
and Cleunicus, the professional soldier,
and we were all having a bit of a drink
at my place in the country. I'd killed us
a brace of chickens, and a sucking-pig,
and broached them some Bibline – as exquisite,
at four years old, as on the day it was pressed.
And I'd got in some cuttlefish and snails.
It was a fine spread. As we tucked in,

it was decided that all should drink a toast
to anyone they fancied; but names had to be named.
So we drank, and called them out, all as agreed.
But she, though I was there, said nothing.
How do you think I liked that? 'Lost your tongue?'
someone joked. 'Seen a wolf?'
'Very clever,' she replied, and her face burned.
You could easily have lit a candle from it.
There is a wolf: a wolf indeed, my neighbour Labas' son,
a tall lad, soft-skinned, whom many think handsome.
It was for him, this famous passion which consumed her.
It was whispered in my ear one day, on the quiet,
but, of course, I never asked any questions –
some use my having a grown man's beard!
Anyway, we four had drunk deep by this time,
and that Larissan, the bastard, started up
some Thessalian song called 'Wolf, My Wolf'.
At that Cynisca burst into tears, blubbing
like some six-year-old for her mother's lap.
So I – you know what I'm like, Thyonichus –
I fetched her one across the ear, and then
another. She hitched up her skirt, and was off
like a scalded cat.[37] I shouted after her:
'So I'm not good enough, you bitch?
There's someone you'd rather cuddle, is there?
You go and kiss him, then, this someone else.
May your tears for him be as big as apples!'
Now a swallow can bring her young some crumbs
in their nest beneath the roof, and be off again,
quick as a wink, to fetch some more.
Well, Cynisca was faster than any swallow
to be up from her seat, through the porch,
and out that door – wherever her feet took her.
The bull was fled to the wood, as the saying goes.
Let's see now: twenty days, then eight, nine, ten . . .
ten more, and today's the eleventh. Add two,
and it's two months since we parted.[38]
I may have been and had a Thracian haircut[39]

for all she knows. It's all Wolf now;
for Wolf her door is open every night.
I'm out of the reckoning, not worth a thought –
like wretched Megara,[40] bottom of the list.
If I could stop loving her, I wouldn't mind.
But how? I'm like the mouse in the proverb,
who tasted pitch, Thyonichus.[41] And I've no idea
what the cure for helpless love may be.
Except that Simias, who fell for that girl,
that brazen one, sailed off overseas and came back cured.
And he was much my age. That's what I'll do:
I'll go abroad like him. A soldier's life
is not the worst, nor indeed the best,
but it's as good as any other.

THYONICHUS
I wish things had gone your way, Aeschinas.
But if your mind's made up,
and you're off abroad, Ptolemy
is the best paymaster a free man can have.

AESCHINAS
And what's he like apart from that?

THYONICHUS
One of the best. Considerate, gallant,
a lover of the arts, the kindest of companions.
He can recognize a friend, and even more an enemy.
He's generous to many, as befits a king,
and turns down few requests. But don't ask too much.
So you fancy clasping a battle-cloak
on your shoulder, and standing firm
on both those legs to meet an enemy's attack?
Then take yourself to Egypt. We're all growing old:
a touch of grey at the temples, and snowy Time
soon turns us white, hair by hair, down the cheek.
We must all keep going while our joints still bend.

XV. *The Adonia*

GORGO
Is Praxinoa at home?

PRAXINOA
She is, Gorgo dear!
Such a time since I saw you:
it's quite a surprise to have you here!
A chair for her, Eunoa, and a cushion.

GORGO
Don't worry. I'm fine as I am.

PRAXINOA
Do sit down.

GORGO
Silly me! What a day to try and come!
I scarcely got through alive, Praxinoa,
what with all the people, all their chariots,
knee-boots everywhere, men in uniform –
that street is endless; and I'm sure,
every time I come, you've moved further
   away.

PRAXINOA
That's that crazy husband of mine.
He comes here, to the ends of the earth,
and buys this cowshed – call it a home? –
just to stop you and me being neighbours.
All out of pure spite, the jealous brute –
he was always the same.

GORGO

Now you mustn't talk of your Dinon
like that, my dear – not in front of the child.
See how he's staring at you, woman.
There, Zopyrion darling, never mind.
She wasn't talking about Daddy.

PRAXINOA

Good God, the child understands.

GORGO

Nice Daddy! Good old Daddy!

PRAXINOA

Well, that *nice* Daddy the other day ...
Just the other day, I said to him:
'Dad, get me some soap and some rouge
from the shops.' He came back, did Daddy,
that giant of a man, carrying a pack of salt.[42]

GORGO

Mine's just the same. Old Diocleidas
is a financial wizard. Just yesterday
he paid seven drachmas for five fleeces –
five motheaten dogskins, more like,
pickings from faded old purses,
nothing but filth, just work and more work.
But come, get your dress and cloak on,
and let's go to King Ptolemy's palace
and take a look at this Adonis.
The Queen, I hear, is doing things in style.

PRAXINOA

Oh, nothing but the best. Well, they can keep it.[43]

GORGO

But when you've seen it, just think,
you can tell those who haven't all about it.
Come on, it's time we were off.

PRAXINOA

Every day's a holiday for the idle.
Eunoa, pick that spinning up. Leave it
lying around once more, and you'll regret it.
The cat would love so soft a bed.
Now get a move on. Bring me water quickly.
I ask for water, and she brings soap.
Never mind, let's have it. Not that much,
you robber. Now pour the water. Idiot!
You've spilt it all over my slip.
That's quite enough. I must be thankful,
I suppose, I've got that much washed.
Now where's the key of the big wardrobe?
Bring it here.

GORGO

Oh, Praxinoa, that dress. So full. It's just you.
Tell me, what did you pay for the cloth?

PRAXINOA

Oh don't remind me, Gorgo. I paid
more than two whole minas of good money.
And I put my very soul into making it.

GORGO

Well, it's a triumph. And that's the truth.

PRAXINOA

Bring me my cloak and hat, Eunoa.
And put them on properly this time.
No, baby, I can't take you.
Boo hoo! The bogey man would catch you!
You can cry as much as you like;
I'm not having you crippled for life.
Let's go.
Phrygia, take baby and play with him.
Call the dog in and lock the front door.

[*Out in the street.*]
Ye Gods, what a crowd! The crush!
How on earth are we going to get through it?
They're like ants! Swarms of them, beyond counting!
Well, you've done us many favours, Ptolemy,
since your father went to heaven.
We don't get those no-goods now, sliding up to us
in the street and playing their Egyptian tricks.[44]
What they used to get up to, those rogues!
A bunch of villains, each as bad
as the next, and all utterly cursed!

Gorgo dear, what will become of us?
Here are the king's horses! Take care,
my good man, don't tread on me.
That brown one's reared right up!
Look how wild he is! He'll kill his groom!
Eunoa, you fool, get back!
Thank God I left that child at home.

GORGO
Don't worry, Praxinoa.
We've got behind them now.
They're back in their places.

PRAXINOA
I'm all right now.
Ever since I was a girl, two things
have always terrified me – horses,
and long, cold snakes. Let's hurry.
This great crowd will drown us.

GORGO
You coming from the palace, grandma?

OLD WOMAN
I am, children.

GORGO
Then we'll get in all right?

OLD WOMAN
By trying, my dears, the Greeks took Troy.
Try hard enough, and you can manage anything.

GORGO
The old girl's vanished –
she just spoke her oracles and went.

PRAXINOA
Women, Gorgo, know everything.
Even the story of Zeus and Hera.[45]

GORGO
Look, Praxinoa! What a crowd at the door!

PRAXINOA
Fantastic! Gorgo, give me your hand.
And you, Eunoa, hold on to Eutychis.
Take care you don't lose each other.
We must all go in together. Stay close by us.
Oh no! Gorgo! My coat! It's been ripped
clean in two! My God, sir, as you hope
for heaven, mind my coat!

STRANGER
It wasn't my fault. But I'll be careful.

PRAXINOA
What a herd! They push like pigs.

STRANGER
Don't worry, madam, we'll be all right.

PRAXINOA
And may you, sir, be all right
forever and beyond, for looking after us.

What a charming man! Where's Eunoa?
She's getting squashed! Come on, girl, push!
That's it. 'All safely in',
as the bridegroom said when he locked the door.

GORGO

Praxinoa, come here! You must look
at these tapestries before anything else.
What grace! What delicacy!
The work of a god, don't you think?

PRAXINOA

By Athena, what craftsmen they must have been
to make these, what artists to draw such lines.
Those figures stand, they move around,
like living things! They can't be just figures.
What a marvellous creature man is!
And there's Adonis; how superb he looks,
lying there in his silver chair,
the first down spreading from his temples –
thrice-loved Adonis, adored even in Hades!

ANOTHER STRANGER

Oh do be quiet, you stupid woman.
Stop that ceaseless prattling.
Like two turtle doves! I swear
their oohs and aahs will be the end of me.

PRAXINOA

Well! Where did he spring from?
What concern is it of yours, pray,
if we do prattle? You must buy
your slaves before you order them about.
And it's to Syracusans you're giving your orders.
If you must know, we're of Corinthian descent,
like Bellerophon himself. We speak Peloponnesian.
Dorians, I presume, may speak Dorian?
We have one master, by Persephone,
let's have no more. Don't waste your time on us.[46]

GORGO

Shush, Praxinoa! She's about to start!
The Argive's daughter is going to sing
about Adonis – that girl with the lovely voice,
who sang the best lament last year.
She'll be worth hearing, I'll bet.
Hush, she's just getting ready.

SINGER

My lady, lover of Idalium,
of Golgi and of Eryx' mountain slopes,
great Aphrodite, toying with your gold,
in twelve short months the Hours have brought you back
Adonis from perpetual Acheron's streams,
the well-loved Hours, soft-footed, Heaven's dawdlers,
always missed, much welcomed, free with gifts.
Cypris, Dione's daughter, you – men say –
gave to Berenice, a mortal queen,
immortal life, gracing her woman's breast
with pure ambrosia. And now for you,
Lady of many names and many shrines,
Arsinoë, her child, of Helen's grace,
pampers Adonis with all that's best in life.
She lays, season by season, at his side
fruit from the choicest trees, delicate plants
preserved in silver pots, rich golden phials
of Syrian myrrh, fresh home-made honey cakes
of every kind that ever woman kneaded,
baked with purest flour and smoothest, sweetest oils,
mixtures of finest colour, scent and taste.
Birds and beasts of every kind are there;
they've built green, shady bowers of fragrant dill.
Above them perch and flit the youthful Loves,
hopping from branch to branch like nightingales
making first trial of their new-grown wings.
The ebony, the gold! The eagles, there,
carved from white ivory, bearing to Zeus,

son of Cronos, a boy to pour his wine.
Above are crimson rugs, softer than sleep.
Miletans, Samian shepherds, both might say,
'Fair Adonis' bed is spread with rugs we made.'
See, Cypris reclines in his rosy arms,
and he in hers. The groom is young: eighteen,
or nineteen, golden down still on his lip:
his kiss is soft. But now, as Cypris lies
in her man's embrace, we'll say farewell.
At dawn, amid the dew, we'll carry him to the shore,
washed by the beating waves. We will bare our breasts,
untie our hair, and let our garments fall;
then, with one voice, we may raise our song:
'Beloved Adonis, you alone, they say,
alone of demigods, visit both earth
and Acheron. This grace was not allowed
to Agamemnon, no, not to great Aias,
heavy-tempered hero, nor to Hector,
first of the twenty sons of Hecuba;
no, not to Pyrrhus, coming home from Troy,
nor Patroclus, nor old Deucalion's race,
nor to the Lapiths all those years ago.
The House of Pelops never earned this right,
nor even Argos' great Pelasgian kings.
Grant us your grace, Adonis, one more year.
Your coming now has blessed us; take our love,
and at your next, you'll find true welcome here.'

GORGO

Praxinoa, this woman's quite something. A genius!
To know so much, to have so sweet a voice!
But it's time for home. Diocleidas will want
his supper; that man's all vinegar.
Keep well clear of him when he's unfed!
Farewell, Adonis, beloved one:
may we be happy when you come again!

XVI. *The Graces*[47]

It is for the daughters of Zeus, and for poets,
forever to hymn the immortals, forever
to sing hymns of heroes and glorious deeds.
But the Muses are gods who hymn the divine,
so we that are men must sing of mortality.

Who is there living by day's steely light
that gladly will open his door to my Graces,
and not send them home empty-handed? Say, who?
They'll come back barefooted, indignant, and chide me
for sending them off on a wild goose chase;
then again they'll relapse, heads sunk on cold knees,
and – the usual end to abortive excursions –
they'll languish deep down in my empty box.
Where can one find such a man these days?
Who gives a damn for the poet who's praised him?
I know of no one. It's not like the old times
when men were intent to win praise for their virtue;
now they are all overcome by mere greed.
Every one, with his hand on his wallet,
looks only for ways of increasing his wealth.
He'll even deny friends the rust from his coppers,
answering quickly, 'What's in it for me?
Remember true charity starts in the home,'[48]
or 'The gods, my good man, are a poet's true patrons,'
or 'Homer's enough. Who needs any more?'
or even, 'My favourite poet,' he'll say,
'is the one who gets nothing at all out of me.'
What use is a fortune in gold, you poor fools,
if you hoard it away in great piles in some chest?
Men with more sense will say profit is gained
by first furnishing all the desires of the soul,
then, say, those of a poet – by generous gifts

as much to mankind as to family and friends;
by regular offerings at heavenly shrines,
and by liberal conduct as host to all guests.
Never refuse a meal to a stranger; let him sit down,
then bid him farewell when he begs leave to go.
Respect above all the Muses' interpreters, holiest of men,
so that even when death hides you deep in dark Hades
your name will live gloriously on; otherwise,
you must languish, forgotten, on cold Acheron's banks,
bewailing your fate like some starveling son,
his hands blistered by spadework,
bemoaning his father's bankruptcy.

There were many slaves in the house of Antiochus;
many drew monthly rations in Aleuas' employ;
there were hundreds of calves and vast herds of cattle
driven, lowing, to the Scopas family's sheds;
on the plain of Crannon countless prize sheep
were watched by the shepherds of the kindly Creons.
Yet their joy in such wealth was abruptly ended
when the wine of their lives was drawn to the dregs
and poured into grim-faced Charon's barge.
Their riches behind them, they'd all be forgotten,
left to moulder for years with the desolate dead,
had it not been for a man inspired, the poet of Ceos,[49]
who matched fine words to his well-tuned lyre
and immortalized their names here on earth;
so the horses that won them the holy games
won their colours, through him, lasting glory in song.
Who would have heard of the heroes of Lycia,
who known of Priam's great long-haired sons,
who of Cycnus, with his woman's skin,
had the poets of old not sung their battle-cries?
Odysseus would have wandered the world those ten years,
would have reached deepest Hades while still alive,
finally fleeing the cave of murderous Cyclops,
and his glorious tale might never have been told.
Names such as those of Eumaeus the swineherd,
of Philoetius, keeper and herder of cattle,

and even of princely Laertes himself,
might have languished forever shrouded in silence
had they not been proclaimed by Ionia's bard.

So the Muses may keep a dead man's name alive,
but his wealth will be squandered by those that survive him.
It is easier to number the waves of the sea,
thrown up on the beach by wind and grey water,
or to wash a clay brick in the clearest of pools,
than to win back a man corrupted by greed.
Good-bye and good riddance to him and his like;
may countless vast fortunes happen their way
and may they always be hungry for more.
For myself, I would choose the respect of mankind,
and men's love, before fortunes in mules and in horses.

Now I am scouring the earth for a man
in whose home we'd be welcome, my Muses and I;
for the road is long and hard to the poet
who travels without Zeus the Counsellor's daughters.
The tireless heavens bring round months, bring years;
their horses will set many more days' wheels turning.
There'll be many a man needing me for his poet
when he's equalled the feats of courageous Achilles,
or those of dread Aias on Simois' plain,
near where Ilus the Phrygian rests in his tomb.
At this moment Phoenicians are quaking with fear[50]
as the sun goes down on the Libyan coast;
Syracusans are taking tight grips on their spears
and fastening their wicker-work shields on their arms,
and among them, like one of the warriors of old,
a plume trimming his helmet, great Hiero prepares.

Now I pray to Zeus, our far-famed Father,
to holy Athena, to the maid and her mother,[51]
who rule the great city of the rich Ephyreans
by the waters of Lysimeleia: my prayer
is that cruel compulsion may scatter our enemies
out of this land, may drive them back over
the sea of Sardinia, to wives and to children
with news of the death of the men that they loved;

may these messengers be the mere dregs of their host.
May the towns which these enemies razed to the ground
be restored to their truly traditional rulers,
the land that they work now be blessed with rich harvests,
their fields with the bleating of countless fat sheep,
and the twilight traveller be hurried along
by the homeward drift of vast cattle herds.
May the shepherds plough over the fallows for seed-time,
working towards their noon rest from the sun,
as the crickets sing high in the trees overhead.
May spiders shroud weapons of war in fine cobwebs,
and battle-cries henceforth be never more heard.
And let poets take up the great glory of Hiero
and noise it abroad past the Scythian sea
to the stonewall bounds of Semiramis' realm.
I am one of these poets, just one of the many;
great numbers are loved by the daughters of Zeus.
May they all sing of Sicily, hymn Arethusa,
her warrior tribes, and her champion, Hiero.
You Graces, goddesses Eteocles loved,
who cherish Minyan Orchomenus –
hated once by the Thebes of old –
when no man calls, I will stay at home;
but when bidden, in confident spirits I'll go,
my Muses beside me, wherever I'm summoned.
Never, I say, will I leave you behind.
For without the Graces a man has nothing,
nothing worthwhile. May they ever be with me.

XVII. *In Praise of Ptolemy*

With Zeus let us begin, Muses, and with him end,
the supreme immortal, in our poems of praise.
But when singing of men we must name Ptolemy
first, last and throughout; for he stands above all.

The ancient heroes, children of demigods,
found true poets to tell of their glorious deeds.
But I, masterly poet of praise, must celebrate Ptolemy;
hymns are the only reward even gods demand.

The woodman climbing to the forests of Ida
looks round him, surveying those plentiful rows,
to decide where to start; and what's my first line?
Which should begin this immense list of qualities
granted by heaven to this king among kings?
Some are family blessings. For as Lagus' son,
Ptolemy boldly achieved such grand schemes
as no man but he could have ever conceived.
Now the Father has placed him among the immortals,
equally honoured with all the blessed; in Zeus' own house
a throne of gold was established for him.
Beside him in friendship sits great Alexander,
bane of the Persians, in a glittering crown.
Close by is the throne of Heracles, Centaur-killer,
fashioned from obstinate adamant. Here,
with his fellow-gods, he feasts and makes merry,
rejoicing above all in the sons of his sons
from whose limbs great Cronos has lifted old age,
numbering all his family among the immortals.
Both these kings were descended from Heracles' son,
both trace back their line to the hero himself.
So he, after drinking his fill of sweet nectar,
returns from the feast to his dearly-loved wife.
To one he hands over his quiver and bow,
to the other his great, knotted club, strong as iron,
which they carry beside him, Zeus' rough-bearded son,
as he goes to pure Hebe's ambrosial chamber.[52]
How clearly among the most modest of women
renowned Berenice stood out, such a gift to her parents.
Our Lady of Cyprus, holy daughter of Dione,
blessed her with the touch of her slender finger,
laying her hand on the child's soft breast.
Never, they say, has woman pleased man
so much as through this she delighted Ptolemy;

and yet he was never more loved than loving.
With such as this, any man may go
in love to the bed of his loving wife,
and safely pass on all he has to their children.
But a wife who is neither loving nor loved
will set her heart on others, elsewhere,
and her children won't mirror their father's face.
Aphrodite, queen of beauty as of heaven,
she was your charge. It was through you
that fair Berenice was spared Acheron,
her beauty rescued from the vale of tears;
for before she reached grim Charon's grimmer barge
you took her up to sit in your own temple,
sharing with her many of your holy rights.
Her breath is gentle on all mankind,
inspiring their hearts with the purest love,
easing the cares of rejection, of loss.
You, dark lady of Argos,[53] bore Tydeus of Calydon
a son, Diomedes, killer of men; and deep-bosomed Thetis
bore the warrior Achilles to Peleus, son of Aeacus;
so renowned Berenice bore warlike Ptolemy
a warlike son, another Ptolemy: yourself, my liege,
taken from your mother soon after birth,
and nursed into the light of day by Cos.
For it was there Antigone's daughter had laboured,
had called for Ilithyia to loosen her girdle.
The goddess stayed by her and saw her through,
relaxing the pain from her every limb;
and the child was born, the beloved son,
the very image of his father. Cos, at the sight,
took the boy in her arms, and shouted for joy.
'God bless you, my child. May you bring me honour
as Phoebus Apollo graced dark-shrouded Delos.
Bring like honour as well to the Triopian hill,
with equal regard for my Dorian neighbours.
Lord Apollo gave as much to Rhenaea as to Delos.'
As the island spoke, the heavens opened
and echoed thrice to an eagle's mighty cries,

a bird of omen, a sign from Zeus;
for he, son of Cronos, has special regard
for formidable rulers, but especially blessed
are those that he loves from their moment of birth.
Wealth and good fortune are his in abundance;
he will master great tracts both of land and of sea.
There are numberless countries with countless tribes
who harvest rich crops thanks to rain sent by Zeus,
but none quite so fruitful as Egypt's broad plains
where the floods of the Nile soak and soften the soil
and every last town has a highly skilled work-force.
In that land there are three hundred cities established,
with three thousand more, and three tens of thousands,
twice three and thrice nine; and Ptolemy rules all.
And he's taken a share of Phoenicia, Arabia,
of Syria, Libya and the dark Ethiopians,
he has the command of the whole of Pamphylia,
of Cilicia, Lycia, and Caria's troops;
he even has charge of the isles of the Cyclades,
thanks to his navy's control of the sea.
The whole ocean, the land and its rushing rivers
all bow to King Ptolemy's absolute rule.
Great armies of horsemen are clustered around him,
great hosts of foot-soldiers in burnished bronze arms.
Were all the world's princes to pool their vast wealth,
his would outweigh it, such riches arrive
each day from all sides at his sumptuous palace.
His people can go about their business in peace;
no enemy infantries cross the rich Nile
to disturb alien towns with the clamour of battle,
nor jump to the shore from their speedy longboats
to scatter the cattle with violence of arms.
Nor could they ever, while such a man
as golden-haired Ptolemy sits on the throne,
a warrior guarding wide Egypt's plains;
he concentrates, as a wise king should,
on preserving his heritage, building it up.

The piles of gold in that wealthy house
never stand idle, like ants' hard-won riches;
vast amounts go as gifts to the holy temples,
where he always sends first-fruits, and much more besides.
He is generous with gifts to his subject kings,
generous to cities and to loyal friends.
No talented singer who brings a clear voice
to Dionysus' holy contest goes home empty-handed;
Ptolemy gives him the gift he deserves,
and his kindness is praised by the voice of the Muse.
What nobler quest has a prosperous man
than pursuit of undying fame here on earth?
It's that fame which keeps alive Atreus' house,
not the boundless fortune they captured in Troy
from the halls of King Priam; that now lies hidden,
deep in the darkness whence no one returns.
Of the men of old, and of those whose footsteps
are still warm in the dust where they trod,
Ptolemy alone has laid up shrines, rich with incense,
for the mother and father he so much loved,
and has raised their statues, in ivory and gold,
to help and inspire those left here on earth.
The months go by, and those altars have glowed
with the flames of many a fat ox's thigh
as he makes his regular sacrifice; he and his wife,
that noble woman, than whom none finer
ever embraced a lord at his hearth;
she gives her whole heart to her husband and brother.[54]
Just so were marriages made in heaven
for those borne by Rhea to be its rulers,
and virgin Iris with perfumed hands
prepares the one bed for Zeus and for Hera.

And so, Lord Ptolemy, farewell. I will sing
of you no less than of other demigods,
and I fancy my words will live on among men.
But for virtue you must pray to Zeus.

XVIII. *Helen's Bridal Hymn*

In Sparta once, in golden-haired Menelaus' palace,
twelve virgins, the flower of all the town's beauties,
each with hyacinth blooms in her hair,
danced outside the newly-painted bridal room.
For Atreus' younger son had closed the doors
on himself and Helen, Tyndareus' daughter,
whom his wooing had won. They sang together,
the twelve virgins, one song with one voice,
threading their feet in and out in time,
filling the palace with their wedding hymn.

Asleep so soon, sweet groom? So quickly gone?
Can you be so heavy-limbed? So fond of dreams?
Perhaps too much drink has laid you low?
So keen to sleep so early should have slept
alone, and left the virgin with her friends,
to pass the hours until the dawn in play
at her loving mother's side ; for, Menelaus, she
tomorrow and tomorrow, year on year,
will always be your bride.

When bringing all your noble band of friends
to Sparta here, you had fortune on your side ;
some good man sneezed, bridegroom, and brought you luck.
For you alone of all of them have Zeus,
Cronos' great son, as father of your bride.
It is the child of Zeus now shares your bed,
a woman of Achaea, the like of whom
has never walked the earth. How truly great
her child will be, if it be like herself.
And we, her friends, who ran her race with her,
anoint ourselves beside Eurotas' pools
the way men do – a youthful band of girls,

four times sixty of us, not one of whom
can rival Helen's grace.

The face of rising Dawn, my lady Night,
is fine, as clear as spring when winter ends:
so, from among us, Helen's gold shines out.
As some tall cypress can enhance the field
or fertile garden it towers above,
or some Thessalian horse its chariot,
so Helen's rosy face is Sparta's crown.
No woman from her basket winds such wool
as she, nor at her ornamented loom
weaves such shuttlework, or cuts her thread
so close to its tall beams. No one can play
the lyre, can sing such hymns to Artemis,
or to Athena's breast, as Helen does –
desire lives in her eyes.

For all your beauty, Helen, all your grace,
you are a housewife now. We, your friends,
will go down early to our running place
and to the flowery meadows, where we'll pick
sweet-smelling garlands, and we'll think of you,
we'll miss you as a lamb her mother's teat.
But first we'll bind for you a clover crown
and set it on a plane-tree in the shade;
then we'll draw smooth oil from the silver urn
and pour our offering beneath that tree.
And on its bark we'll write, in Dorian,
for every passer-by to read: 'Bow down,
for I am Helen's tree.'[55]

Farewell now, bride, farewell now, noble groom.
May Leto, queen of nurses, grant to you
fine children, holy Cypris mutual love,
and Zeus, the son of Cronos, untold wealth
through every generation of your race.

Now sleep, breathe love into each other's breasts,
and breathe desire. Be sure to wake at dawn,

for we'll be here again before the day,
when the very first song-bird wakes, and raises his neck
of colourful feathers, to crow.

Hymen, O Hymenaeus, bless and rejoice in this match!

XIX. *The Honey-Thief*

A bee once cruelly stung the god of love
as he was stealing honey from the hives.
His fingertips, each pricked, began to smart,
and with the pain he blew upon his hand,
he stamped and danced. Then Eros showed his wound
to Aphrodite, and he made complaint
that bees, such tiny things, should be the cause
of such great pain. His mother laughed. 'Aren't you,'
she said, 'just like the bee, in being so small,
yet with your sting inflicting such great pain?'

XX. *The Young Herdsman*

Eunica scorned me when I tried to kiss her.
She laughed at me, and said, 'Be gone!
Would you, a goatherd, offer me your kisses?
You are rough; and I am used to gentle city lips,
not those of rustics. Never bring your kisses
to lips as sweet as mine – no, not even in your dreams.
What a face, what language, and what boorish ways![56]
Your mouth is diseased, your hands are black
and your breath foul. Be gone, before you dirty me!'
With this she spat three times upon her breast,
from top to toe she looked me up and down,
her eyes glaring, a sneer on her lips;

she played the lady, she grinned, and pompously
she mocked me. At once I felt my blood boil,
my face grow flushed with anguish, as a rose with dew.
At last she went away, she left me. But in my heart
I nurse a deep-felt grudge – that so fine a man
should be the butt of such a faithless woman.

   Shepherds, bear me witness. Am I not handsome?
Or has some god just changed me to another man?
There was a time I flowered with beauty:
my chin was thick with beard, as a tree with ivy;
my hair curled richly, like parsley, round my temples,
and my white forehead gleamed above dark brows;
my eyes were brighter than Athena's grey ones,
my lips softer than cream, and from them flowed
a voice sweeter than honey from the comb.
My playing is fine, whether on flute
or cross-flute, whether pipe or reed.
The women on the hills all say I'm handsome;
they love to kiss me. Yet this city thing would not,
for I'm a herdsman. So me she passes by, ignores.
Yet noble Dionysus herds his cattle in the vales.
She cannot know that Cypris lost her mind
over a herdsman, that in the Phrygian hills
she tended sheep, and loved Adonis in the woods,
and in them wept for him. Who was Endymion
if not a herdsman? And as he drove his stock
was he not sighed for by Selene, coming from Olympus
down through the woods of Latmus to share her lover's
   bed?
You too, Rhea, you mourn a herdsman.
And, mighty Zeus, was it not for a shepherd boy
you became a wandering bird?[57] But Eunica,
and she alone, will never kiss a cowherd.
And who are Cybele, Cypris and Selene
compared with Eunica, the greatest of them all?
Grant, Cypris, that she may never
in city or on hill, kiss her darling,
but let her sleep throughout the night alone.

XXI. *The Fishermen*

It is poverty alone breeds craftsmanship,
Diophantus; she teaches men to work.
The labourer is kept even from his sleep
by a troubled heart. If, for one brief moment,
he dozes off, anxieties will fill his sleeping mind
and disrupt, quite suddenly, any chance of rest.

Two old fishermen lay together in their wattled cabin
beneath its wall of leaves, on a bed
they had made themselves from dried seaweed.
Near by lay the tools of their strenuous trade –
baskets, rods, hooks, baits thick with weed,
lobster-pots and traps of woven rush, ropes,
a pair of oars, a battered skiff upon its props;
with the tiny mat beneath their heads, and their coats
as rugs, this was all they had –
their entire wealth. No key, no door, no watchdog:
all these they would have thought excess,
for poverty watched over them and theirs.
They had no neighbours; the sea lapped gently
at their very walls, hemming their homestead in.

Now the Moon's chariot had not yet reached mid-sky
when their familiar tasks awoke the fishermen.
Rubbing the drowsy sleep from their eyes,
each told the other what was in his heart.

ASPHALION
They lie, my friend, all those who say the nights
grow short in summer, when they bring long days.
It's not yet dawn, and I've already dreamed
a thousand dreams; there's no forgetting them.
Just how much longer will this night go on?[58]

118

HIS COMPANION
Asphalion, you can't go blaming our friend the summer.
It's not time, somehow overrunning its course,
that disturbs you, but anxiety, cutting short
your sleep, making the night seem long.

ASPHALION
Can you interpret dreams? Have you ever learnt?
Mine have been fine tonight, and I'd like you
to have a share in what I've seen.

COMPANION
Yes, let's share our dreams as we do our catch.
I may perhaps have to search my mind, and guess,
but all the best interpretations are homespun.
Besides, we've plenty of time to chat.
What's a man to do as he lies, unsleeping,
on his bed of leaves? It is, they say,
the ass among thorns and the town-hall lamp
that never sleep. But come, tell me all.
For friends should always share their dreams.

ASPHALION
After our hard day at sea, I fell asleep
early last night – and not through over-eating,
for you'll remember we supped promptly
and spared our stomachs all excesses.
I saw myself perched on a rock, just sitting,
watching for fish, dangling the treacherous bait
from my rod. And I got a good bite –
as hounds dream of foxes,[59] so I of fish.
He was firmly hooked, and began to bleed;
the rod bent and strained in my hand
as he struggled. I leant over the water,
but could see no easy way to lift
so large a fish with such light tackle.
I pricked him gently, just to remind him
of his wound; then I gave him slack,

but tightened when he didn't try to run.
In the end, however, I won my prize, and landed
a golden fish – yes, every scale pure gold.
It had me terrified. What if this fish
should be some favourite of Poseidon's?
Or specially treasured by sea-green Amphitrite?
Slowly, and very carefully, I took out the hook
lest its barb rip any gold from that mouth.[60]
I was converted, there and then, to life ashore.
I swore I'd never go near the sea again;
I'd stay on *terra firma* and lord it with my gold.
That woke me up. Now it's all yours,
my friend: you put your mind to it.
For that oath I swore has unnerved me.

COMPANION

Don't worry. There's nothing to fear.
You swore no oath. Nor did you catch
that golden fish you saw. That dream
was a pack of lies. But if you'll spend
all your waking hours in search of those fabulous fish
then there's hope in what you saw. When you cast,
cast for fish of flesh and blood: or golden dreams
and an empty stomach will be the death of you.

XXII. *The Dioscuri*[61]

I sing of the sons of Leda and shield-bearing Zeus.
Castor was one, the other fierce Polydeuces,
tough with his fists when he strapped on the gloves.
I sing two and three hymns of the brothers
born in Sparta to Thestius' daughter,
saviours of men on the razor's edge,
of horses that bolt from the blood of war,
of ships that defy the signs in the stars

and founder amid ferocious storms,
dashing their timbers with mighty waves
from in front, or behind, or wherever they please,
crashing them into the vessel's hold, bursting its sides,
till the sail and the rigging hang tattered, useless,
and the night brings yet heavier rain and tempest,
the broad sea crashes beneath the blast,
the buffeting winds, the inexorable hail.
Yet even so they live: these ships,
these crews that thought they were dead,
dragged by you, by you alone, from the depths.
The winds at once die; the sea lies calm, glistening;
the clouds disperse, this way, that; the Bears appear;
between the Asses emerges the Manger, half seen,
signalling that all is fair again for sailing.

　　Saviours of men, beloved brothers,
horsemen and harpers, athletes and singers,
shall my first song be of Castor or Polydeuces?
Let it be of both; but begin with Polydeuces.

The Argo was safely through the Clashing Rocks
and into the snowy Pontic's dark mouth,
and now, with the dear Sons of Heaven aboard,
reached the land of the Bebryces. Down the ladders,
on either side of the ship, swarmed the heroes,
and started across the sheltered bay's broad beach
to make themselves beds and rub sticks for fire.
But ruddy Polydeuces and swift-riding Castor
took a different path from their comrades together
to look at the various wild woods on the hill.
Beneath a smooth boulder they found there a spring,
eternally flowing, bubbling to the brim with purest water,
the pebbles in its depths like crystal or silver.
Tall pines grew close by, poplars, and plane-trees,
leafy cypresses; and fragrant flowers, thick in the meadows,
a labour of love, as spring dies, for rough bees.
There, in the open, sat an ogre of a man,
fearful to behold, his ears crushed by fist-blows,

his huge chest and broad back one great sphere of iron
    flesh,
like some colossus from the forge; beneath his shoulders
the muscles stood out from his mighty arms like rocks
rounded and polished in a winter torrent's pools.
Across his back, round his neck, hung the skin of a lion
fastened by its paws. Polydeuces the champion spoke first:

'Greetings, stranger, whoever you may be.
What people, tell me, own this land?'

AMYCUS
Greetings, indeed, from men I never saw before?

POLYDEUCES
Don't worry. We're not criminals. Nor were our fathers.

AMYCUS
I'm not worried. And I don't need you to tell me.

POLYDEUCES
Are you some savage – always arrogant, resentful?

AMYCUS
I am what you see. It's *you* who trespass here.

POLYDEUCES
Come with us, and you'll return with gifts of friendship.

AMYCUS
Give me no gifts. You shall have none of me.

POLYDEUCES
What, man, won't you even let us drink this water?

AMYCUS
You will know when your parched lips are dry with thirst.

POLYDEUCES
What's your price? Silver? Say, how can we win you?

AMYCUS
Put up your fists and face me, man to man.

POLYDEUCES
Just boxing? Or kicking too? My eye is good . . .[62]

AMYCUS
Fists alone, and pull no punches. Give it all you've got.

POLYDEUCES
Who then? Against whom do I put on my gloves?

AMYCUS
Him you see before you. He's no woman. Call him The
    Boxer.

POLYDEUCES
And is there some prize, fit for us to fight for?

AMYCUS
I'll be yours. Or if I win, you mine.

POLYDEUCES
That would be no more than a red-crested cock-fight.

AMYCUS
Whether we fight like gamecocks or lions,
it'll be for no other prize than this.

Amycus, with that, took his hollow shell, and blew,
and in answer the long-haired Bebryces came
to gather beneath the shade of the planes.
So Castor, second to none as a fighter, went off
to fetch all the heroes from the Magnesian ship.
When both men had gloved up with leather,

winding the length of the thongs round their arms,
they stepped forward, each breathing death against the
    other,
launching straight into the fiercest of struggles
over which one should fight with the sun at his back.
But your cunning, Polydeuces, outwitted that huge man
and Amycus had the sunlight full on his face.
In a rage he lunged forward, jabbing with his fists;
but the son of Tyndareus met his attack
with a blow to the chin. He was all the more angry,
and took to all-in battle, charging with head down.
The Bebryces cheered; the heroes, too, shouted,
urging Polydeuces on, more and more afraid
that in so confined a space this Tityus of a man
might overwhelm and destroy their gallant comrade.
But the son of Zeus stood up to him, on this side,
now on that, bruised and cut him, with his left,
now with his right, and checked the attack of Poseidon's
    son,
for all its great power. Stopped in his tracks,
Amycus stood punch-drunk, spitting crimson blood.
The heroes' shouts grew louder as they saw
the ugly wounds around his mouth and jaws;
his eyes narrowed as his face grew swollen.
Then the prince confused him with feints and passes
on every side; when he had him at his mercy,
he hammered a blow on his brow, above the nose,
laying bare his face, skinning it to the bone,
leaving Amycus on his back among the flowers.
Soon he was up again. The fight grew fiercer;
with brutal leather punches they were battling to the death.
The Bebrycian chief aimed his fist attack
below the neck, upon the chest, while Polydeuces,
the invincible, kept pummelling his face, disfiguring it.
Amycus' flesh contracted with the sweat; the giant
seemed a midget. But Polydeuces' muscles strengthened
in the heat of the violence, taking on a bolder colour.
    How did Zeus' son lay low that hog of a man?

Say, goddess, for you know. And I shall be your voice;
I the interpreter, with your guidance, of your will.

Amycus, looking for a breakthrough, dropped his guard,
seized Polydeuces' left hand with his left,
and leaning forward, shifting his weight to the right,
swung a massive hook right up past his belt.
It would have all but killed Amyclae's king,
had it made contact. But Polydeuces dodged,
cocking his head aside, and landed a huge punch
beneath the other's temple, his whole shoulder behind it.
Dark blood soon gushed from Amycus' gaping face-wound.
Then Polydeuces piled another left onto his mouth,
rattling the gritted teeth, then showered his cheeks with
    blows,
crushing his face, beating it to pulp. Amycus,
at last, collapsed to the ground, scarcely conscious,
holding up his hands in surrender, near to death.
Then you, Polydeuces, boxer, though the winner,
did not take unfair advantage of the man,
but simply demanded a solemn oath,
in the name of his father, Poseidon of the sea,
that he'd cause no more trouble to innocent strangers.

Now, my lord, I have sung your praises,
I will turn to Castor, also son of Tyndareus,
horseman, spearsman, armoured in bronze.

The two sons of Zeus had snatched Leucippus' two
    daughters,
and were carrying them off, most closely pursued
by Aphareus' two sons, Lynceus and manly Idas,
who had been about to become their bridegrooms.
When they reached dead Aphareus' tomb, they all jumped
from their chariots, and went for each other,
laden with spear and shield. But Lynceus began to speak,
to shout at them all from beneath his helmet:
'Why, sirs, are you so keen for a fight?
Why so presumptuous with other men's brides?
Why are these naked swords in your hands?

Leucippus pledged these his daughters to us
long since; he named us in his bridal oath.
You've no right to empty other men's beds
by winning him over with cattle and mules
and whatever else, bribing us out of our brides.
I am not a man of many words, but again
and again I have told you to your faces:
"It ill becomes men of quality, my friends,
to woo brides whose grooms are waiting at their door.
Sparta's a big place; so is Elis, with its horses;
Arcadia, with its sheep; Achaea, Messene, Argos;
Sisyphus, with its long coastline. Girls by the thousand
are growing up there, in their parents' homes,
all of them lacking neither looks nor intelligence.
And you could both easily have your pick of them,
for fathers are always happy to find their girls
good husbands – and you indeed are of the best,
the cream of the heroes of this or any age,
you and your fathers and your family of old.
Come then, friends, let us marry our brides
and we'll all help you find your own somewhere else."
I've said that so often; but each time my words
were blown on the winds to the rolling waves.
Stiff, stubborn men that you are, you took no notice.
But listen this time, if only as our cousins.'[63]

[*A lacuna in the text: the beginning of Castor's reply is lost.*]

CASTOR

... but if your hearts are set on a fight,
on a family feud, if our spears must swim in blood,
then Idas and my brother, manly Polydeuces,
must keep their hands out of this hateful dispute.
Let Lynceus and me, the two younger brothers,
submit this thing to the harsh judgement of war.
That will spare our fathers a part of their grief;
one death in one family shall be quite enough.
The others shall then be the toast of their comrades,
bridegrooms not corpses, and shall marry the girls.
Thus the least harm will come of this family feud.

The god acted on his words. For the two elder brothers
both took off their armour and laid it on the ground.
Lynceus stepped forward, gripping his sturdy spear
beneath the rim of his shield, and Castor brandished his;
proud plume-feathers nodded on both their crests.
At first they set to work with their spears,
lunging at any glimpse of exposed flesh;
but before either was wounded, both weapons
stuck fast in the other's grim shield, and were smashed.
Then each straight away had his sword from his scabbard
to do his enemy to death. The struggle seemed endless.
Castor landed blow after blow on his shield,
on his plumed helmet; Lynceus, with his eagle eye,
pierced his shield back and clipped his crimson plume.
Then Lynceus thrust his sword-point at Castor's left knee;
Castor dodged back, and sliced off his fingers.
Lynceus was beaten; he dropped his sword, turned,
and ran off swiftly to his father's tomb,
where mighty Idas lay watching the duel.
But the son of Tyndareus was quickly after him,
and plunged his broad blade deep into his side,
and then through the navel. The metal spilt his entrails.
Lynceus slumped, collapsed on to his face;
the deepest of all sleeps had soon sealed up his eyes.

But Laocoosa was not to see even her other son
happily married at his father's hearth. For Idas
had quickly ripped up Aphareus' tombstone
and was making to hurl it at his brother's killer.
But Zeus defended Castor; he dashed the carved stone
from the brother's hands, and destroyed him with a
    thunderbolt.
To take on the sons of Tyndareus at war
is no light thing. Sons of the supreme,
they are themselves supreme among men.

And so, farewell, sons of Leda.
Send down blessings on all my hymns,
make them immortal. All singers are dear
to the sons of Tyndareus, to Helen,
and to the heroes who sacked Troy with Menelaus.

Your fame was won by the singer of Chios,
in his hymns on Priam's city, the Achaean ships,
the battles won at Troy, and on towering Achilles.
Here I, too, offer you the Muses' soothing songs,
as far as both they and my talents allow.
For such hymns of praise are a god's most precious right.

XXIII. *The Lover*

A lover once pined for a heartless youth
whose looks were charming, but whose ways not so.
He hated his admirer, showed him no sympathy,   .
knew nothing of the kind of god Love is –
of the deadly bow he carries in his grasp,
of the cruel arrows he shoots into the heart.
So in talk behind his back, or even face to face,[64]
this boy was adamant; he gave the man
no comfort for his raging fires: no flicker of the lip,
no twinkle in his eye, no rose in his cheeks,[65]
no word, no kiss, to ease the lover's heart.
He eyed this poor wretch as a woodland beast
glares up at its hunters. His lips wore a sneer,
and his eyes betrayed a compulsive cruelty.[66]
His anger at such moments transformed his face;
haughty feelings drained all colour from his cheeks.
But despite all this his rare beauty was constant;
his lover was aroused all the more by his rage.
At last he could stand the flames no longer, so fierce
was Cytherea's fire, so he went along to that forbidding
    house
and wept, and kissed the doorpost, and cried aloud:
'Pitiless, sadistic, nursling of some brutal lioness,
stone-hearted, unworthy of any human love,
I come to your door with the last of my gifts:
my corpse in its noose. I wish no longer,

my dear young friend, to trouble you with the sight of me.
I'm off on the road you've condemned me to,
where lies, men say, the common cure for one-way love:
the road to oblivion. Yet if I take the cup,
and put it to my lips, and finally drink it dry,
my desire shall not even then be quenched.
Now at last, my love, I bid your door farewell.
I know what is to be. A rose may have beauty,
but time will wither it; likewise, the snowdrop
may blossom in spring, but will quickly age.
The lily is white, but it fades in its time;
the snow too is white, but it melts in the warmth:
so the beauty of childhood is fine but short-lived.
There will come a day when you too will love,
when your heart will burn, and you'll weep salt tears.
So I ask you, boy: do me one last favour.
When you leave your house, and find a poor wretch
hanging in the doorway, don't pass him by.
Stay a moment, and weep a little. Offer your tears;
then untie the rope and cover me up
with something you're wearing. Give me one last kiss,
grant the touch of your lips to my corpse at least.
Have no fears; I can do you no further harm;
one kiss, and you'll be rid of me.
Dig me a grave, where I may hide my love;
and before you leave, say three prayers for me:
"My friend, lie still." And, if you will,
this too: "My noble friend is dead."
Then write this epitaph I scratch here on your wall:
"Love killed this man. Traveller, pass him not by.
Rest here, and say: He had a heartless friend."'

    With this he took a stone, a fateful stone,
and placed it on the threshold of the door
from whose lintel he slung his rope;
he looped the noose around his neck, and kicked away
the stone support beneath his feet. He hung there, dead.

Soon after, the boy came through the door.
He saw the corpse, hanging in his very entrance,

but didn't even look twice. He shed not one tear
over the body, still warm, but just wiped himself on it,
smeared his boy's clothes in blood, and went his way,
regardless, to wrestle at the gymnasium,
and, unmoved, to swim at his favourite pool.
He approached the god he had insulted, climbed
onto his shrine, and dived into the water.
The statue, too, dived in, on top of him,
killing the heartless boy. His blood stained the water;
and a child's voice floated over it, saying:

Now rejoice, all those in love,
for he that hated is dead.
Now love, all those who hate,
for the god sees justice done.

XXIV. *The Infant Heracles*

One night, when Heracles was ten months old,
Alcmena of Midea bathed him and Iphicles,
his younger brother by a night, as usual;
she suckled them, and laid them in that same bronze shield
Amphitryon stripped from the dying Pterelaüs.
Gently she stroked her children's hair, and said:
'Sleep, my babies, sleep sweetly and wake refreshed.
Sleep in peace, little brothers, your mother's soul.
Blest be your rest and blessed your awakening.'
She rocked the great shield; and they fell asleep.
But at midnight, when the Bear swings west
against the mighty shoulder of Orion,
fiendish Hera[67] dispatched two deadly monsters
to slide across the broad-beamed threshold of the house,
two glistening snakes, weaving their ice-blue coils,
with orders to devour the baby Heracles.
Coiling and uncoiling, they slithered forward
on their hungry bellies, their eyes glinting

with an evil fire, their gaping mouths spitting poison.
But when they were near, and their forked tongues
flickered over the sleeping children, a sudden light
filled the house – for great Zeus knew all –
and Alcmena's little children woke up.
Iphicles looked up, and saw the deadly creatures,
their cruel jaws leering over the shield's rim;
he screamed, and kicked off the woolly blanket,
desperate to get away. But Heracles faced them,
and took them in his hands, and gripped their necks,
keeping tight hold on those throats with their deadly
   poison,
hated and feared even by the gods. At that, the snakes
wound their coils tight around the child,
this boy, this suckling babe that never wept,
tightened their knot, then relaxed it again,
easing the pain in their twisted spines.

   Alcmena was the first to be awakened by the cry.
'Get up, Amphitryon. I'm too terrified to move.'
'Quick, get up, don't stop to put your sandals on.
Can't you hear our little boy screaming?
Can't you see this light all around the walls,
like dawn, though it's still the dead of night?
There's something wrong in this house, my lord.'
While still she spoke, he was out of bed;
he snatched his mighty sword, hanging as ever
above their cedar couch; then he seized his scabbard
of sturdy lotus-wood, and with his other hand
strapped on his new baldric. Suddenly the room
was plunged back into darkness, so he called
to his slaves, who lay snoring, deep asleep:
'Bring lights, men, quickly, bring torches from the fire!
Break down the door! Burst through its iron bolts!'
A Phoenician housemaid, sleeping by the corn-mill,
heard him and cried: 'Get up men, quickly!
The master's calling!' All were up in a moment.
They lit their torches and came out headlong;
soon the house was full of running people.

When at last they saw Heracles, the baby,
clutching the two serpents in his tiny hands,
there were cries of amazement. But the baby boy
held the creatures up to Amphitryon's eyes,
then danced with childish joy, and laughed,
and laid the monsters, slumbering now in death,
at his father's feet. Iphicles was in a frenzy,
stiff with terror; Alcmena clutched him to her breast.
Amphitryon laid Heracles back beneath his blanket
and so returned to bed, to resume his rest.

   The cock's third crow was just proclaiming dawn
when Alcmena summoned Teiresias the prophet,
man of truth, and told him the whole mystery.
She asked what would come of it, saying:
'Do not, if the gods have some curse for us,
hide it from me. For there's no way at all
that man can escape what Fate weaves at her loom.
But forgive me, son of Eures; I teach wisdom to the wise.'
'Take heart,' Teiresias replied, 'Seed of Perseus,
mother of the great, take heart, be mindful now
of the better things among those that are to come.
By the sweet light that deserted my eyes long since,
I say that many a woman of Greece, as each night
she cards the soft wool about her knees,
shall sing of Alcmena; you, my lady, will be worshipped
by the women of Argos. For this son of yours,
this mighty man, a broad-chested hero,
supreme of all creatures, whether man or beast,
shall rise among the stars to a throne in heaven.
It is decreed he will fulfil twelve tasks,
then take his place above in the House of Zeus;
a pyre in Trachis[68] shall have his mortal remains.
And he shall be called a son of the immortals
in his marriage, of those same immortals
who sent those monsters to destroy the child.[69]
Now, my lady, you must prepare a fire
beneath those ashes. You must collect dried twigs
of wild pearwood, parched and windblown,

of thorny paliurus, of brambles and briars.
And on this firewood you must burn those snakes
at midnight, the hour they tried to kill your child.
Then tell one of your maids to gather the ashes
before first light, and to carry them off
over the river to the rugged cliffs,
there to throw them away, every last speck,
fling them beyond your borders, then return;
but not once on the way may she look behind her.
For your house: first, to fumigate it,
burn pure sulphur; mix fresh water with salt,
as the custom is, and sprinkle it around
from a young twig bound in wool. Last, sacrifice a boar
to Zeus the Master, and you will master all your enemies.'
Despite the weight of his many years,
Teiresias left his ivory throne, and was gone.

So Heracles, nourished by his mother's care,
grew up at her side like a sapling in a vineyard
and was dubbed the son of Amphitryon the Argive.
Reading and writing he learnt from old Linus,
a tireless guardian, heroic son of Apollo;
Eurytus, born to the wealth of great estates,
taught him to draw a bow and aim an arrow;
but Eumolpus it was, the son of Philammon,
made him a singer, shaping his hands
to the boxwood lyre. Every last trick
by which the Argive wrestlers with their supple hips
bring each other down, with all the devices
known to boxers and their leather gloves,
each ploy and movement practised in the art
of hand-to-hand combat, the young boy learnt
from Hermes' son, Harpalycus of Panopeus,
the man whom none dared look at
from far off, much less face in the ring,
so dark was the frown that furrowed his grim brow.
Amphitryon himself fondly taught his son
to drive and lead the horses of his chariot,
and safely steer his wheel-nave round the post,

for he'd brought home many a valuable prize
from the fast-run races in Argos, land of pasture;
and only time destroyed the chariots he drove,
the years alone slackened their leather harnesses.
Then how to cover his shoulder with his shield,
how to go for a man, with spear at the ready,
how to fend off a sword-stroke, draw up troops,
assess the strength of advancing enemies,
lead a cavalry troop – all this he learnt
from Castor the horseman,[70] then an exile from Argos
where his whole estate had been seized by Tydeus
whom Adrastus had given that horse-loving land.
No demigod rivalled Castor in the field
until the years had worn away his prime.

Such was the training devised for Heracles
by his loving mother. For his bed,
a lion skin was placed close by his father's –
an honour in which he deeply rejoiced.
His evening meal was some roasted flesh
and a massive Dorian loaf in a basket:
more than enough to fill a farmhand's belly.
By day he ate little, never anything cooked.
He wore a simple robe, reaching just below the knee . . .

[*The text breaks off here.*]

XXV. *Heracles and the Lion*

The old man in charge of the cattle
took his hand from the plough, and replied:
'With pleasure, friend, I'll tell you all you ask,
for I revere the awesome powers of Hermes of the Roads.
Men say that he of all gods is most angered
if you deny a traveller who asks you the way.
King Augeas' fleecy flocks don't all graze together,
in one pasture, or even in one place; some are shepherded

along Helisos' banks, others by Alpheus' sacred stream;
some beside Buprasium's vineyards; and others here.
Each flock has its own, quite separate, fold.
But there's enough to eat for all his herds,
despite their massive numbers, in Menius' great marsh,
for the water-meadows and the fens are rich
in the honey-sweet grass on which horned cattle thrive.
That's where they sleep – see, over there on the right,
beyond the stream, where the dense planes spread
   themselves,
and the wild olive grows green: a holy place, friend,
shrine of a formidable god, Apollo of the Pastures.
Close by are the farmworkers' spacious quarters;
we keep a careful watch on the king's great wealth,
beyond me to describe. Often we'll re-sow fallows
we've ploughed three, four times in a year.
The boundaries of his land are known to those that dig it,
hard-working men, who look after his vines
and bring the fruit in to the vats when summer wanes.
For this whole plain belongs to Augeas:
all those acres of wheatfield, those crowded vineyards,
right down to the furthest edge of Acrorea,
with all its rivers. He's nobody's fool.
And we spend all our days busy working his land;
that's the way life is for a country retainer.

   But tell me now, for I'm sure I can help you,
who've you come here after? Is it Augeas himself
you've come to see, or one of his slaves?
I know, and will tell you, the lot; for I see
you're no ordinary man, nor of humble birth,
cutting so fine a figure as you do: indeed,
the sons of the gods on earth are such men.'

   'That's right, old man,' Zeus' mighty son replied.
'It's Augeas I want to see, lord of the Epeians.
It's need of him that has brought me here.
If he's down in town among the people
dispensing justice and seeing to their needs,
then take me, friend, to his highest steward,

so I can tell him why I'm here, and have his reply.
It's the will of the gods that one man help another.'

'It must have been their will, stranger, led you here today,
so quickly is your wish fulfilled,' replied the old ploughman.
'Augeas, beloved child of the Sun, is here
with his own son, the good and manly Phyleus.
It was only yesterday he returned from the town,
after a long stay, to inspect his great estates,
his immeasurable wealth. For I reckon kings, at heart,
are just like other men, and feel their interests
are best protected if they watch them themselves.
But let's go to him. I'll take you down
to our farms, where I'm sure we'll find the king.'

And so he led the way, much puzzled in his mind
by the stranger's lion-skin, the huge club in his hand,
and where he might be from. Again and again
he thought of asking him, but held himself back,
checking the words on his lips, for he feared,
in the stranger's haste, he might speak out of turn.
It's no easy thing to read another man's mind.

The dogs sensed their approach from a distance
by their scent and then by the sound of their footsteps;
they barked at them angrily, and from all sides attacked
great Heracles, son of Amphitryon. The old man
they barked at, too, but in futile excitement;
they were wagging their tails and soon licking him.
He picked up a handful of stones from the ground
and sent the dogs packing, scurrying off; with curses
and swear-words he silenced their barking,
happy at heart that his home had such good guards
in his absence. And, 'Well, well,' he said.
'What a rash creature indeed the gods, our rulers,
have given man as his friend. So impetuous!
Were the beast's wits as sharp as his tongue,
and he could tell who to lose his temper with,
and who not, no creature on earth could rival him.
But he's altogether too hasty, too hot-tempered.'
And so they hurried on, and at last reached the farm.

THE TOUR OF INSPECTION

The sun turned his horses towards the west,
bringing evening on. The flocks of fat sheep
had left the pastures for their farmyard folds.
Next came the cattle, herd after herd, in thousands,
lumbering on like rain clouds across the sky,
driven by a southern gale, or a northerly from Thrace.
Numberless, without end, they roll on through the heavens,
in such profusion does the wind billow them up
one after the other, crest heaving after crest.
Just so the cattle thronged home, more and yet more,
until the whole plain was thick with them,
and all the paths, and the luxuriant meadows
were filled with their lowing. They rolled into the barns,
soon full, and the sheep settled in their folds.

Then not one of the countless farmhands
stood idle; there was something for each to do.
This one donned heavy shoes on his feet, pulled tight
with slender straps, to get near them for milking;
another put the calves beneath their mothers
to quench their thirst on the warm milk they loved;
this man held the pail; that prepared a rich cheese;
another drove the bulls back away from the cows.
Augeas meanwhile moved among them, checking every stall,
inspecting the care his men lavished on his stock.
Heracles, with earnest face, accompanied the king
and his son as they surveyed his vast wealth.
Amphitryon's son, for all his great self-control,
was amazed beyond all measure as his eyes took in
the god's enormous gift. For no mind could imagine,
no tongue explain how so many head of cattle
could belong to just one man – or even to ten:
no, not if they were richer than all other kings together.
But the Sun had granted his child this unique gift –
to be richer in cattle than any other man on earth.
And he saw to it himself that the cows always thrived
and fattened; they were free from all the sicknesses
which waste a herdsman's time, and increased

from year to year in number and in quality,
always granted easy births, and always bearing heifers.
With them, moreover, went three hundred white-legged bulls
with curving horns, and two hundred reds besides,
all fully grown, ready to mount and mate.
Twelve more, sacred to the sun, were pastured there;
glistening white, like swans, they stood out
from the common herd, and grazed apart,
keeping alone among the lush pastures of the plain,
such a lofty pride did they take in themselves.
Whenever wild beasts ventured out of the woods
to chase the livestock at large around the plain,
these would be the first to scent and to charge them
with ferocious bellows, and with slaughter in their eyes.
Far supreme both in courage and strength was Phaeton,
a bull of massive power, whom the herdsmen called Star
as he shone out so brightly among the herd.
There was no mistaking him. Now he caught sight
of Heracles' lion-skin, taut-dry, menacing,
and threw his whole weight, full face, at his ribs.
But the hero was watching, and met the charge
by snatching the left horn in a fearsome grasp
and straining that solid neck down, down to the ground,
forcing the animal back with heaves of his shoulder
till the muscle stood quivering on his arm, like a rock,
hunched over the sinews. The king, his warrior son
and all the herdsmen looked on in silent wonder,
stunned by the prodigious strength of Amphitryon's son.

Phyleus and mighty Heracles were heading for the town,
the rich fields far behind them. With sure feet
they picked their way along the narrow path
often hidden by the undergrowth, which took them
through the vineyard from the farms. When they reached
the road, and started out along it, Augeas' son
turned his head back slightly, over his right shoulder,
to speak to the son of Almighty Zeus behind him:
'There's something I can't get out of my mind –

a story I once heard, long since, about you;
if indeed, friend, it was about you. I was still young;
a stranger arrived here from Argos one day.
He was a Greek, from the coast, a native of Helice,
and he told this tale all over Epeia:
how he'd seen some Argive kill a wild beast,
a ferocious lion, the plague of the country,
that lived in a cave near Nemean Zeus' shrine.
He couldn't be sure if this chap was from Argos,
he said, or from Tiryns, or maybe Mycenae.
But he knew for certain, if I remember right,
that the stranger was a descendant of Perseus.
No other man on the coast, I reckon, but you
could have dared such a thing, only you.
And this animal skin you dress yourself in
is a clear enough sign of the strength in those hands.
Come now, hero, I need to know. You tell me
if I've guessed you right. Are you that man?
The one the Achaean from Helice spoke of?
Have I found you out? Then tell me, too,
how you managed to kill such a fearsome beast
single-handed. And how it came to be in Nemea,
with all that water. You'd find no such monster
in Apia – not that you'd want to.
Nothing like that could survive out there:
only bears and boars and murderous wolves.
For this very reason those that heard the story
could scarcely believe it. Some said he was lying,
telling cock and bull stories to raise a cheap laugh.'

    With that, Phyleus stepped to the edge of the path
that there might be room to walk side by side,
and a better chance to hear Heracles' reply.
The hero stepped up beside him, and said:
'Your first question you've answered yourself,
son of Augeas, quick enough, and quite correctly.
And since you've asked, I'll tell you in detail
about this monster, and how it all happened –
except where it came from. For none of the Argives,

despite their numbers, can be sure about that.
We can only guess that some god was angry
about our sacrifice, and sent down this curse
on the sons of Phoroneus. And savage it was:
for the beast, raging like a river in flood,
plundered the lowlands, massacring the people –
especially those of Bembina, whose land bordered his;
those people endured most intolerable suffering.

To kill this grim beast was the very first task
Eurystheus set me. So I took my supple bow,
a full quiver of arrows, and set off after him;
in my other hand a sturdy club of olive-wood,
its bark still fresh, its stem still moist, fashioned
from a spreading tree which I'd found by sacred Helicon,
and wrenched from the ground, twisted roots and all.
When I came to the lion's most familiar haunts,
I prepared my bow and lined up an arrow, tipped
with death, running the string through its rounded notch.
Then I scanned the horizon, first this way, then that,
in search of the cursed creature, hoping to sight him,
before he saw me. By the time it was noon
I'd still found no footsteps, nor heard any roar.
And in all those ploughed fields, among all those herds,
there was not one single man to be seen
about his work, not one I could ask:
sheer pallid terror kept them all in their homes.

So I went on searching the hills, and the undergrowth,
never thinking of letting up till I'd found him
and put my strength to the test. Towards evening,
he was on his way back to the cave, well fed
on flesh and blood, his tongue licking his chops,
with congealing gore spattered over his chest,
his bristling mane, his ferocious face.
Quickly I hid in the shade of a bush
by the side of the track, and as he went by,
let loose an arrow. It hit his left side,
but had no effect; for the sharpened point
couldn't pierce his flesh; it just fell to the ground.

The beast at once threw up his gory head
in angry surprise, to seek me out,
and bared his greedy teeth with a snarl.
I drew my bow and shot another arrow,
worried indeed that the first one had failed.
It struck him hard on the chest, right over the lungs,
but the deadly thing couldn't so much as prick
his skin; it fell, quite futile, at his feet.
  Now I was in trouble, for I was drawing my bow
in anxious haste a third time, when he saw me.
The merciless creature, rolling his eyes around
in a glare, had spotted me, and lashed his great tail
around his rear end, ready at once to attack.
His whole neck stiffened with rage, his tawny mane
seethed in his passion, and he arched his back
like a bow, hunching up his sides and his loins.
You know how a skilful wheelwright heats,
then arches wild fig-boughs into a curve,
to bind them into a chariot wheel; and sometimes,
as he's bending the smooth branch, he loses his grip,
and in one great leap it is far away: well,
that's how he threw himself at me, a massive jump,
hungry to sink his cruel jaws in my flesh.
I covered my quiver with my cloak, and held it out
in front of me; with the other hand, I raised
my rock-solid club high above my head
and smashed it straight down on his skull;
it struck the invincible beast's mere fur,
and split clean in half. The lion had fallen,
before he could reach me, from high in mid-air
to the ground between us, where he stood
on shaky feet, his head clearly dizzy;
the strength of the blow had rattled his brain,
plunged his eyes into darkness. It was then
I saw the pain had dulled his reactions
and seized my chance before he recovered.
Throwing down my quiver and bow, I grabbed
that trunk of a neck by the nape, and tightened,

tightened my grasp with all of my strength,
to strangle him. I attacked from behind,
for fear he should claw me and tear my flesh.
I stood on his hind feet to hold them down,
and straddled him, keeping firm grip with my thighs,
till at last, as I heaved, his body fell back
in my arms. He was dead. I laid him out on the ground;
his soul was gone to the depths of hell.

Now it was over, I began to wonder how best
I might strip the dead beast of his bristly skin –
no easy task, for I just could not cut it
with iron, with stone, indeed with anything.
Then one of the gods blessed me with the idea
of piercing the skin with the lion's own claws;
with these I made quick work of the skinning
and wrapped it around me, a sure defence
against the gashes and wounds any battle may bring.

That, my friend, is how the lion of Nemaea
came to his death; who, while he had lived,
inflicted great suffering on both man and beast.'

XXVI. *The Bacchanals*

Ino, Autonoë, apple-cheeked Agave,
three themselves, led three bands to the mountain.
There they cut wild leaves from thick oak-boughs,
gathered living ivy and earthy asphodel,
to build twelve altars on the open grass –
three for Semele, for Dionysus nine.
Then they took from their caskets holy offerings,
hand-made by themselves for the sacred altar,
where now they laid them in reverent silence.
This Dionysus had taught them to do;
this was the god's pleasure. But high on a cliff,
not far away, hiding in a mastich bush,

Pentheus watched them and all they did.
Autonoë was the first to see him.
Her scream was fearful; and with her feet
she scattered in chaos the god's holy relics
which only the initiate may ever behold.
She was already maddened; soon the others, too, raged.
Pentheus, terrified, tried to escape them,
but they chased hard behind him, their skirts
hitched up, with their belts, round the thigh.
'What do you want with me?' shouted Pentheus;
Autonoë replied, 'You'll soon see: before I can tell you.'
Then his mother, roaring like a lioness over her brood,
pulled her own son's head from its neck;
while Ino made firm her foot against his belly
and wrenched his arm clean off at the shoulder;
Autonoë followed on his other side. The rest,
meanwhile, tore apart what was left of him,
and returned in blood-stained triumph to Thebes,
bringing pain, not Pentheus, down from the hills.[71]
But I feel nothing for him. Those against Dionysus
are not to be pitied, whatever they suffer,
no, not even if only a child of nine or ten.
I pray simply to be pure, and to please
those with purity. The eagle is so honoured
by the Shield Bearer, Zeus. Through him
blessing comes only to the sons of the pure.

Farewell, Dionysus, born on Dracanus,
laid in the snow from the mighty thigh of Zeus.
Farewell, fair Semele; farewell to your sisters,
daughters of Cadmus, honoured among women.
Dionysus commanded, and you killed this man:
the question of blame can never arise.
Let no man dispute the will of the gods.

XXVII. *The Seduction*[72]

GIRL
It was Paris, a goatherd like you, who made off
with Helen – for all her wisdom.

DAPHNIS
More likely she set out to win her goatherd
deliberately – with a kiss.

GIRL
Don't be so sure of yourself, little satyr.
Kisses, they say, are empty things.

DAPHNIS
Even in empty kisses there is fond delight.

GIRL
I wipe your kiss from my lips. I spit it out.

DAPHNIS
You wipe your lips?
Then give me them again for another kiss.

GIRL
You should keep your kisses for your cattle,
not for unmarried girls.

DAPHNIS
Don't be so sure of yourself;
your youth, like a dream, will swiftly be gone.

GIRL
That's true. But what if I am growing older?
Life at the moment is all milk and honey.

DAPHNIS
Grapes become raisins. Roses wither and die.

GIRL
Keep your hands to yourself.
Any more, and I'll bite your lip.

DAPHNIS
Come under those wild olives with me.
There's something I want to tell you.

GIRL
No thanks. I've heard your smart stories before.

DAPHNIS
Come beneath this elm with me then.
I'll play my pipe for you.

GIRL
Go and play it to yourself.
There's no fun in your morbid songs.

DAPHNIS
Ssh! You'll rile Aphrodite unless you're careful.

GIRL
She doesn't worry me. I pray only to Artemis.

DAPHNIS
Quiet! She'll strike you down!
Once Aphrodite traps you, there's no escape.

GIRL
Let her do her worst. Artemis will look after me.

DAPHNIS
No girl has ever avoided Love. And you won't be the first.

GIRL

By Pan, I shall. It's you he'll enslave. And for good.

DAPHNIS

I'm worried that he'll give you to a lesser man than me.

GIRL

Many men have chased me. Not one has touched my heart.

DAPHNIS

Well, add me to your list. I've come to join the queue.

GIRL

Oh Daphnis! Dear heart, what can I do?
Marriage brings nothing but trouble.

DAPHNIS

No, there's no pain, no sorrow, at weddings.
People just dance for joy.

GIRL

And wives, they say, then fear their bedmates.

DAPHNIS

No, they run them. What have wives to fear from men?

GIRL

I'm afraid of the pangs of childbirth.
The stabs of Ilithyia are cruel.

DAPHNIS

But it's Artemis, your very own queen,
who eases the pain of women in labour.

GIRL

I'm afraid that childbirth will lose me my looks.

DAPHNIS

But if you love the children you bear
You'll see your youth dawn again in them.

GIRL
And if I accept: what gifts would you bring
to show how you value my hand in marriage?

DAPHNIS
You'll have my whole herd, all my groves, all my pasture.

GIRL
Well, swear that, once married, you'd never desert me,[73]
you'd never leave me without my consent.

DAPHNIS
Never, by Pan, I'd never leave you,
not even if you wanted to throw me out.

GIRL
Will you build me a bedroom? A house and a farm?

DAPHNIS
I'll build you a bedroom. I'll cherish your flocks.

GIRL
But my old grey father? What am I to tell him?

DAPHNIS
He will bless your marriage when he hears my name.

GIRL
Then tell it me. There's often much in a name.

DAPHNIS
I am Daphnis, son of Lycidas. My mother was Nomaea.

GIRL
A noble family. But mine is no worse.

DAPHNIS
I know; you're Acrotime, daughter of Menalcas.

GIRL
Show me the glade where you make your home.

DAPHNIS
Come, then. See how tall my cypresses grow.

GIRL
Graze on, my goats.
I'm off to see where this herdsman works.

DAPHNIS
Feed well, my bulls.
I'm going to show this girl my land.

GIRL
What are you up to now, little satyr?
Your hand in my dress, fondling my breasts . . .

DAPHNIS
Your little apples, soft with down . . .
I'm giving them their first lesson in love.

GIRL
By Pan, I shall faint. Keep your hands to yourself.

DAPHNIS
Don't worry, my love.
There's nothing to fear. Don't tremble so.

GIRL
Now look where you've thrown me!
This ditch is muddy, You've spoilt my pretty dress.

DAPHNIS
I'll lay my soft sheepskin beneath your clothes.

GIRL
No, no! Now you've torn my slip!
Why have you undone it?

DAPHNIS

I make my first offering to Aphrodite.

GIRL

Stop! Someone's coming. I heard a noise.

DAPHNIS

That's the cypresses whispering about your wedding.

GIRL

You've ripped my dress to tatters. I am naked.

DAPHNIS

I shall give you another dress, even finer.

GIRL

You are full of promises. Yet soon, perhaps,
you'll refuse me even a grain of salt.[74]

DAPHNIS

It will all be yours. I would give you my soul.

GIRL

Forgive me, Artemis. I have disobeyed you.

DAPHNIS

I will sacrifice a heifer to Eros,
to Aphrodite herself a cow.

GIRL

I came here a virgin. I go home a wife.

DAPHNIS

A wife, a mother, a child's nurse:
a girl no more.

And so they rejoiced in their fresh young bodies;
they murmured softly, and it was over;

their secret bridal love was fulfilled.
She arose, and returned to tending her sheep,
her eyes downcast, her heart glad within.[75]
And he, delighting in the joys of marriage,
took himself off to his cattle herds.

Take the pipe, shepherd; it's yours again;
let's think of another country song.

XXVIII. *The Distaff*

Come, distaff, friend of spinners, come with me,
grey-eyed Athena's gift to all earth's housewives,
share my joyful journey to Neileus' Miletus,
that glorious city, home of Cypris' shrine,
green and lush amid the slender reeds.
Thither we set our sails, and ask of Zeus
an easy passage; once there, I shall rejoice
to feast my eyes on my beloved friend,
on Nicias, the Graces' sacred son,
and feel the welcome of his mutual love.
And there, my gift of exquisite ivory,
I shall present you to his wife. With her,
you'll work to fashion many coats for men,
and many of those sleek gowns women wear;[76]
for every mother sheep might just as well
be shorn of her ample fleece even twice a year
for all that slender Theugenis would care,
such busy hands she has, such thrifty ways.
I'd never introduce you to the house,
be sure, of a slovenly or lazy wife;
for we are fellow countrymen, we share
old Archias of Ephyra's great town,[77]
the very cornerstone of Sicily,
birthplace and home of many honoured men.

Now you're to live among Ionians,
at fair Miletus, in the home of a doctor
whose skill with drugs can cure mortal disease.
There you're to win great fame for Theugenis,
to be, distaff, the envy of all wives,
that often she may fondly call to mind
her friend the poet. For all who look at you
will say to her: 'Great love lies in small gifts.
The precious things are those that come from friends.'

XXIX. *For a Boy*

In vino veritas,[78] they say, my boy,
so we too in our cups we must speak the truth.
I'll tell you then what occupies my mind:
it's you, that you'll not love me with all your heart.
I know it's so. Half this life I live
I owe to your beauty; the rest is nothing.
When it is your will, I pass a day
among the blessed; when not, all is darkness.
To plunge a lover into misery
is surely roughest justice. You are young:
listen to me, then, learn from your elder;
the gain will be all yours, and you'll be grateful.
It's best to make one nest in one sole tree,
out of the reach of all creeping creatures.
But you: today you're on one branch,
tomorrow another, always looking for the next.
Whoever sees and praises your fine face
is your friend for life; he who loved you first
is left among those on mere nodding terms.[79]
Men most like himself should be a man's best friends.
Live your life by this rule, and you'll always have
respect among men, and indulgence from Eros,
the nonchalant master of mortal hearts,

who has melted down what was once my iron nerve.
By your gentle lips, I beg you recall
that you were younger twelve months ago:
before a man can spit, we're old and wrinkled.
And youth, once lost, can never be regained;
it has wings on its shoulders, and all that flies
is well beyond the reach of mere men.
Think on my words, and show more kindness;
return the love of a man who is true.
Then, when you've grown the beard of manhood,
we'll be like Achilles and his friend.
But if you throw my words to the wind,
and say in your heart, 'Stop bothering me!'
though now I'd go fetch you the golden apples
or Cerberus, keeper of the gates of death –
if still you reject me, then love will die.
Were you ever to come, and stand at my door,
and call my name, I would not reply.

XXX. *For Another Boy*

Ah, the pain of this cursed disease!
It's more than a month I've suffered love's quartan.[80]
The boy's looks are mediocre,
but he leaves such a path of grace in his steps,
and the smile on his lips is sweetness itself.
Just now the pain doesn't come every day;
it eases at times. But already it's changing;
soon I'll have no relief: no, not sleep.
For yesterday, as he passed me by,
he gave me a sidelong glance, too shy
to look me in the face – and he blushed.
At once love tightened its grip on my heart,
and I hurried home, my new wound smarting.
I called my soul to account, asked myself:

'What can it be you're after now?
Is there never an end to your stupidity?
Your hair's grey at the temples. Or had you forgotten?
It's time you saw sense. Your youth is long gone.
Your looks are lost, so stop behaving
as if you were taking your first taste of life.
And another thing: as a man grows old,
he should steer himself clear of the love of young boys.
They are far too cruel. Life bears some along
as a swift hoof a deer; they can change tack tomorrow,
quite alter their course, and the flower
of their youth smells as sweet as before.
But the man in love can feed only on memory
as desire consumes him to the very bone.
His every night is plagued by fantasies,
and a year's not enough to shake off the disease.'
With these few home truths I reproved my soul,
and with others beside; then came the reply:
'Whoever's intent on mastering Love and his tricks
must first count the numberless stars above.[81]
Now, like it or not, I must stretch my neck
beneath the hard yoke, and must bear its load;
for such is the will, my friend, of that god
who cheated even omniscient Zeus,
laid low mighty Cypris. With a single breath
he picks me up, then carries me off,
like a leaf that lives on the wind one short day.'

THEOCRITUS

The Epigrams

I

Those dew-moist roses and that bushy thyme
are sacred to the Muse of Helicon.
But yours, Apollo, is the dark-leaved bay
which sanctifies your shrine on Delphi's height;
this horned white goat chewing the terebinth
shall stain your holy altar with his blood.

II

Daphnis the fair-skinned, who plays country songs
upon his well-tuned pipe, now gives to Pan
his flute, his staff, his javelin, a skin
and this, the pouch in which he carries fruit.

III

You sleep here, Daphnis, on the leafy ground,
resting your tired limbs, now your nets are staked
high on the hills. But Pan is after you;
and Priapus, too, with ivy-gilded brow . . .
together they approach your cave. Now run!
Shake off this drowsiness! Wake up and run!

IV

Along that footpath, shepherd, past the oaks,
you'll come across a statue, newly carved
from fig, its bark still fresh. You'll see it's lost
its legs and ears, but still has all it needs
to procreate, to do great Cypris' work.
It's in a sacred grove, close by a spring

forever flowing from the rocks round bays
and myrtles and sweet-smelling cypresses.
A vine spreads out its tendrils there, and bears
its fruit; in spring, the clear-voiced blackbird sings
his lively tune and lilting nightingales
return the song in honeyed notes. Go there;
sit down, and pray to gracious Priapus
that I may lose my love for Daphnis. Say,
should he grant this, at once I'll offer him
a fine young goat. Should he refuse,
I'll make three offerings to win my love:
a goat, a heifer and a hand-reared lamb.
Now may the god receive and grant my prayer!

V

Come on now, by the Nymphs, let's have a song.
Play something pretty on your double-flute;
then I will take my lyre, and I'll strike up
and Daphnis, too, the cowherd, will join in
and charm us, with the breath of his waxed pipes.
Let's stand among the oak-leaves, by the cave,
and rob old Pan, goat-lover, of his sleep!

VI

What do you gain, poor Thyrsis, by these tears?
Why weep your eyes away? It's gone, your kid,
your pretty love, it's dead and gone, caught up
and savaged in the cruel jaws of the wolf.
Your dogs still bark; but when death comes, and bones
and ashes both are gone, what do you gain?

VII

You left behind, Eurymedon, an infant child
when, in your prime, death took you to your grave.

Now you are with the godly; but your son is shown
respect, in memory of his father's name.

VIII

Miletus welcomes now the Healer's son,[1]
come here to share the home of Nicias
the doctor, who burns offerings each day
before his cedar statue; he indeed
commissioned it himself. Eetion,
the sculptor, was rewarded handsomely –
the just deserts of master craftsmanship –
and on this work he lavished all his art.

IX

Take, friend, Orthon of Syracuse' advice:
never sail on a stormy night when drunk.
I did; and now lie here abroad, short-changed,
deprived of richer burial at home.

X

This marble altar Xenocles set up
for you, Muses, in honour of all nine.
His music's made him famous, as all know,
but he does not forget the gift was yours.

XI

This is the grave of Eusthenes the wise,
a physiognomist, whose eye could read
a man and know the nature of his mind.
His friends have buried him with honour here,
a foreigner in foreign soil, a poet
loved dearly by his fellow men. The sage

died destitute, but now has all he should –
for such a man, help was not hard to find.

XII

Damomenes the choirmaster set up
this tripod, Dionysus, and this bust
of you, most gracious of the blessed gods.
He was in all a modest man; his sense
of seemly beauty won his choir the day.

XIII

This goddess is not Cypris of the People.
When you pray, call her The Heavenly,
set here to share the home of Amphicles,
just as he did his children and his life.
This I have done, Chrysogona the chaste.
Since, Holy Lady, first they worshipped you,
from year to year their happiness has grown.
For mortal men who bear the gods in mind
find that their service is its own reward.

XIV

This bank makes welcome citizen and foreigner
alike. Deposits and withdrawals strictly depend
upon the state of your account. No haggling here.
Caicus will change your money even after dark.

XV

Now, traveller, I shall know if you esteem
a worthy man, or count him a mere wretch.
For you shall say: 'God bless this tomb; it lies
so lightly on Eurymedon's sacred head.'

XVI

This girl was in her seventh year when death,
untimely death, took her, so full of life.
Poor child, she died of grief; her brother too,
just twenty months, had tasted cruel death.
Ah! How, Peristere, you've suffered! How
God sets despair and death so near at hand!

XVII

Look on this statue, traveller; look well,
and then, when back at home, 'In Teos,' say,
'I saw an image of Anacreon,
the greatest of the songmakers of old.'
And, if you seek the essence of the man,
then say of him, 'He gave joy to the young.'

XVIII

The words are Doric, Doric too the man:
the poet Epicharmus, pioneer
of comedy. To honour you, Bacchus,
his fellow citizens have raised in bronze
what once was flesh and blood. Our debt is paid.
We men of Syracuse remember here
the wisdom of his words, the way of life
he taught our children. Here we offer thanks.

XIX

Here lies the poet Hipponax. Do not,
unless quite pure of heart, come near his tomb.
But if you are a worthy man, and true,
feel free to sit, and sleep here if you will.

XX

Here, by the road, this monument was built
by young Medeius for his childhood nurse;
and here he wrote her name: Cleita of Thrace.
The love she showed him has its just reward,
for now she always will be called The Good.

XXI

Stand here and look upon Archilochus,
the old iambic poet, known from east
to west. The Muses surely cherished him,
Apollo loved him well – so full was he
of music and of words, so rarely skilled
in playing, and in singing to the lyre.

XXII

This is Peisander of Camirus, first
to chronicle the son of Zeus, in verse:
his lion-fights, the swiftness of his hand,
the labours he performed. Now many months
have passed, and many years, but here
the poet stands in bronze for all to see.

XXIII

What tomb this is and whom it holds
are clearly written: 'I am Glauce's grave.'

XXIV

These offerings Apollo had of old;
the bases here are younger – twenty years

for this, for this one five, this twelve,
and here two hundred, as the dating shows.

XXV

Think, traveller, have a care; do not set sail
now, out of season. Life is short enough.
You, poor Cleonicus, set out in haste
from Lower Syria, eager to do trade
in Thasos – oh, Cleonicus, for trade!
You sailed just as the Pleiads set; and so,
as they sank beneath the ocean, so did you.

XXVI

[*For a collection of pastoral poems.*]

The pastoral Muses once were scattered; now
they are together in one fold, one flock.

XXVII

I am Theocritus of Syracuse,
not he of Chios; mine's the greater town.
Son of Praxagoras and Philinna,
I am the author of these pastorals.
It is no alien Muse I have espoused.[2]

BION

The Poems and Fragments

1. *Lament for Adonis*

I weep for Adonis, cry, 'Fair Adonis is dead';
'Fair Adonis is dead,' the Loves echo my grief.
Sleep no more, Cypris, shrouded in purple,
awake to this grief, and put on mourning,
beat your breast and tell all mankind:
'Fair Adonis is dead.'

I weep for Adonis; the Loves echo my grief.

Fair Adonis lies high in the hills, his thigh
holed by a tusk, white into white.
Cypris despairs as his breathing grows softer;
the blood flows red down his snow-white flesh,
the eyes beneath his brow grow dark,
the rose flies from his lip, and on it dies
the kiss that Cypris shall never know again.
Now the goddess longs for the kiss of the dead,
and he cannot feel the live touch of her lips.

I weep for Adonis; the Loves echo my grief.

Cruel, cruel was the wound in his thigh,
but crueller still the wound in her heart.
Loud is the baying of his faithful dogs,
loud the weeping of the Nymphs on the hill.
Aphrodite unbraids her hair, goes barefoot,
in tears, around the wood, her curls in tatters.
The undergrowth tears at her sacred flesh,
the brambles spill her holy blood, but on she runs,
her cries the louder, the length of the glades,
screaming for her Assyrian boy,
forever calling on her lover's name.
A dark pool of blood congeals round his navel,

the purple spreads up his breast from the thighs,
discolouring the nipples, once white as snow.

'Alas, Cytherea,' the Loves cry again.

Her gracious man has perished, and with him
her beauty. When Adonis lived,
Cypris was fair; her looks died when he did.
'Alas, poor Cypris,' from every summit;
from all the woods, 'Alas, poor Adonis.'
The rivers weep for Aphrodite's grief,
Adonis is mourned by the mountain streams;
all nature's flowers grow red with sorrow.
Cythera's island is everywhere filled,
its ridges, its glens, with songs of lament:
'Alas, Cytherea. Fair Adonis is dead,'
and Echo replies, 'Fair Adonis is dead.'
Who would not weep for Cypris' luckless love?

She saw, she took in Adonis' mortal wound.
It was not to be checked; she saw his thigh
drowning in blood, flung up her arms, crying,
'Wait, Adonis, my lost love, wait,
stay till I am with you one short last time,
till I have you in my arms, pressing lip on lip.
Awake, Adonis, just one brief moment,
for a kiss, last kiss, a kiss to live
as long as you have breath; breathe your last
into my mouth, breathe your soul into my heart,
till I've sipped the sweetness of your poison
to the dregs, drunk the lees of your love.
That kiss I will cherish as I would
the man himself, now fate takes you,
Adonis, takes you into exile,
distant exile on Acheron's shore,
within the domain of that harshest of kings:
while I, a god, live on behind you,
a wretched god, unable to follow.
Take him, Persephone, take my lover;

you have far greater powers than I,
and all that is loveliest falls to you.
For me all that's worst, all that's saddest,
unending; again I weep for my dead Adonis,
and I live, Persephone, in fear of you.
You are dead, my one love, dearest of men,
you are gone like a dream. Cytherea is widowed;
her girdle of love lost its magic with you;
Love is lying idle and stays indoors.
Why were you rash? Oh, why went hunting?
How, oh how was so perfect a man
enticed to take on the wildest of beasts?'
So Cypris lamented; Love echoes her grief:[1]
'Alas, Cytherea. Fair Adonis is dead.'

Aphrodite sheds tears as Adonis blood,
drop matches drop; on the ground
they mingle, and bring forth flowers.
From the blood grows a rose,
from the tears an anemone.

I weep for Adonis; fair Adonis is dead.

Enough tears now, Cypris, enough for your man
as he lies in the woods. But it isn't right
to leave him there, alone among the leaves;
give him your bed, in death as in life.
For in death, Cytherea, he still has his beauty,
a beauty in death as a beauty in sleep.
So lay him now where he used to lie
on those same soft sheets, in that same gold bed,
where he shared your sacred sleep all those nights;
it is longing to bear his weight again.
Strew him with garlands, with flowers,
then leave them to die. Let all nature die,
now Adonis is dead. Anoint him
with Syrian perfumes, with oils;
let all fragrance fade, let perfumes all die,
for he was your perfume, and he now is dead.

There lies Adonis, wreathed in purple,
graceful Adonis. Love mourns; Love weeps;
the Loves have cut off their hair in sorrow.
Here someone has laid his bow at his side,
another his arrows, another his quiver.
One lays a feather. One looses his shoe.
Some bring water in a golden pail,
and bathe his thigh. One stands behind
and fans fair Adonis with his feather wings.

'Alas, Cytherea,' the Loves echo their grief.

Hymen has lit every torch at the door,
and sprinkled marriage garlands around it.
He sings no longer of wedding joys
but rather of grief, of Adonis' death.
The Graces weep over Cinyras' child,
saying one to the other, 'Adonis is dead.'
Their cries of sorrow have a sharper note
than their songs of praise. Even the Fates
weep for Adonis, and call out his name.
In their songs they weave him a life-giving spell
but it falls on deaf ears. Not by his own wish;
Persephone has him, and won't let him go.

Enough tears, Cytherea, enough for today.
No more wailing now or beating your breast.
There is time enough to come for your grief,
time to weep, time to sorrow, as year succeeds year.

11. *Myrson and Lycidas*

MYRSON

Come, Lycidas, sing me some pretty Sicilian song,
something graceful, moving, some love serenade
such as Polyphemus might have sung Galatea.

LYCIDAS
Very well, Myrson. I feel like a song. You name it.

MYRSON
That pretty Scyros love-song we envy –
Achilles' stolen kisses,[2] his stolen bride,
the tale of a boy dressed up as a woman,
of the tricks he played while in his disguise,
and of how he was spotted by Deidameia
in the bedroom of Lycomedes' daughters.

LYCIDAS
One day long ago, a black day for Oenone,
the herdsman snatched Helen and took her to Ida.
The whole of Achaea was summoned to arms:
not a man of Mycenae, of Elis or Sparta
would hide in his home from the dread call of war.
There was one, one alive, stowed away among women –
Achilles, who learnt how to spin, not to fight,
how to practise the arts of Lycomedes' girls,
how to live like a woman. He became quite a she.
In his dress, in his looks he was every inch female;
he rouged his white cheeks till they blushed dark as flowers,
he walked like a girl, wore his hair in a bow.
Yet his heart was a man's; he bore male desires;
and each day he would sit beside Deidameia
from dawn until dusk. He would kiss her white hand;
he would hold up her weaving and praise its rare grace;
at meals he would choose no companion but her.
Every move was a step on the path to her bed.
'All the others,' he'd say, 'sleep together like sisters,
but still you and I, virgins both, go each our own way.
We are friends, we are women, we share our good looks,
yet we sleep quite alone, each in separate beds.
It is cruel Nysa's plotting that keeps us apart . . .

[*The text breaks off here.*]

171

III. *Cleodamus and Myrson*

CLEODAMUS
Spring, Myrson, or winter, autumn or summer,
which do you prefer? To which most look forward?
Summer, when our labour is all behind us,
or rich autumn, when men have most to eat?
Or winter, when work's out? Those lazy days,
when men take their ease, make winter a favourite.
Or is it the freshness of spring that you love?
Come, tell me. We've plenty of time for a chat.

MYRSON
To arbitrate on the work of the gods
is not man's place. All four of the seasons
are sacrosanct, all equally fine.
But I must confess there is one I prefer:
I'll tell you, Cleodamus. It isn't summer,
when I'm always burnt by the heat of the sun,
nor is it autumn, the time of disease.
I can't stand winter – all that frost and snow.
No, give me the springtime all year round,
free from excesses of heat or of cold.
In spring all is love-making, everything blossoms,
the nights are as long and as fresh as the days . . .

[*The text breaks off here.*]

IV

A young fowler was once in the depths of a wood
out searching for birds, when he saw Love hiding
on a box-tree branch. He rejoiced at his luck
to have found, as he thought, so handsome a specimen;

slotting together his catching-rods,
he lay down in wait for his frisky prey.
The boy waited, and waited, it seemed, without end.
At length he grew angry; he threw down his rods
and ran out of the woods to find the old ploughman
who'd taught him his trade. He told him about it
and showed him Love's perch. Then the old man smiled
and he shook his grey head. 'Leave this one alone,'
he said to the boy. 'This bird's not for catching.
He's made of pure evil. You keep well away.
You'll find it's a blessing to let this one go,
for there'll come a day, when you're grown to a man,
when suddenly he'll be the one chasing you,
and whenever he pleases he'll perch on your head.'

V

I dreamt great Cypris stood before me
holding the hand of her little child, Love,
his eyes on the ground. And she said to me:
'Shepherd, dearest of men, take this boy,
and teach him to sing.' With that, she was gone.
So, fool that I was, I taught little Love,
a most willing pupil, all about music:
how Pan made the cross-flute, Athena the flute,
how Hermes the lyre, sweet Apollo the harp.
But he paid no attention to all of this detail,
just wrote his own love songs and sang them to me.
Then I became pupil; he talked of his mother,
her art, the lusts of both gods and men.
Before long I'd forgotten all that I'd taught him,
and could only remember the songs he taught me.

VI

The Muses are never afraid of cruel Love.
They make him their friend, settle him in their hearts,
and follow him closely. Whenever a song

is sung by a man with no love in his soul,
they abandon him, and will teach him nothing;
but if some lover sings sweet melodies,
they all flock to him, race to be first at his side.
Every word, as God is my witness, is true:
for if I sing of any other, god or man,
but Lycidas, then my tongue always stumbles,
cannot give of its best. But if I sing of him and of Love,
then my voice flows like honey, and my lips rejoice.

VII

... all I know is it's wrong to attempt the unknown.
If my little songs may be said to have beauty
then my fame, while I live, will rely on the past,
on what Fate has allowed me, and on that alone.
But if they are worthless, why try to go on?
Say Zeus, or even capricious Fate,
were to grant mankind two lives to live –
the one for the high life, the other for work –
one might perhaps get the work over first,
then live the second to reap the rewards.
But as Heaven only allows the one span,
and that too brief for all we would do,
how long must we wretches grunt and sweat,
how long labour and slave to pile more upon more,
to glut the desires of insatiable greed?
Can we all have forgotten we're only mortal?
That Fate has allowed us so short a time?

VIII

Happy are lovers whose love is returned.
Happy was Theseus in comfortless Hades,
for Peirithous went through its depths at his side.
Happy Orestes among the barbarians,[3]
for Pylades shared every step of his way.

Achilles was blessed while his friend was alive[4]
and happily died when his death was avenged.

IX

Evening Star, golden light of Aphrodite,
dear Hesperus, sacred crown of blue night,
as fainter than the moon, so brighter than all stars;
tonight, friend, you must light my way
as I go to serenade my shepherd love –
you, not the moon, who was new last night
and will dim too soon. It's not for robbery
or highway hold-ups I ask you
to light my path tonight: but for love.
And the course of true love is most worthy of light.

X

Gentle Cypris, born of Zeus or the sea,
why so unkind to gods and to men?
And again why so cruel to your very self
as to bear so evil a child as Love?
So inhuman, so pitiless, so quite unlike you
to behold or to know. Why these wings,
gentle Cypris, why these deadly arrows,
so we've no escape when he's tracking us down?

XI. *To Hyacinthus*

Seeing your pain struck Phoebus dumb.
He tried every cure, sought expert skill;
he anointed the wound with ambrosia,
with nectar; he bathed it all over;
but there's nothing can cure the decrees of Fate.

XII

So now I will go my way to the hill,
whispering to the sands of the shore
the prayers I pray to harsh Galatea.
I will not abandon my dearest hopes
until I am all but past old age.

XIII

It's not right, my friend, to go to experts
for all that you want, to approach other men
for everything. You make your own pipe.
It's the simplest of tasks.

XIV

Let Love summon the Muses, and the Muses bring Love.
And may the Muses eternally grant me song
whenever I wish it, most exquisite song,
the pleasantest cure for a man's every ill.

XV

Enough little drops of water, they say,
can dig a channel in a stone.

XVI

Don't leave me, I beg you, without some reward,
for even Phoebus is paid for his singing,
and recognition improves anything.

XVII

A woman's quality lies in her beauty,
a man's in his courage.

XVIII

Everything blessed by heaven is possible.
There's nothing a man may not do,
may not easily do, with the will of the gods.

MOSCHUS

The Poems

1. *The Fugitive Love*

Cypris was calling everywhere for her son Love:
'Anyone who sees one Love lingering at crossroads –
he is my runaway. I'll give a reward for information.
Anyone with word of him will have a kiss from Cypris.
And if you bring him in, you'll get more than a kiss.
The boy is easily recognized. You'd know him in a crowd.
His face is not white, more the colour of fire.
He has burning eyes, which pierce you right through.
He's an ill-tempered soul, yet most suavely spoken:
he never means a word he says. A voice of honey,
but a heart of gall; boorish, deceitful, an inveterate liar,
fond of childish pranks, and cruel practical jokes.
A fine head of hair, and an arrogant brow.
His hands are a baby's, but shoot a long way –
they can carry beyond Acheron to the kingdoms of Death.
His body is naked, his mind well endowed.
He has bird-like wings, and is always in flight
among both men and women – now to this one,
now that: he makes his perch on their hearts.
And he has a small bow, ready armed with an arrow,
the tiniest of darts, but it travels sky-high.
On his back a gold quiver, well stocked with these darts,
with whose venomous points he will wound even me.
It's a barbarous weapon, but far worse is his torch:
with its tiny flame it can kindle the sun.
If anyone catches him, bring him in chains.
Don't show any pity. If you find him weeping,
be sure it's no trick; if laughing, just drag him in.
Above all, if he ever starts trying to kiss you,
get out of his way. His kiss bears a curse,
his lips are pure poison. If he says to you:
"Here, take this and welcome. My armour's all yours,"
don't touch it. It's deadly. He's dipped it in fire.'

11. *Europa*

Europa once dreamed a true dream, sent by Cypris.
It was almost dawn, the night three parts gone,
when relaxing sleep steals down, honey-sweet,
to rest on our lids, gently seal up our eyes,
the hour when true dreams are all shepherded forth.
As chaste Europa, daughter of Phoenix,
slept safe and sound in her rooftop room,
she dreamt that two nations, one this side,
one that, were fighting the fiercest of wars over her.
They were both dressed as women; the one as a native,
the other a foreigner. The native woman clung to her girl,
claiming she'd borne her and raised her herself;
but the foreigner dragged her away by force.
And she wasn't entirely unwilling to go,
for the woman was saying: 'Fate gives me the right.
Zeus the Shield Bearer says that Europa is mine.'

Europa was frightened. She leapt from the bed
where she'd lain, her heart pounding.
The dream she had seen was a waking vision
for both women remained there in front of her eyes
as she sat in silence a long, long time.
At last she found her frightened, girlish voice:
'Which of the gods sent such ghostly visions?
I was deep asleep on my bed, in my room . . .
what could such strange dreams signify?
Who was that foreign woman I saw as I slept?
How did my heart feel such desire for her?
And why did she in her turn embrace me
with such love, as if I were her own child?
I pray that the gods breed no harm from this dream.'

Then she got up and went to find her friends,
those her own age, all from good families,

those with whom she loved to play: whether they danced,
or bathed their lovely bodies in the stream,
or gathered fragrant lilies around the fields.
And there suddenly they were, all on their way
to the seaside meadows, each with her flower-basket,
to be together again in their favourite place,
to share the fresh roses and the sea-sounds they loved.

   Europa's basket was fashioned from gold,
an object of wonder, of startling grace,
made with painstaking care by Hephaistus, a gift
for Libya when the Earthshaker bedded her,
passed on by her to the radiant Telephassa
because they were of one blood. Now it belonged
in all its beauty to Telephassa's daughter, chaste Europa.

   There was much fine work on the basket's bright gold.
First to meet the eye was Io, Inachus' daughter,
not yet returned to her female form,
a heifer swimming across the salt ocean,
thrashing her feet. The sea was blue lacquer.
On either side, high on carved clifftops,
a massive crowd watched the cow out at sea.
The second picture was Zeus, son of Cronos,
beside the seven-mouthed Nile, laying gentle hands
on Inachus' heifer, and lifting her horns,
restoring the girl to her true woman's shape.
Beneath the basket's rim lay Hermes,
stretched out beside Argus, whose eyes never sleep;
from his purple blood there emerged a bird
with wings the colours of flowers, a proud plumage,
spreading its tail round the golden cup's lip
as a ship spreads its sails when gathering speed.
This, then, was lovely Europa's basket.

When the girls reached the meadows, thick in blossom,
they shared with delight their deep love of the flowers –
the fragrant narcissus, the dark hyacinth,[1]
the violet, thyme – for the fields were rich:
spring filled the air and its blossoms the earth.

Then the girls had a crocus game, to see
who could pick most of its fresh yellow buds;
only their queen, in the midst of them,
gathered the flame-red rose, in its glory.
She was to them as Aphrodite to the Graces.

But her joy in the flowers was to be short-lived,
and her virgin girdle not long undefiled.
For Zeus, son of Cronos, the moment he saw her,
succumbed to a venomous arrow from Cypris,
who alone had power over him. How his heart suffered.
Now he had to avoid his jealous wife's anger
and he hoped to bewitch the young girl's tender heart,
so he hid his godhead by becoming a bull –
not a common bull, who feeds at the trough,
nor a worker, pulling a heavy cart, or dragging
the curved weight of a plough through the earth;
no, he was no bull to graze with the herd.
His flesh was tawny, and bright on his brow
stood a pure white circle; his grey eyes beneath
flashed lightning glances of desire; on his head
two horns had grown high to a perfect match,
as if he had pared the horned rim of the moon.

He moved into the meadow. The girls, unabashed,
were seized by desire to approach, and to touch
this ox, this creature of beauty and fragrance;
even the luxuriant breath of the meadow was freshened
by its unearthly scent. So the ox moved among them,
and soon he was standing beside chaste Europa;
to weave his charm, he began licking her neck.
So she stroked him in return, and with gentle hand
wiped away the heavy foam from his mouth;
and she kissed the bull. He lowed, peacefully,
with as tender feeling as sweet Mygdony's flute.
He knelt at her feet, and beckoned her
with a toss of his head, to mount his broad back.
'Come on,' she called to her rich-haired companions,
'dear ones, friends, let's go for a ride on this bull.
Such fun! We can all fit on his back at once.

He won't mind. He looks so meek and mild,
so gentle, not at all like other bulls.
He seems to be blessed with a man's understanding,
lacks only a tongue to speak his mind.'

    The rest would have followed. But the bull was aroused,
seized by his desire, and he charged away,
making with speed for the open sea.
Europa looked back and called to her friends,
reaching out to them, but they were far behind.
The bull reached the shore, and ran on, out to sea,
treading the waves with undaunted hoof,
taking to the water with the ease of a dolphin.

    At his coming, the sea grew calm;
its creatures gambolled in great Zeus' path.
The dolphins jumped the waves for joy,
the Nereids surfaced from the depths
and escorted him on the sea-beasts' backs.
At the head of all, the thundering Earthshaker
cleared his brother a path through the waves,
and guided his way. Then the Tritons gathered
to attend him, lusty trumpeters of the deep,
playing marriage hymns on their tall spiral-shells.
Europa, meanwhile, on Zeus the bull's back,
with one hand grasped his mighty horn
while gathering her purple dress in the other,
for fear it should drag in the deep salt sea.
Its folds at the shoulder billowed wide in the wind,
like a ship's full sail, making her a light cargo.

    Soon she was so far away from her father's land
she could see neither wave-beaten shore nor high mountain,
only the wide sky above an endless sea.
She looked around herself, and asked
'Godlike bull, where are you taking me?
And won't you tell me who you are?
How can you voyage where bulls never tread?
The sea is for ships to cross under sail –
not for oxen, who always dread salt-water.
What is there here you can drink? What food

can you get from the sea? You're some god.
You must be; only a god could do this.
For bulls no more venture out into the sea
than dolphins on land. But to you
sea and land are all one. You've no fear.
You speed on your way; your hooves are just oars.
Perhaps before long you'll be up in the blue,
soaring over the clouds, like a bird on the wing.
What a fool, what an ill-fated fool I was
to abandon my home and to follow this bull
on so strange a journey, to be led so astray!
Pity me, Earthshaker, lord of the waves,
as I see you guiding our way, grant me mercy.
Be gracious, watch over me during this voyage.
For I know it's some god has me out here at sea.'

    As she finished, the broad-backed bull replied,
'Take heart, my girl. Have no fear of the waves.
Though I look like a bull, I am Zeus himself.
I can take on whatever shape I please.
It's love of you has led me to this,
to becoming a bull, making far out to sea.
Soon you will be in Crete, which nursed me,
there to be married. And from our love
will be born to you sons who'll be famous men,
all of them sceptred kings on earth.'
So he spoke; and all he said was fulfilled.
Crete came into sight, and Zeus once more
assumed his own shape. The Hours made them a bed,
Zeus untied her girdle, and so it was
that the virgin became the bride of Zeus
and the mother of the children of Cronos' son.

III. *Lament for Bion*

Join, glades, my hymn of mourning;
Dorian waters, lament with me;
weep, rivers, weep for Bion, for his beauty.
Now orchards, sorrow with me; sigh, groves;
flowers, breathe grief from your tight clusters;
now roses, deepen your red in mourning; and yours,
anemones; now hyacinth, let your lettering speak,
your leaves chatter their grief.
The beautiful flute-player is dead.

Sing, Sicilian Muses, raise your song of grief.

Nightingales, as you sing, deep among thick leaves,
tell Arethusa, Sicily's stream, that Bion
is dead, Bion the shepherd; that, with him,
music has died, and all Dorian song has perished.

Sing, Sicilian Muses, raise your song of grief.

Swans of Strymon, lament; raise your song
at the water's edge, your song of sorrow;
sing as you would at death's approach. Tell
the Oeagrian maidens, tell all the Bistonian Nymphs:
the Doric Orpheus is dead.

Sing, Sicilian Muses, raise your song of grief.

Now he will be heard no more
he that tenderly cared for his stock;
no longer will he sit and sing
alone among the oaks; but in the house of Hades
now must raise the song of Lethe.
And so the hills are silent; the cows,
wandering among the bulls, low mournfully,
and will no longer graze.

Sing, Sicilian Muses, raise your song of grief.

Bion, your sudden death brought tears
even to Apollo; the satyrs wept, and every Priapus
dressed in black; each Pan mourned your music;
all the springs bewailed it in the woods;
the waters changed to tears. Echo, too, is weeping
in the rocks, for she is silent, she may imitate
your voice no more. At your death
trees threw down their fruit, flowers
all wasted away. Now flocks no longer yield
rich milk, nor hives sweet honey.
In the honeycomb it dies of grief, and may no more
be gathered, since the day your honey perished.

Sing, Sicilian Muses, raise your song of grief.

Never before was the Siren's song so sad
along the beach, the nightingale's among the rocks,
the swallow's around the long hills;
never so sad was Ceyx' lament
for poor Halcyon, never the seabird's call
across the grey waves, the bird of Memnon's,
hovering in the vales over the son of Dawn's tomb:
never so sad as when mourning Bion's death.

Sing, Sicilian Muses, raise your song of grief.

The nightingales and all the swallows,
to whom he would give joy, and whom
he taught to sing, now sit among the branches
and sing alternately. The second choir replies:
'Birds, raise your mourning-hymn
and we will join it.'

Sing, Sicilian Muses, raise your song of grief.

Thrice-beloved, who now will play your pipe?
Who will put your flute to his mouth?
What man would dare? For your lips and your breath
live on; the sound of your music still echoes

in those reeds. Shall I carry your pipe to Pan?
Yet even he, perhaps, would fear
to play, lest he prove second to you.

Sing, Sicilian Muses, raise your song of grief.

And Galatea: she too sighs for your music,
she who would love to sit beside you
at the water's edge. The Cyclops' song
could not compare; from him she turned away,
lovely Galatea, but on you she looked
more happily than on the sea. And now,
its waves forgotten, she sits alone
upon the sand; but still she tends your herds.

Sing, Sicilian Muses, raise your song of grief.

All the Muses' gifts have died with you,
my herdsman; the sweet kisses of young girls,
the lips of boys. Around your corpse
the Loves weep pitifully; and Cypris longs for you
much more than for that kiss
she gave Adonis as he, that day, lay dying.

This, most tuneful of rivers, is for you
a second grief; this for you, Meles, another pain.
Homer, that first rich voice of Calliope,
has long been dead; men say that your great streams
were tears for your sweet son,
and that your grief quite filled the sea.
Now Bion: now you mourn another child,
and grief again dissolves you.
Both were cherished by fountains:[2] for one drank
at Pegasus' spring, the other at Arethusa's.
One sang of Tyndareus' lovely daughter,
of Thetis' great son, and of Atreus' Menelaus;
the other sang neither of war nor tears,
but of Pan. His was a herdsman's voice;
he sang as he tended his cattle;
he would carve his pipes, and milk

his gentle heifers; he taught the young to kiss;
he nurtured Love as his own child
and roused the passions of Aphrodite.

Sing, Sicilian Muses, raise your song of grief.

Every glorious city, Bion, mourns you,
every town: Ascra weeps for you
more than for Hesiod; Boeotia yearns for you
more than for Pindar; lovely Lesbos
grieved less for Alcaeus, Teos less for Anacreon;
Paros misses you more than Archilochus;
and Mitylene, who sorrowed for Sappho,
now grieves for your song. To Syracuse
you are a Theocritus; and Ausonia's lament
is this hymn of mine. For I am no stranger
to pastoral song, but a pupil of yours,
an heir to your Dorian style,
honoured, when others inherited
your wealth, to be left your music.

Sing, Sicilian Muses, raise your song of grief.

Ah, when the mallows perish in the orchard,
or the green parsley, or the thickly blossoming dill,
they grow again, and live another year;
but we who are so great and strong, we men
who are so wise, as soon as we are dead,
at once we sleep, in a hole beneath the earth,
a sleep so deep, so long, with no end,
no reawakening. And so it is for you:
in the earth you shall lie, shrouded in silence;
whilst, if it pleases the Nymphs, a frog
may sing forever. I do not envy them
his music: there is no beauty in it.

Sing, Sicilian Muses, raise your song of grief.

Poison, Bion, poison came to your lips,
and you took it. How could it touch
such lips without becoming nectar?

And what man on earth could be so vicious
as to mix poison and give it you
when you asked? He has poisoned music.

Sing, Sicilian Muses, raise your song of grief.

But justice comes to all. For me, this song
shall be my mournful elegy upon your death.
Had I been able to descend to Tartarus,
as Orpheus did, Odysseus, and once Alcides,
then perhaps I would have come
to Hades' throne, and, if you sing for him,
listened to you, and to what it is you sing.
Let it be some song of Sicily,
for Persephone, some sweet country song,
for she too is Sicilian, she once played
on Etna's shores; she knows Dorian music;
your singing would not go unrewarded.
As once she granted Orpheus, for the rhythms
of his harp, the return of his Eurydice,
so shall she return you, Bion, to the hills.
Could my pipe ever match the magic of his harp,
I would myself have sung for you to Hades.

IV

When the wind lightly ripples the dark blue sea
my cowardly heart is aroused, and my love of the earth
gives way to a powerful desire for the ocean.
But when the deeps roar, when they turn to grey,
and the surface foams, arching and bucking,
and the waves grow long and break with a crash,
then I turn my eyes back to the land, to its woods.
I run from the sea; and the earth more than ever
is welcome to me, the wood's shade refreshing,
where even when gales blow the pine will just sing.
The sailor's is a hard life: a ship for his home,
the sea his workshop, fish his elusive prey.
Give me sweet slumber beneath a leafy plane,

with murmuring water well within hearing:
the music true countrymen love, never shun.

V

Pan loved his neighbour, Echo;
Echo loved a sprightly satyr,
and the satyr was mad about Lyda.
As Pan's flame was Echo, so Echo's was the satyr,
and his Lyda. Love all round. And all got their due.
For anyone who pooh-poohed the heart of his lover
was rejected in turn by the heart that he loved.
Let this be a lesson to those yet to love:
love those that love you if you'd have your love returned.

VI

Alpheus, leaving Pisa and setting out to sea,
brings with him Arethusa, by whose water olives grow,
and fine wedding gifts: leaves, pretty flowers, holy dust.
He runs deep into the sea, flowing far beneath the waves,
so that water with water, fresh with salt, may never mix;
and the ocean never knows that the stream is passing
    through.
It's that setter of traps, that preacher of troubles,
that boy Love, weaving one of his spells,
has even managed to teach a stream to dive.

VII

Once tyrant Love put aside his bow, his torch,
and took up an oxherd's rod. With pouch on back,
he'd harnessed and yoked himself a tough pair of steers
and was ploughing and sowing Demeter's wheatfields,
when, looking up, he called to Zeus, 'Give me good
    harvest,
or I'll yoke my plough to Europa's bull.'

THE PATTERN POEMS

Two of the following six pattern poems, possibly more, cannot be understood without the help of the notes at the back of this volume, pp. 222–7.

Theocritus' *Syrinx* and Dosiadas' *Altar* are both entirely couched in riddles, and are so translated; the notes contain a full exegesis of these riddles. It will also be seen that Vestinus' *Altar* is built on an acrostic, which I have rendered into English; and that Simias' *Axe* and *Egg* both have to be read as the lines are numbered – from each end alternately, meeting in the middle. The poets vary in their concept of the pattern (or, more familiarly, concrete) poem, and the printing of the poems here is not designed to impose a specifically literary role upon them. The *Syrinx*, for instance, may well have been written purely for inscription on a pipe, never intended for the page; the same may be true of *Axe* and *Wings*. Both *Altars* are obviously purely literary in intent and form. But *Egg*, equally obviously, was not intended for inscription on anything but an egg. The reader must therefore grant a literary indulgence, and make his own transposition.

THEOCRITUS. *Syrinx*

The bedmate of Nobody, mother of The Warmonger,
bore the nimble pilot of The Stone-swapped's nurse;
not The Horned One fed by the son of a bull
but The Once-heart-burning for the P-less itys,
named whole, but double, lover of girlish
Split-voice, wind-carried child of sound,
who made a sharp sore for the Muses,
violet-crowned, to hymn his hot desire,
conquered parricide-like armies,
drove them out of Tyre's girl,
to whom this Simichid Paris
gives the blind's fond blight
which enjoy, man-treading
gadfly of Lydia's queen,
thief-son,   fatherless,
box-legs, delight in it,
play sweet tunes
to your mute girl,
a Calliope,
u n s e e n .

SIMIAS. *Axe*

1   To Athena, man-goddess, for her puissant advice, Epeius of Phocis

3   when with fire-breathing Doom he consumed all Troy,

5   not numbered among the Achaean vanguard

7   And now he goes the way of Homer,

9   Thrice blessed is the man

11   His every breath

12   is a happy one.

10   on whom you smile down.

8   thanks to you, Pallas, holy, wise.

6   but a murky stream drawn from that pure source.

4   the sacred city, drove gilded lords from their thrones,

2   has given this axe, with which he cut down high heaven-built towers,

SIMIAS. *Wings*

Look on me, lord of deep-bosomed Earth, overthrower of Acmon's son.
Have no fear, at such a beard on the chin of one so small;
for I was born long ago, when Necessity held sway,
a sullen regime, making every creature,
whether of Air or of Chaos,
keep itself
to itself.
Not so I, swift-flying son
of Cypris and Area; I won and now wield
my power not by force, but by gentle persuasion,
and all alike yield to it: land, deep sea, brazen heaven.
I make their ancient sceptre my own and lay down the law to the gods.

SIMIAS. *Egg*

The Dorian

1   The Dorian
3   a chirruping mother,
5   accept it graciously. For she was chaste,
7   Hermes, thundering herald of the gods, picked it up
9   among the tribes of men, with orders to increase, increase its pace
11   From the top he fattened the steep-slanting slope of its wandering feet,
13   swapping his legs for those of swift fawns, the nimble children of fleetfoot stags.
15   over topmost hillcrests with far-flying feet they follow the tracks of that nourishing nurse
17   till some bloodthirsty beast hears the echo of their cries in his den's deep recesses, and suddenly
19   listening, following the noise of their cries, dashing at once through the bushy glens on those snowclad slopes:
20   flying on feet as swift as theirs the great god made quick work, hurrying along the complex measures of the song.
18   leaps up from his sleep in the rocky lair, at once makes after the dappled mother's children, chasing a straggler,
16   past the caves of countless mountain-pasture-feeding sheep, past the caves of slender nymphs,
14   Immortal desire for their much-loved mother, for her precious teat, quickens their pace;
12   striking as he went all manner of notes in a song of Pierian harmony,
10   from one foot a line to ten, keeping proper rhythm all the way.
8   from beneath its fond mother's wings, thrust it out
6   the mother who shrilled its labour throes.
4   has spun this thread;
2   nightingale,

DOSIADAS. *Altar*

> I was built by a twice-young man,
> the husband of a transvestite jade;
> not the ash-bedded son of Empusa, the fate appointed
> to a Trojan herdsman and a bitch's pup, but the lover
> of a golden one; when the Man-boiler calmed
> the bronze-limbed wind, raised by the twice-wed
> Virgin-born,   mother-rejected.
> When he saw me erected here,
> the   murderer   of   Theocritus,
> the   burner   of   Three-nights,
> he screamed, he howled in pain;
> the belly-crawling Age-shedder
> had   crippled   him   with   poison;
> but as he made moan in the wave-washed isle,
> Two-life, the robber, Pan's mother's bedmate
> came, with the cannibal's son, to take him off, and his
> Ilus-piercing arrows, to Teucer's thrice-ravaged daughter.

VESTINUS. *Altar*

       Sacrificial juices, as dark purple
       As the trickling flux-drops of the
       Cuttlefish, never flow over me.
Raised high above, the knife spares all Pan's property
Its Naxos rock-honed blade; nor am I ever blackened as
Fragrant oils drip, thick fumes curl up, from Nysian twigs.
     In me you see no altar built from gold, no
     Construct of bricks or Alybean silver nuggets;
     Even less did that Cynthus-born race of two make
       Me from the horns of those bleaters
       Around the smooth Cynthian ridges,
       Nourished by its mountain pastures.
       Yet I may match any in the balance.
       You look on an altar built by the
       Earth-born Nine, with Heaven's daughters'
       Aid; the supreme lord of the undying
       Rendered their skill here immortal.
       So now, drink deep from the spring
       Of the Gorgon's child's hoof; pour
       Libations freely, make me sacrifice;
     Your prayers merit offerings far richer than those
     Made by the young girls of Hymettus. Come now,
     Proceed, approach boldly, for I conceal no
Impurities, no poisonous creatures such as hid in that
Altar set up by the purple ram thief at Neae of Thrace,
Near Myrine, to you, holy daughter of three fathers.

NOTES

These notes cover details of text, translation, authorship and exegesis, with other points of incidental interest. All further background detail concerned with proper names may be found in the glossary.

Editions, studies and papers referred to are:

Gow, A. S. F., *Theocritus*, Cambridge University Press 1950, revised 1952 edn.

Cholmeley, R. J., *Theocritus*, G. Bell, 1930.

Edmonds, J. M., *The Greek Bucolic Poets*, Loeb Classical Library, 1912, revised edn 1928.

Wilamowitz-Moellendorf, U. von, *Die Textgeschichte der Greichischen Bukoliker*, Berlin, 1906.

Legrand, M., *Étude sur Théocrite*, Paris, 1898.

Gercke, A., *Alexandrinische Studien*, Rheinisches Museum: 42, 1887; 44, 1889.

Lang, Andrew, *Theocritus, Bion and Moschus*, London, 1880.

Ribbeck, O., *Theokriteische Studien*, Rheinisches Museum: 17, 1862; 18, 1863.

Meineke, A., *Theocritus, Bion, Moschus*, Berlin, third edn, 1856.

Ahrens, H. L., *Bucolicorum Reliquiae*, Leipzig, 1855. *De Dialectis Aeoliis*, Gottingen, 1839.

Bergk, T., *Poetae Lyrici Graeci*, Leipzig, 1843.

Fawkes, Francis, *Theocritus, The Idylliums*, London, 1767.

THEOCRITUS
The Idylls

I. THYRSIS' LAMENT FOR DAPHNIS

1. I have accepted the emendation οὐ (the Greek negative) for οὗ (the conjunction 'where') which is the MS reading. This form would not have been used in Doric dialect. The text as it stands finishes with an aposiopesis – 'to avoid', as Gow puts it, 'an indelicacy'. Literally, then: 'Do men, talking about Cypris, not tell how the herdsman . . .' This phrasing is here dismissed as too coy.

2. The text specifies 'Lycaon's son', without mentioning Arcas by name. Lycaon was a mythical king of Arcadia.

II. THE SORCERESS

It is generally agreed that much of the structure and apparatus of this situation have been borrowed by Theocritus, if not directly imitated, from a mime of Sophron, which has eluded dating.

3. κατάδεσμος, 'binding', was a traditional magic remedy for errant lovers. The various herbs and materials (bay-leaves, wool, etc.) are listed in much the same spirit as those of Shakespeare's witches in *Macbeth*; all have their origin as magic charms in myth.

4. There are a number of islands referred to as Dia, but this of course is the one otherwise known as Naxos, and so identified by Callimachus and later authorities.

III. THE SERENADE

5. A Dorian version of 'He loves me, he loves me not'. The leaf of τηλέφιλον, literally 'love at a distance', has been identified as that, perhaps, of the poppy. Three substantial suggestions have been made about the ritual: (1) that the omen was read from the mark left on the arm after the leaf had been slapped on it by the hand; (2) that the omen was decided by the noise of the slap; and (3), which I have adopted here, that if the slap makes the leaf stick to the arm, he loves me; if it falls away, he loves me not.

6. Another such traditional omen: this time characteristic of the belief in involuntary physical movements heralding the lover's approach.

IV. THE HERDSMAN

In Idylls IV and V, Theocritus' style is at its 'lowest'; hence the coarseness of the dialogues, hence the obscenities. A doggedly purist translator would attempt to reproduce the two shepherds' language in respective regional dialects; it has been done. I have been content to keep the tone strictly colloquial.

7. Physical exercise and hearty appetites were two pre-requisites of athletic training periods. Digging was a commonly practised part of the athlete's limbering up; the twenty sheep would have been Aegon's rations during his thirty-day stint.

8. i.e. and devour the twenty sheep. The insinuation is that their sacrifice for the athlete's belly will achieve little more.

9. The township founded by Lampriadas has not been identified, so it is unclear at whom Battus is sneering. Edmonds suggests that Lampriadas is Milon's father; Gow makes a very full analysis which remains inconclusive.

V. THE GOATHERD VERSUS THE SHEPHERD

The singing match is a convention of pastoral poetry which Theocritus pioneered. In Idylls VII, IX and X there are sung dialogues which are not directly in competition (despite the MS title of IX); in V, VI and VIII there are specific judgements made on the singers' respective merits. But no criteria for victory in these contests are anywhere outlined, and the poet is clearly going to write the opposing songs to as evenly matched a standard as he can. Thus there is nothing not in the translation to help the reader ponder the final verdict.

10. These lines are generally rendered into Latin, a bizarre form of euphemism, or omitted altogether. As Francis Fawkes put it in a footnote to his 1767 version: 'There was a necessity in this place to omit translating four lines in the original, which are infinitely too indelicate for modest ears.' It is in fact a considerable pleasure to liberate the first line of Lacon's reply – a superb insult, surely.

11. The squill is a plant of the lily family, whose bulb was thought to have diuretic or generally purgative powers, especially effective for combating bile – which is the implication here. These are medically accepted properties, but the 'witch's grave' instruction adds a magical element. Graves were traditionally a setting for the practice of the black arts; those of witches, or sagacious old women, had an especial charisma. (The ritual of flogging Pan's statues with squills is referred to in Idyll VII; see n. 19.)

12. This necessarily fails to recreate an allusion in the original: literally, 'If I don't castrate you, may I be Melanthius instead of Comatas.' Melanthius was, like Comatas, a goatherd; his death, among the suitors and the reprobate women, at the hands of Telemachus and Odysseus, is described in *Odyssey* Book XXII: 'Melanthius was dragged out across the court and through the gate. There with a sharp knife they sliced his nose and ears off; they ripped away his privy parts as raw meat for the dogs, and in their fury they lopped off his hands and feet' [trans. E. V. Rieu]. Comatas, in other words, is vowing to castrate himself if he doesn't get the ram.

VI. THE SINGING MATCH

13. One of several examples in the Idylls of spitting as a means of averting evil spirits or curses. Admiring one's own reflection in water was a traditionally hazardous pastime; such vanity was not usually allowed to pass unpunished by the nymphs or sea-spirits, as Narcissus would testify.

VII. THE HARVEST FEAST

14. Simichidas is generally assumed to be a deliberate self-representation by Theocritus. This poem is thought to retell a true incident in the poet's past, and the other figures to be various of his friends. If it is true, this is a unique example of the *mascarade bucolique*, the city poet's pastoral charade, which is initially – as here – a deeply rooted literary device, but has its more ludicrous descendants in Marie-Antoinette's pastoral party games in the Petit Trianon at Versailles.

The argument as to the identities of the dramatis personae has been fiercely fought, but is not directly relevant to the qualities of the poem. The hypotheses are ably marshalled by Gow, who summarizes the theories about Lycidas as follows: Aratus (Bergk), Astacides (Ribbeck), Callimachus (Gercke), Dosiadas (Wilamowitz), Leonidas (Legrand) and Rhianus (Legrand).

15. Homer. For an explanation of these lines, see Introduction p. 15.

16. These birds were supposed to demand a calm from nature for their nesting at the time of the winter solstice. The Kids stood in the sky at the end of November.

17. The story is based on that of Comatas, a mythical goatherd whose master locked him in a chest, and opened it two months later to find him still alive and the chest filled with honeycomb. It has been suggested that Theocritus intends to draw a parallel with the savage treatment of the poet Sotades by Ptolemy Philadelphus, who is said to have thrown him in such a chest into the sea for criticizing his incestuous marriage. (See Introduction p. 16 and n. 54.)

18. Sneezing was regarded as an omen of good luck. But in the case of love, as here, its flavour could be bitter-sweet; the implication is that the poet, happily or unhappily, is *deeply* in love.

19. A reference to the ritual flogging of Pan's statues, dating from the occasion on which Arcadia's young musicians – who needed full stomachs to sing well – found he had denied them sufficient rations. (For squills, see n. 11.)

VIII. THE SECOND SINGING MATCH

The authenticity of this poem is questioned, largely on grounds of language, prosody and metre, with reference to various uncharacteristic shapings of the tale. The MS is not under any suspicion; all the questioning is internal. Gow concludes: 'I cannot believe that the Idyll is by the same hand as Theocritus' genuine bucolic poems. If not by him, it is by an imitator, but by an imitator of considerable independent talent.'

20. My own adaptation, not strictly accurate, of a corrupt line.

21. I have taken a liberty with ἰσομάτωρ, which literally means that the lamb is 'the same as its mother', i.e. as big, or perhaps of the same quality. 'The word does not occur elsewhere,' Gow tells us.

22. This song, down to 'I love them, so do you', marks a unique use of elegiac metre by Theocritus amid hexameters, which has been advanced as an argument against his authorship of this poem. The entire passage is textually disputed, and it is clear that the jump from line 52 to 53 means Daphnis' reply is missing; I have adopted Gow's reconstruction of the remainder.

23. This line, and its echo in the next stanza 'Both man and beast decay' I have generalized; for although the Greek specifies the particular shepherd, pasture, neatherd and cattle, the sense is universal.

24. One of many examples throughout the Idylls of a character invoking a divine precedent to prove the nobility of country occupations. The most frequent example, as here and throughout – for instance, I and XX – is the listing of gods who have adopted pastoral disguises to pursue their love affairs, or who have otherwise been involved by their amours in the country scene. It is a sound defence for the countryman rejected by his class-conscious beloved.

IX. THE THIRD SINGING MATCH

The authenticity of this poem is also in doubt. Scholars have suggested that it is an amalgam of disparate fragments, and its movement is certainly at times eccentric. The most commonly agreed resolution is that it is in fact a unity, but a less than mediocre unity, and well below our poet at his best.

25. This is more than the schoolboy belief, as in Idyll XX, that spots grew on a liar's tongue. There are various explanations of the blisters here; the two most commonly accepted are (1) that they

grew on the tongue which spoke of an absent love, or (2) that they grew on the tongue which concealed a truth entrusted, and vanished when the trust was betrayed. For those who accept the second thesis, of course, the blisters are the very opposite of a punishment.

X. THE REAPERS

It is worth noting that the landscape of this poem is more agricultural than pastoral, and that it is unique among the Idylls in this respect.

26. That χόριον means 'leather' is a conjecture with fairly wide acceptance, but 'skin', 'guts' and 'pudding' (Edmonds) have been suggested. The proverb, anyway, clearly points the dangers of one taste leading to addiction.

27. The Greek μάντις clearly implies that this creature is of the preying mantis variety. The 'grasshopper' reproach must be a reference to Bombyca's skinniness.

XI. THE CYCLOPS

28. Nicias was a doctor-poet, clearly a close friend of Theocritus. It is the same Nicias to whom Idyll VIII is addressed, and to whose wife the poet carries the gift of a distaff in Idyll XXVIII. Epigram VIII is a dedication for a statue of Asclepius he has set up.

29. Polyphemus' mother was Thoosa, daughter of Phorcys, a sea deity. She was a sea-nymph, and bore the Cyclops to Poseidon.

XII. THE BELOVED BOY

Scholars have had their doubts about the authenticity of this Idyll, not least because the Ionic hexameters in which it is written are not normally the vehicle for such emotional content. But the mystery which surrounds its presence in the MS has never been satisfactorily resolved.

30. The poem's title is ’Αίτης, meaning 'lover' or 'beloved'. This is a Doric word literally meaning 'hearer'. See n. 32.

31. It has been suggested that Theocritus is deliberately insulting Arsinoë, wife of her brother Ptolemy Philadelphus, as she had previously been married to Lysimachus and Ptolemy Keraunos. But Theocritus' praise of Ptolemy, his patron, in such Idylls as XVII make this unlikely; it seems more probable that he is joining in the general abuse of Helen's promiscuity, if indeed he means to specify at all.

32. The terms in the text, εἰσπνηλος and ἀίτης, in fact mean 'inspirer' and 'hearer', referring to their respective positions in the

homosexual relationship. These, at any rate, are the meanings deduced by Gow from the various traditions. Their implication is not disputed.

33. Lydian stone was famous for its use as a touchstone for testing gold. Gow, commenting that the ancient method of testing is nowhere precisely described, quotes the *Chambers's Encyclopaedia* (1904) definition of 'assaying': 'To compare the appearance of a streak made with the metal on a hard basaltic stone of dark colour with those produced by certain touch-needles, the composition of which is known, after all the streaks have been subjected to the action of nitric acid.' The ancient process is likely to have been similarly conceived, probably without the acid test.

XIII. HYLAS

34. Literally, in the text, 'flaming' star. The fall of such a star presaged wind; hence the ensuing two lines of the simile.

35. My own reconstruction of two and a half disputed lines.

XIV. AESCHINAS AND THYONICHUS

36. Part of the Pythagorean's staple diet was a daily loaf of bread, but specifically barley bread. The insinuation is that he demanded his loaf to be not merely of superior quality, but more elaborately prepared.

37. The movement of the verse is here akin to that accelerated in English by clichéd proverbs, so I have allowed myself the indulgence of vulgarizing the Greek adverb θᾶσσον, literally 'quickly'.

38. There has been much argument over the various mathematical sequences suggested by these numbers. I have adopted the generally accepted 'days', which is not actually in the text; and have rather smoothed the issue over, being content that my version totals sixty days, which is close enough to two months to satisfy the reader more interested in pastoral poetry than statistics.

39. The force of this remark is clear; but there has been some scholarly discussion as to the exact style of a Thracian haircut. Their practice was, it seems, either to shave the head completely bald; or, more exotic and so here preferable, to shave it bald with the exception of the crown, which was tied in a top-knot. The common Thracian epithet ἀκρόκομοι, used by Homer in *Iliad* IV, implies as much, and may – I think – be accepted. But compare Cholmeley: 'The Thracians as a barbarian tribe wore their hair long and ragged'; he marshalls Lucian to his defence.

40. Tradition – later enshrined in a proverb of Callimachus (Epigram XXV) – had it that the Megarians sent to Delphi to ask the oracle which was the most noble city in Greece. Back came the reply that Argos had the best soil, Thrace the best horses, Sparta the best women and Syracuse the best men ... 'but you, Megara, come neither third nor fourth, nor even twelfth; you just don't enter the reckoning'.

41. An ancient version, it seems, of 'curiosity killed the cat'. The formula of a mouse tasting something bitter had several variations as a proverb for getting oneself into trouble entirely through one's own fault; here the implication is that the mouse climbed the pitch-pot and fell in. It appears to have quite the opposite force of the literary reference it recalls to modern readers: *Macbeth*, I, vii, 44–5,

> '... Letting "I dare not" wait upon "I would"
> Like the poor cat i' th' adage?'

The cat hesitated to eat the fish as it would have to get its feet wet (Heywood, *Three Hundred Epigrammes*); Lady Macbeth is urging her husband to wade in.

XV. THE ADONIA

This festival was held in honour of Adonis and usually lasted two days, the first – as here – being spent in lamentation, the second in joyful anticipation of his second coming. In parts of Greece and Egypt it lasted eight days. There was traditionally a superstition that the first day on which it fell was one of bad luck.

42. See n. 74.

43. A rather free version of, literally, 'Everything is rich in rich houses.' The Greek phrase does contain a sneer, and imply a refusal to go, which a constrained English translation cannot mirror.

44. The Egyptians, with whom there was a long-standing hostility, had a bad reputation in moral matters, and it is historically noted that Ptolemy's reign did much to curb their behaviour.

45. Praxinoa is referring to the original seduction of Hera by Zeus. Although there were various legends, supplemented by considerable background detail in Book XIV of the *Iliad*, it was always supposed that much had been left unpublished about the incident, which became a favourite subject for gossip. It thus also became an apt prey for feminine intuition.

46. The Greek has, 'Don't level an empty (vessel)', a reference to the practice of smoothing surplus grain from the top of a filled

jar before sealing it. Levelling an empty jar may thus be understood as a proverb for wasting time.

XVI. THE GRACES

47. The poet makes use of the double meaning of the word Charites: either, the Graces, ladies-in-waiting to the Muses and a symbol of beauty and high quality; or, gratitude for generosity of the kind shown by patrons. This may have been the title poem of a now lost collection (see Introduction, p. 12).

48. Another anglicization, this time perfectly precise, of a clumsy Greek proverb: The knee is closer than the ankle. The line continues: '(Rather) may something come *my* way.'

49. Simonides.

50. The reference to the imminent Carthaginian wars dates the poem at 274 B.C.

51. The maid is Persephone, her mother Demeter. The city is Syracuse.

XVII. IN PRAISE OF PTOLEMY

52. Hebe is literally described as 'white-ankled'.

53. Deiphyle, daughter of Adrastus, king of Argos.

54. Gow explains: 'The incestuous marriage of Arsinoë with her full brother cannot have caused any surprise to their Egyptian subjects, for in Egypt such marriages were common both inside and outside the royal family, and, in it, had the advantage of securing for the children a double share of the royal blood.' But the marriage 'offended Greek sentiment', and the death by which Ptolemy punished Sotades for his crude criticism is intriguingly similar to the incarceration of Comatas in Idyll VII. See n. 17.

XVIII. HELEN'S BRIDAL HYMN

55. The famous Helen of the *Iliad* and the *Odyssey* was also worshipped as a goddess, and was as such closely associated with trees. There was a famous tree-cult at Rhodes, mentioned by Pausanias, and there was a legend that she was hanged on a tree. This line is famous for associating Helen's tree-cult with Sparta.

XIX. THE HONEY-THIEF

There is little doubt that this poem is not by Theocritus, but was included among the Idylls by editors because of its similarity to Moschus' *The Fugitive Love*.

XX. THE YOUNG HERDSMAN

The authenticity of this poem is in doubt. The arguments against
it line up behind the contention that similar themes are better
treated elsewhere in the Idylls, and this has the look of a poor
imitation. Gow summarizes the theories as to true authorship:
Cyrus of Panopolis (fifth century A.D.) (Ahrens), Bion or Moschus
(Meineke), School of Bion (Wilamowitz and Legrand). Cholmeley
comments: 'The language belongs to a later writer.'

56. This line is followed in the MS by two which have been
generally rejected. I have elected to omit them, as they intrude a
sudden reversal of Eunica's sentiments, which could only stand
rather speciously as a momentary hesitation in her dismissal:

> How daintily you coax me, how sweetly you beguile;
> that silky beard ... those gentle curls ...

57. Rhea, alias Cybele, loved a herdsman named Attis; he, like
Aphrodite's Adonis (quoted in this poem and Idyll I, 105), was
killed by a boar. The love of both goddesses was unrequited. Zeus
loved the shepherd boy Ganymede, to whom this is a reference;
the god changed himself into an eagle, and carried the boy up to
heaven to be his cup-bearer, or – as Shakespeare has it (*As You
Like It*, II, i, 127) – 'Jove's own page'.

XXI. THE FISHERMEN

The authenticity of this poem is in doubt, primarily on linguistic
and metrical grounds. Cholmeley quotes Andrew Lang: 'There is
nothing in Wordsworth more real, more full of the incommuni-
cable sense of nature, rounding and softening the toilsome days of
the aged and the poor, than the Theocritean poem of the Fisher-
man's Dream'; but then decides 'a piece worthy of Theocritus is
not necessarily a Theocritean piece'. He argues Leonidas of
Tarentum's case, but the notion is dismissed by Gow, who with
Wilamowitz is worried by the 'moralizing tendency'. He also
misses 'the continual reminiscence of earlier writers' and finds the
vocabulary 'bald and undistinguished, where Theocritus's is rich
and full of associations'.

58. This line and a half is my own resolution of one in the
Greek which has evaded satisfactory explanation.

59. I have supplied foxes, as creatures which hounds pursue and
may therefore be presumed in this sense to dream of. The text has
ἄρτος, a loaf of bread, which is clearly absurd, and does not sug-
gest any obvious misreading. The most common suggestion, ἄρκτος

(bear), is – rightly, I think – dismissed by Gow as equally unlikely.

60. I have omitted the following line, which is hopelessly corrupt.

XXII. THE DIOSCURI

This poem is thought to be an amalgam of various separate entities, probably two or three. One reason is that the Castor section is a strange story to choose for a panegyric. The separate sections – (1) the introduction, (2) Polydeuces and Amycus, and (3) Castor and Lynceus – are in themselves satisfactory, but the poem as a whole hangs together rather shakily.

61. Dioscuri means 'the sons of Zeus'. Theocritus takes the first part of the poem, the fight of Polydeuces with Amycus, from Apollonius' account in the *Argonautica*, improving on it in purely dramatic terms, without significantly changing details of the story. The entire opening section, and the conversation passage, are his own invention and appear a masterpiece of imaginative structure when set beside Apollonius' bald version.

The second section of the poem, Castor's fight with Lynceus, differs slightly from the narrative in *Cypria*, an epic poem of the eighth century B.C. variously attributed to Homer (wrongly) and to Stasinus of Cyprus. The tradition was that Idas and Lynceus, sons of Aphareus, reproached Castor and Polydeuces for having paid no dowries for their intended brides, Phoebe and Hilaeira, daughters of Leucippus (and so the Apharidae's cousins). The Dioscuri stole the Apharidae's cattle and handed them to Leucippus as payment. Battle commenced, in which Idas killed Castor, Polydeuces killed Lynceus and Zeus killed Idas with a thunderbolt; Castor and Polydeuces were later immortalized and placed among the stars. In Theocritus' version, the girls are betrothed to the Apharidae, the fight is not over the cattle, and Castor of course is not killed.

62. Another corrupt line. The first half is generally agreed, and the second half as I have adopted it makes sound sense.

63. The lacuna is best placed here, where we may accept Lynceus' speech as complete. One may assume that Castor's reply began with a formal statement of their claim to the girls, leading naturally into a fight as the only solution to the deadlock.

XXIII. THE LOVER

This poem is so uncharacteristic of Theocritus that it may confidently be rejected, as its claim is not substantiated by any ancient authority. It was known to the Latin poets, and imitated by them. It has echoes of Theocritus, and reminiscences of Bion. The Aesop-like moral with which it ends is unique in the canon, and seems (suggests Gow) to be borrowed from Moschus.

64. In both speech and intercourse, literally. Intercourse, that is, in the sense of chance encounters.

65. i.e. He did not blush.

66. Both lines are corrupt, but have been satisfactorily patched up to indicate some such meaning.

XXIV. THE INFANT HERACLES

The poem is now thought a satisfactory whole, as the Antinoë manuscript contains fragments of thirty-two lines which seem to complete it in the form of a prayer to Heracles for victory. But they are not sufficiently intact to be rendered.

67. Hera's enmity for Heracles pursued him throughout his life, leading to many adventures – of which this is as such the most famous, with the later murder of his wife Megara and their children in a fit of madness the goddess put upon him. The Twelve Labours were not directly connected with her. As the hero's name, however, means 'Hera's glory', his case seems most apt for questioning the manifold stories concerning Hera's jealousy for the children of Zeus; many theories are advanced to explain her vindictiveness, but all are more assumptive than substantial.

68. Heracles was burnt on a funeral pyre on Mount Oeta, in the country of Trachis, whose capital city adopted his name when he retired there after killing Eunomus; he was received by Ceyx, its king. Heracles' wife, Deianira, trying to win back his love after he had brought Iole home with him from Oechalia, sent him a cloak smeared in blood which she thought was a love-charm. But the blood had been given her as such by the centaur Nessus, whom Heracles had killed when he tried to rape Deianira; it was Nessus' own death-blood, and it was poisonous. Heracles put on the cloak, and it killed him.

69. There follow two lines which I have rejected, with most editors, as intruders. Gow translates them: 'That day shall be when the jag-toothed wolf shall find the couching fawn and shrink from harming it.' They both interrupt the narrative, and impute to Heracles a pacifist role which certainly is quite out of place.

70. There is no evidence to suggest that this is the Castor of the Dioscuri, brother of Polydeuces. The information within the poem about his land being resettled on Tydeus bears no relation to any

legends. Despite the distinction of all Heracles' tutors, therefore, this may well be another Castor, otherwise unidentified.

XXV. HERACLES AND THE LION

Both the completeness and the ascription of this poem have been questioned. It falls naturally into its three parts, and is likely – if it cannot be accepted as it stands – to be part of a longer piece. The authorship has only been questioned because of lack of external evidence, and efforts to refute Theocritus' case have been rather half-hearted. It is necessary simply to understand that Heracles has performed his labour of cleansing the stables between the poem's second and third parts, as implied by the heading inserted in the MS between parts one and two.

XXVI. THE BACCHANALS

Although the poem is poor by Theocritus' standards, no convincing refutation of his authorship has been made, despite a vigorous attempt by Wilamowitz. The narrative, which follows the familiar lines of Euripides' *Bacchae*, is similarly advanced to that of XXII and XXV; suggestions have been made that the poet is describing a painting of the incident, which was a standard text for artists. Edmonds suggests that it 'was probably written in honour of the initiation of a boy of nine into the mysteries of Dionysus by a mock slaying-rite'. It would seem from the use of the first person that the piece is clearly a fragment.

71. A perennial problem for translators of this poem and of Euripides is that the name of Pentheus is used as a pun on the Greek word for 'grief', in this case πένθημα. The only solution is to abandon the pun altogether, or to make – as I have here – an inevitably feeble attempt. For 'pain', sense-wise, read 'sorrow'.

XXVII. THE SEDUCTION

As this poem 'is by the commentators generally attributed to Moschus', says Francis Fawkes, 'I may well be excused from translating it,' and he does not do so. The poem is generally rejected, and is certainly incomplete; Edmonds argues that the missing part 'comprised the lines introducing the match, the whole of the rival's piece, and the prelude of the shepherd's piece'. But we need only assume, for our present purpose, that in the lines preceding the opening Daphnis has stolen a kiss.

Fawkes takes the opportunity for a swipe at Dryden, whose translation of this idyll has been often cited as obscene: 'Dryden generally improves and expatiates upon any subject that is ludicrous, and therefore the tenor of his translation will be found very different. The last five lines in Greek, he has expanded into fourteen.' But I quote at the relevant lines below two extracts from Dryden's version, which must surely seem very tame to a modern audience. One measure of Dryden's hunt for the obscene is that he converts Idyll XXIII into a heterosexual poem.

72. This is my title. (MS: *The Lovers' Conversation*.)

73. Dryden: Swear then you will not leave me on the common
            But marry me, and make an honest woman.

74. The use of salt as the humblest of commodities has a worthy pedigree in Homer (*Odyssey* XVII, 455 ff.): 'You wouldn't give so much as a pinch of salt from your larder to a retainer of your own, you that sit here at another man's table and can't bring yourself to take a bit of his bread and give it to me, though there's plenty here' [trans. E. V. Rieu]. Compare also Theocritus' Idyll XV, 17: 'He came back, did Daddy, / That giant of a man, carrying a pack of salt.'

75. Dryden: Her down cast eyes beheld her print upon the grass.

XXVIII. THE DISTAFF

76. The text implies that they are in fact not merely 'sleek' but see-through.

77. Syracuse. It is described, literally, as 'the very marrow of the three-cornered island'.

XXIX. FOR A BOY

The last two Idylls, like XXVIII, are ostensibly modelled in metre, dialect and substance on the lyrics of Sappho and Alcaeus. These last poems capture some of the delicacy of the Greek sense of homosexuality, and are of similar sentiment to our own Elizabethan love poetry. In 1767, however, this obviously would not do, and Fawkes – as Dryden with XVIII – changes the title to *The Mistress*, explaining, 'I have taken the liberty to make a change in the application of (the poem), which renders it far more obvious and natural.'

78. I hope I may be forgiven this latinism; it is too appropriate a translation to set aside, as is *terra firma* in XXI.

79. Literally: 'your three-year friends' and 'your three-day friends' respectively.

XXX. FOR ANOTHER BOY

80. A fever (malaria has been suggested) which strikes every fourth day. Alternatively, it has been seen as an intermittent illness which lasts seventy-two hours when it strikes. The clearest solution is that it is a fever which produces a paroxysm every fourth day.

81. Literally: 'must first reckon how many times nine the stars number'.

THEOCRITUS
The Epigrams

The authorship of the epigrams has been exhaustively discussed, in both collective and individual terms. We may accept I to XXII as authentic, with the authority of the MS; the others must be considered separately.

I

An inscription for a painting.

II

An inscription for a painting.

III

An inscription for a painting.

IV

This poem is scarcely an epigram, and is the only one of this collection which cannot be an inscription – except, at a stretch, on some sort of milestone or roadside notice. Its inclusion is obviously due to its pastoral nature, and the epigrammatic point made in the closing lines.

V

Possibly an inscription for a painting.

VI

Again, possibly for a painting.

VII

An epitaph, seemingly on the same tomb as XV.

VIII

For a statue of Asclepius set up by Nicias (of Idylls XI and XIII).
1. The Healer is Apollo.

IX

An epitaph.

X

Inscription on an altar to the Muses.

XI

Epitaph on the tomb of Eusthenes the physiognomist.

XII

Inscription for a tripod and a bust of Dionysus.

XIII

Inscription for a statue in Chrysogona's domestic shrine.

XIV

A trade sign or advertisement for a money-changer.

XV

Epitaph.

XVI

Epitaph on the tomb of a young girl, possibly shared with her
young brother.

XVII

Inscription for a statue of the poet Anacreon.

XVIII

Inscription for a statue of the poet Epicharmus, probably modelled
on his own metre. See Glossary.

XIX

Epitaph on the tomb of Hipponax, written in his honour in the
scazon iambic metre.

XX

Epitaph for the tomb of a nurse.

XXI

Inscription for a statue of the poet Archilochus.

XXII

Inscription for a statue of the poet Peisander at Camirus.

XXIII

Epitaph for the tomb of Glauce. Not in the bucolic collection, but attributed to Theocritus in the Greek Anthology.

XXIV

Inscription for a new base to Apollo's shrine. Again not in the bucolic collection, but attributed to Theocritus. It appears in the Greek Anthology.

XXV

Not in the collection. Probably by Automedon; but I include it because of its relevance to the corpus of the epigrams as a whole.

XXVI

Not in the collection. Probably by Artemidorus, another Alexandrian. Included here for the same reason as XXV.

XXVII

Dedication for a collection of Theocritus' poems. It is thought by some to be by Theocritus himself, but by more to be the work of a later author, not least because we have no evidence that Theocritus ever collected his work. Peter Jay, editor of *The Greek Anthology* (Allen Lane, 1973), prints this version of the poem (ix. 205), but attributes it to Artemidorus.

2. My translation, adopted in part from his note, braves Gow's verdict of 'ambiguous', as I accept this poem to be distinguishing our poet from the Theocritus of Chios, the rhetorician. If the Chian is meant to be Homer, says Gow, the line means 'I have not aped the style of any other poet'. If it is the other Theocritus, he goes on, '(it) might still have that meaning, or (it) might mean that the poems in this particular collection were uniform in kind (e.g. Sicilian, that is to say, bucolic). If the author is an editor . . . (it) might more plausibly be understood to mean "This collection contains nothing but my own works."' Gow concludes that the

last interpretation is 'on the whole . . . the most probable'. But I prefer, assuming Theocritus' authorship, to accept his proud raising of the pastoral standard.

BION

The Poems and Fragments

I. LAMENT FOR ADONIS

Generally accepted as the work of Bion, clearly under the influence of Theocritus' *Thyrsis' Lament for Daphnis* (Idyll I) and related to Moschus' *Lament for Bion* (III). But problems of chronology confuse who influenced whom; little can be gleaned on that score from the poems themselves, which in fact form part of the meagre apparatus used for dating.

1. Here, and at 'Love mourns, Love weeps', I have substituted the singular for the text's 'the Loves'.

II. MYRSON AND LYCIDAS

A fragment, probably by an imitator of Bion.

2. Achilles is not named in the text, but referred to as Peleus' son.

III to XVII

are all fragments, some possibly complete poems, preserved in quotations made by Stobaeus, and attributed to Bion with varying certainty. Stobaeus (*floruit* 405 A.D.) has the sad fate of being remembered largely for those he quoted.

VIII

3. The implication, specified in the text, is of the barbarians' inhospitable ways.

4. A reference to Achilles' love for Patroclus. The next line refers to Patroclus' death at the hands of Hector, who in his turn was killed by Achilles.

XI. TO HYACINTHUS

The dedication in the title is preserved in the MS. Hyacinthus, whose death the fragment describes, was loved by Apollo (Phoebus) but killed by Zephyrus, who also loved him and was jealous of his attentions to Apollo.

XV

This fragment, aptly titled *Persistence* by Edmonds, has the water literally 'wearing' the channel in the stone. I have strengthened it to help the piece stand alone.

XVIII

A fragment quoted by Orion the grammarian.

MOSCHUS

The Poems

These are all that remain of Moschus' output, and only border on the pastoral. But they have important affinities with much of this collection.

I. THE FUGITIVE LOVE

The similarity of this poem to Theocritus' Idyll XIX influenced the inclusion of the latter, though highly dubious, in the bucolic collection.

II. EUROPA

1. Liddell and Scott: 'The hyacinth of the Greeks seems not to have been the same as ours, but to have comprehended the iris, the gladiolus and larkspur.'

III. LAMENT FOR BION

The only really pastoral poem in the Moschus canon, but now accepted as the work of a pupil of Bion. It has obvious affinities with Bion's *Lament for Adonis* (I) and Theocritus' *Thyrsis' Lament for Daphnis* (Idyll I).

2. An important expression of the fountain's central place in the pastoral code. Arethusa, fountain of Sicily, was literally the source of pastoral poetry.

IV

Quoted, with V and VI, by Stobaeus. They may confidently be assumed to be the work of Moschus.

V

Compare the moral and its use with that of Theocritus' Idyll XXIII.

VII

Preserved in the Anthologia Planudea (4.200) and attributed – apparently wrongly – to Moschus because of the reference in the last line to Europa's bull, to which Moschus II is devoted.

THE PATTERN POEMS

The *Technopaegnia*, as these poems have commonly been named, are assumed to have passed from some self-sufficient collection into the Palatine Anthology, in which they have come down to us. One or more of them occur in various bucolic collections, and their ascriptions have been the subject of much debate.

THEOCRITUS *Syrinx*

The most substantial objection to this poem's ascription to Theocritus (which it makes itself), is that the shepherd's pipe in this shape was not of Grecian, but of Etruscan origin. The Greek syrinx was generally made of reeds of equal length. Edmonds suggests that 'the variation in the heard length of the lines would correspond naturally enough to the variation in note of the tubes of the pipe', and contentedly accepts the poem as Theocritean because of the Simichidas cross-reference with Idyll VII. Myself, I doubt the poem's authenticity, and suspect it must be of a considerably later age; its affinities with Dosiadas' *Altar* could help date it. But it is part of the bucolic canon; and is sufficient of a tribute to our poet to accompany any version of his works.

A paraphrase of the poem with the riddles solved will assist an understanding: Odysseus' wife, mother of Telemachus, gave birth to a fleet-footed goatherd; not Comatas, who was nourished by bees, but him whose heart was once on fire for Pitys; namely, Pan, who loved Echo, and invented the syrinx to immortalize his love in music; he also defeated the Persians, expelling them from Europe. To him Theocritus dedicates this pipe: enjoy it, Omphale's favourite, son of Hermes and Odysseus, hoofed one; delight in it, make sweet love-music for your Echo, who cannot speak and is invisible.

The bedmate of Nobody Odysseus named himself Nobody when answering the Cyclops' 'Who is there?' His bedmate, i.e. wife, was Penelope, who was said by various legends to be, as here, the mother of Pan.

mother of the Warmonger Telemachus, son of Odysseus and Penelope, has affinities both in name and character with the epithet 'Warmonger'.

bore the nimble pilot of the Stone-swapped's nurse Zeus, in various legends' versions of various situations, was exchanged for, or changed himself into, a stone. He was suckled by a goat; so the Stone-swapped's nurse's pilot is simply a goatherd. Which is what Pan was, and a nimble – fleet-footed – one at that.

not the Horned One fed by the son of a bull i.e. not the goatherd who . . . A reference to Comatas, the goatherd of Idyll VII, closed in a chest by an angry king, who returned to find him still alive nourished by honeycomb. Bees were often referred to as sons or children of the bull; κεράστης, long-horned, is a pun on Comatas' name. See nn. 17 and 54.

but the Once-heart-burning for the P-less itys Itys, the Greek word, means shield-rim, which is what the MS conveys; the pun is quite untranslatable, so I have settled for a direct transcription in this instance only. Add the P and you have Pitys (Greek for pine), the girl with whom Pan was in love.

named whole, but double, lover of girlish Split-voice Pan's name in Greek means 'whole'. 'Double' refers to his two goat's legs. Split-voice is an obvious pseudonym for Echo, a child of sound, whose replies were swift as wind, thus 'wind-carried'.

a sharp sore for the Muses The Greek word 'syrinx' can also mean an abscess, or suppurating wound, thus 'sore'. 'Sharp' is a pun on the pain of the sore and the timbre of the music.

parricide-like armies . . . Tyre's girl 'Parricide-like' is the common aural pun of such riddles: Perseus killed his grandfather, Acrisius of Argos, and so – through the sound of his name – the armies referred to are those of the Persians. Europa was daughter of Agenor, king of Phoenicia, and is thus 'Tyre's girl'. The riddle thus adopts her for the continent of Europe; and the couplet refers to the part played by Pan in the battle of Marathon (see Herodotus VI, 105).

this Simichid Paris i.e. the poet himself. Despite Theocritus' claim in the anyway dubious Epigram XXVIII, he is often cited as the son of Simichus (hence, for instance, the Simichidas of Idyll VII). Thus Simichid is a frequent nickname for him. He calls himself Paris because his name, Theocritus, literally means 'judge between gods' which is exactly what Paris did at the heavenly beauty contest. The reference is used the other way round (Theocritus to mean Paris) in Dosiadas' Altar.

the blind's fond blight Very contrived. 'Blight' is explained by the note on 'sore' above. It is dear to the blind only because πηρός means blind, and πήρα means wallet, a traditional pastoral trapping. Interchange the words, therefore, and the syrinx becomes a 'blight' dear to wallet-carriers, i.e. pastoral figures, here denoted by 'the blind'.

man-treading gadfly of Lydia's queen Lydia's queen was Omphale, of whom Pan was a particular favourite, thus a 'gadfly' perpetually at her side. 'Man-treading' is explained by the affinity between gadflies and clay, or earth; for Prometheus made men of clay, and so man-treading is used to mean clay-treading.

thief-son, fatherless, box-legs The poem adopts two theories of Pan's parentage simultaneously. 'Thief-son', because the son of Hermes, god of thieves; 'fatherless', because son of Odysseus, or Nobody (see note above on *bedmate of Nobody*). 'Boxlegs' is, again, a very contrived word-riddle; λάρναξ is the Greek word used here for 'box'; χηλός also means 'box', and χηλή means 'hoof'; the words are thus interchanged to suggest Pan's hooves.

your mute girl, a Calliope, unseen Echo is obviously 'mute' in herself; similarly, therefore, 'unseen'. There is a textual problem over 'Calliope'; with a capital initial letter, as I have adopted it, it refers to the Muse of Poetry, with whom Echo is being flatteringly compared; with a small initial letter, it simply means 'beautiful'. Either solution is refreshingly simple.

SIMIAS *Axe*

Simias of Rhodes, generally accepted as the author of the three following poems, flourished about 300 B.C. *Axe* was probably written to be inscribed on a votive copy of the axe with which Epeius made the Wooden Horse, in which the Greeks finally penetrated Troy and ended the war. The original axe was said to be preserved in a temple of Athena. Hence the references to the Wooden Horse and to Athena (Pallas) which form the basis of the poem. The lines must be read from the beginning and end alternately, as they are here numbered.

Axe and *Syrinx* are probably the only two of the pattern poems which were designed for inscription upon the actual physical object they represent. Yet, as is clear, they are equally successful as concrete poems.

SIMIAS *Wings*

The wings represented are those of Love; and the lines may have been written for inscription on the wings of a statue of Love as a bearded boy, a common representation. It is the only one of the pattern poems to make no reference to its own shape, or the figure it represents. It amounts simply to a rather charming expression of Love's arrogance, and his own personal, cheeky brand of god-baiting.

SIMIAS *Egg*

Egg marks a change in Simias' conception of the pattern poem, for it is clearly designed to be written on an egg. From the flat oval shape, I always assumed it must have moved in horizontal bands, until a friend recently executed a handsome version in the form of a spiral on a vertical axis. The poem is in fact about itself, its progression from one-foot to ten-foot lines and the consequent increase in rhythmic speed. The poem is visualized as the nightingale's egg, but there is no suggestion of any dedicatee. It must have been composed, as Edmonds concludes, simply as a *tour de force*, although I find no evidence of the riddle-poem he sees it to be. The lines are again, as with *Axe*, to be read from beginning and end alternately, meeting in the middle. English can scarcely sustain lines as long as those demanded by the central couplets, so any reading must take particular care with the punctuation, which has been specifically deployed to sustain the rhythmic scheme.

   has spun this thread i.e. the poem itself.

DOSIADAS *Altar*

Altar, closely modelled on the *Syrinx*, marks a return to the riddle-poem, and to the deliberately literary concrete form. The poem is in the shape of an altar, not for inscription on one; the genre thus becomes an apt vehicle for votive dedications. This altar was apparently dedicated by Jason to Athena while becalmed on his way to Colchis for the Golden Fleece. Nothing is known about Dosiadas, a well authenticated name, apart from this poem. It is derived from the *Syrinx* and Lycophron's *Alexandra*, and so must be of considerably later date.

twice-young man ... transvestite jade 'Twice-young' refers to Medea's notorious rejuvenation techniques, as also recalled later in the poem in 'Man-boiler'. She is called 'transvestite' as she disguised herself in men's clothing when escaping into Media. The Greek word στήτη contains the sneer mirrored in 'jade'.

the ash-bedded son of Empusa ... Trojan herdsman and a bitch's pup Empusa, a monster in Hecate's power, was able to change her shape; and is thus used here to denote Thetis, mother of Achilles, who had similar powers. Achilles is 'ash-bedded' because Thetis placed him in the fire with a view to immortalizing him. 'The fate appointed' is intended to convey in English the double meaning, both active and passive, of the Greek μόρος: Achilles was killed by Paris, a Trojan herdsman; having himself killed Hector, son of Hecuba, who was changed into a bitch.

lover of a golden one Chryse, Golden One, is another name for Athena; this line constitutes the altar's dedication.

the Man-boiler ... bronze-limbed wind Very involved. 'Man-boiler' means Medea, Jason's wife, who tricked Pelias' daughters into cutting him up and boiling his limbs in the hope of granting him a second youth, as she had so done for Aeson. But Medea is also used as a pseudonym for Athena, who cast down Talos – the 'bronze-limbed' man, protector of Crete – from the Acropolis. The lines only mean that Jason was becalmed. The relevant legends are detailed in Robert Graves' *Greek Myths* (Penguin edition) 92.1 ff.

twice-wed, Virgin-born, mother-rejected The wind has been raised by Hephaistus, who married Aphrodite and Aglaia ('twice-wed'), was the fatherless son of Hera ('Virgin-born') and was thrown by her from Olympus ('mother-rejected').

the murderer of Theocritus Theocritus means Paris (see note on *Syrinx, Simichid Paris*). Paris was killed at Troy by one of the arrows of Philoctetes, to whom 'murderer' therefore refers. (See note on *wave-washed isle* below.)

the burner of Three-nights Three-nights is Heracles, who was supposed to have been begotten on three consecutive nights. Philoctetes set the light to his funeral pyre, is thus his 'burner'.

belly-crawling Age-shedder i.e. the serpent sent by Hera to wound Philoctetes; it sheds its age in terms of skins. The 'poison' here may be a double reference, also suggesting the wound from one of his own arrows by which Philoctetes eventually died.

the wave-washed isle is Lemnos, where Philoctetes was living when Odysseus came to fetch his arrows – once the property of Heracles – which the oracle had decreed as necessary to the end of the Trojan War.

Two-life, the robber, Pan's mother's bedmate Odysseus returned from Hades ('Two-life'), abducted Philoctetes and his arrows from Lemnos ('robber') and was husband of Pan's mother, Penelope. (This reference is made in reverse in *Syrinx*, 1: 'The bedmate of Nobody'.)

the cannibal's son is Diomedes, son of Tydeus, who ate the head of Melanippus.

Ilus-piercing arrows The arrows also caused the destruction of the tomb and body of Ilus (see Glossary).

Teucer's thrice-ravaged daughter i.e. Troy, sacked by Heracles, by the Amazons, and now by the Greeks.

VESTINUS *Altar*

Julius Vestinus is the commonly accepted version of a corrupt MS ascription. He is known from an inscription to have been 'High Priest of Alexandria and all Egypt, Curator of the Museum, Keeper of the Libraries at Rome, Supervisor of the Education of Hadrian and Secretary to the same Emperor'. So this Altar is a copy of Greek models, but has been preserved in bucolic manuscripts, among the *Technopaegnia*. The acrostic is a dedication to the Emperor Hadrian, but has become necessarily cryptic in my translation; a fuller version would read, 'Olympian, may you sacrifice for many years.' The acrostic is the only riddle element in the poem, which is otherwise straightforward, and again specifically self-referential. The pregnant use of certain proper names (Naxos, Nysa, Alybe etc.) is quite Greek in spirit, and all are explained in the glossary. This poem, again, is purely literary, and not for direct inscription; it specifies as much in 'built by the earth-born Nine' (see note).

all Pan's property i.e. sheep and goats as sacrificial animals.

Cynthus-born race of two Apollo and Artemis. (See Glossary.)

Yet I may match any in the balance The MS word ἰσόρροπος has led to this phrase being understood as 'I may weigh the same'; but it implies 'equally balanced' in the fuller sense of the phrase.

the earth-born Nine are the Muses (i.e. I am a work of literature). The Graces (Idyll XVI) are Heaven's daughters.

at Neae of Thrace ... A reference to Dosiadas' *Altar*, which this poem obviously imitates. Myrine is another name for Lemnos, 'daughter of three fathers' (Tritogeneia) a term for its dedicatee, Athena.

APPENDIX

Ptolemy Philadelphus, Patron of Theocritus

Ptolemy Philadelphus was the second Macedonian king of Egypt, becoming joint ruler with his father in 285 B.C. The country he inherited was one whose territory had been established by the campaigns of Alexander, and in whose capital there were already the makings of a literary movement.

His father, who is distinguished by either of two surnames, Lagus or Soter, was the son of Arsinoë by King Philip of Macedon. When pregnant she had been given in marriage to one Lagus, generally described as 'of mean extraction'; he, to conceal her disgrace, exposed the newly-born child in a wood. The baby was rescued by an eagle, who fed and sheltered him, and later readopted by Lagus on account of this miraculous preservation. He called the child Ptolemy, and felt confident of his future greatness.

Recalled to the Macedonian court after Philip's death, and educated there, the young Ptolemy became an intimate of Alexander, and later distinguished himself in the king's campaigns, of which he also wrote a chronicle. After Alexander's death the distribution of empire gave Ptolemy rule of Egypt, with Libya and part of Arabia. He declared himself king nineteen years later in 304, and annexed Palestine, Cyprus and a number of Aegean islands. A rational and clement ruler, he organized effective military power and established a centre of largely philosophic learning in Alexandria. His first wife was Artacama, daughter of a fellow satrap; they were divorced after Alexander's death, and Ptolemy subsequently married Eurydice and later (probably without divorce) Berenice, who bore him Ptolemy II in 308.

The elder Ptolemy played little active part in government after appointing his son joint ruler, and died three years later in 282. Ptolemy Philadelphus, so called by antiphrasis because he killed two of his brothers, threw his energies into securing a lengthy peace by establishing wide political and trade alliances. Most significant was an exchange of ambassadors with the emergent Roman empire, recent conquerors of Pyrrhus and the Tarentines. The peace was shaken by war with Macedonia from 266 to 261, in which he came off marginally worse, and by two Syrian Wars, the first of which (c. 276–71) won him major areas of Syria and Asia Minor, the second (c. 260–53) proving indecisive. The conflict was fomented by his brother Magas, dependent king of Cyrene, who had the support of King Antiochus of Syria in his challenge for Ptolemy's throne. Magas was overcome and put to death, and a makeshift alliance with Antiochus sealed by giving him Ptolemy's daughter, Berenice, in marriage.

Berenice was his child by Arsinoë I, daughter of the Thracian king Lysimachus, whom he had married in 289; he later married his sister Arsinoë, for whom he had always expressed deep love, and to whose memory he built a famous monument. (See also n. 54.) Ptolemy died in 264 B.C., at the age of 64, and was succeeded by his son, Ptolemy Energetes.

His great wealth was famous, and was carefully used for the benefit of the estimated 33,000 cities under his rule. He maintained massive and well-equipped military forces, who acted as much in the protection of trading interests as in territorial defence. But his wealth also subsidized the foundation of the literary school of Alexandria, a haven for men of letters and of learning from the world over. Under Ptolemy's aegis Alexandria's famous library was founded and equipped; at his death it is said to have contained some 200,000 books, which later increased more than threefold before the building was partly destroyed by fire when Caesar burnt his own fleet two centuries later; the restoration was supervised with great success by Cleopatra. To Ptolemy's patronage we owe the work of Euclid, Theocritus, Callimachus, Lycophron and many others (see Introduction pp. 12–13). He is believed to have commissioned the translation of the Old Testament into Greek, the work being undertaken by a team of seventy scholars and thus being named the Septuagint.

GLOSSARY

This glossary is intended also to act as an index of proper names, but only those names which have some existence outside the text. Names used by the poet simply for characters are not listed; nor are those whose mention in the text is self-sufficient or self-explanatory. Details given, apart from parentage, are restricted to those relevant to this particular mention of a person or place. Cross-references, by the abbreviation q.v., are suggested only where further relevant information can be found. The Roman numerals in brackets after each entry indicate the poems in which the name appears. Numbers only refer to Theocritus' Idylls; Ep to Theocritus' Epigrams; B to the poems of Bion; M to those of Moschus; other references are to the pattern poems.

Some of the identities of both people and places in this glossary, and of those related to names listed in it, are hotly disputed. Only where directly relevant do I summarize the different theories; on the whole, I have simply entered the most likely version.

ACHARNAE (VII) A village in Attica, north of Athens. Its people are the subject of a play by Aristophanes.

ACHERON (XII, XV, XVI, XVII, BI, MI) A river in the underworld, always used in Greek literature to signify the river of death.

ACHILLES (XVI, XVII, XXII, XXIX, BII, BVIII) A Greek hero, son of Peleus and Thetis, famous for his part in the siege of Troy. His lover, Patroclus, was killed by Hector, whom Achilles murdered in revenge.

ACIS (I) A stream which rises on Etna. Acis was originally a Sicilian shepherd loved by Galatea, q.v.; he was killed in jealousy by Polyphemus, and turned by the gods into a stream.

ACMON (*Wings*) The most ancient of the gods.

ACROREA (XXV) An upland tract in Elis.

ACROTIME (XXVII) A name, otherwise unknown, assumed for the purpose of this poem by textual scholars.

ADONIS (I, III, XV, XX, BI, MIII) A Greek youth, famous for his beauty, who was loved by Aphrodite. He was killed by a boar while out hunting, and was believed thereafter to spend half of each year on earth with Aphrodite, and half beneath it with Persephone – hence summer and winter. Son of Cinyras, q.v.

ADRASTUS (XXIV) A mythical king of Argos, one of the Seven Against Thebes.

AEGILUS (I) A town in Attica, famous for its figs.

AESARUS (IV) A small river which flowed into the Ionian Sea near Croton.

AESON (XIII) Son of Cretheus; father of Jason, q.v., by Alcimede.

AGAMEMNON (XV) King of Argos and Mycenae, who with his brother Menelaus, led the Greeks to victory at Troy. His murder by his wife Clytemnestra is the subject of Aeschylus' play.

AGAVE (XXVI) Daughter of Cadmus, king of Thebes, and mother of Pentheus. The best-known version of this story is Euripides' play, the *Bacchae*.

AIAS (XV, XVI) The Greek name of Ajax, son of Telamon, another of the Greek heroes at Troy.

ALCAEUS (MIII) A renowned lyric poet of Mitylene, in Lesbos. *Floruit c.* 600 B.C.

ALCIDES (MIII) Heracles, q.v.

ALCMENA (XIII, XXIV) Mother of Heracles by Zeus, and of Iphicles by Amphitryon.

ALEUAS (XVI) A king of Thessaly.

ALEXANDER (XVII) Alexander the Great, king of Macedon 336–23 B.C.

ALPHESIBOA (III) Daughter of Pero and Bias. See Melampus.

ALPHEUS (IV, XXV, MVI) A river which rose in Arcadia and passed through Elis. Its god loved the nymph Arethusa, who was turned into a fountain by Artemis. Used in IV to signify the sports grounds of Olympia.

ALYBE (Vestinus *Altar*) A town in Asia Minor famous for its silver-mines.

AMARYLLIS (III, IV) A traditional name for a girl in pastoral poetry, first used by Theocritus and later by Vergil and Milton.

AMPHITRITE (XXI) Wife of Poseidon.

AMPHITRYON (XIII, XXIV) A prince of Tiryns, son of Alcaeus and Hipponome. He married Alcmena, who bore him Iphicles. Lived in exile in Thebes.

AMYCLAE (XII, XXII) A town in Laconia.

AMYCUS (XXII) Son of Poseidon by Melia, and king of the Bebryces. Famous largely for his death at the hands of Polydeuces.

ANACREON (Ep XVII, MIII) Lyric poet of Teos. *Floruit c.* 530 B.C.

ANAPUS (I, VII) The river of Syracuse, in Sicily.

ANCHISES (I) A cowherd on Mount Ida who was loved by Aphrodite, and became by her the father of Aeneas.

ANTIGONE (XVII) Mother of Berenice. Great-niece of Antipater of Macedon.

ANTIOCHUS (XVI) A king of Thessaly.

APHAREUS (XXII) King of Messenia; father of Idas, Pisus and Lynceus.

APHRODITE (*passim*) Goddess of beauty, mother of Love.

APIA (XXV) The Peloponnese.

APOLLO (*passim*) Son of Zeus. God of all the arts. Among the names by which he was known was Paean, the Healer, used in two of the Idylls and retained in Epigram VIII.

ARATUS (VI, VII) A poet from Soli in Cilicia, *floruit c.* 277 B.C. Son of Athenodorus, he was famous for his *Phaenomena*, a poem about astronomy. His patron was Antigonus Gonatas, king of Macedonia. Both these references, however, may well be to an unknown person of the same name.

ARCADIA (II, VII, XXII) A country in the centre of the Peloponnese, bordered by Achaea, Messenia, Elis and Argolis. Derived its name from Arcas.

ARCAS (I) Son of Zeus by Callisto, daughter of Lycaon.

ARCHIAS (XXVIII) A Corinthian descended from Heracles, he founded Syracuse in 732 B.C.

ARCHILOCHUS (Ep XXI, MIII) A lyric poet of Paros, the first to write in iambics. *Floruit* 685 B.C.

ARETHUSA (I, XVI, MIII, MVI) A fountain in Syracuse, the source of all pastoral poetry. Originally a nymph of Elis, who was changed into a fountain by Artemis to save her from Alpheus, q.v.

ARGO (XIII, XXII) The ship used by Jason and the Argonauts on their quest for the golden fleece.

ARGOS (XIII, XIV, XV, XVII, XXII, XXIV, XXV) The capital city of Argolis, in the Peloponnese.

ARGUS (MII) A creature, son of Arestor, with a hundred eyes. Hera set him to guard Io, but Hermes – on the orders of Zeus – lulled him to sleep and killed him. Hera, it is said, then placed his hundred eyes in the tail of the peacock.

ARIADNE (II) Daughter of Minos, king of Crete. She was loved by Theseus, but abandoned by him on the island of Naxos, though carrying his baby. A disputed legend tells that she hanged herself.

ARSINOË (XV) Daughter of Ptolemy I, she was successively married to Lysimachus, Ptolemy Keraunos and her brother Ptolemy Philadelphus. See n. 54.

ARTEMIS (II, XVIII, XXVII) Goddess of hunting, of childbirth (as Ilithyia) and of the Moon.

ASCRA (MIII) A Boeotian town, where Hesiod was born.

ATALANTA (III) Daughter of Schoenus, king of Scyrus. A fast runner and a reluctant bride, she would only marry the man who could outrun her. Many died in the attempt, as the penalty for losing was death. But Hippomenes threw down golden apples (given him by Aphrodite) in her path; she stopped to pick them up; he won the race and her hand.

ATHENA (V, XV, XVI, XVIII, XX, XXVIII) Goddess of wisdom, born from the brain of Zeus.

ATHENS (XIV) Capital of Attica. Named after Athena.

ATHOS (VII) A mountain in Macedonia, overlooking the Aegean. Still famous for its monastery.

ATREUS (XVII, XVIII, MIII) Son of Pelops, father of Agamemnon, q.v., and Menelaus, q.v.

AUGEAS (XXV) Son of Helios, the Sun, and king of Elis. One of the Argonauts. Killed by Heracles, whom he had refused to pay for cleaning his stables.

AUSONIA (MIII) Properly Southern Italy, but used as an ancient name for Italy itself. Auson was son of Odysseus.

AUTONOË (XXVI) Daughter of Cadmus, king of Thebes. Sister of Agave, q.v.

BACCHUS (Ep XVIII) Dionysus, q.v.

BELLEROPHON (XV) Son of Glaucus, king of Corinth. Rider of Pegasus, killer of the Chimaera.

BEMBINA (XXV) A Peloponnesian town.

BERENICE (XV, XVII) Wife of Ptolemy I, supposedly deified after death by Aphrodite.

BIAS (III) King of Argos, son of Amythaon. See Melampus.

BIBLINE (XIV) The wine of Biblia, a district of Thrace.

BISTONIAN (MIII) Thracian.

BLEMYAN (VII) The Blemyes were an African tribe who lived at the mouth of the Nile.

BOEOTIA (MIII) A district of central Greece.

BUPRASIUM (XXV) A city of Elis; also the name of its country, and of a river flowing through it.

BURINA (VII) A Coan fountain.

BYBLIS (VII) A Miletan fountain.

CADMUS (XXVI) Mythical king and founder of Thebes, father of Agave, q.v., Autonoë and Ino.

CALLIOPE (MIII, *Syrinx*) The Muse of poetry. Daughter of Zeus and Mnemosyne, she is said to have borne Orpheus to Apollo.

CALYDON (XVII) A city of Aetolia in central Greece, ruled by Oeneus, father of Meleager.

CALYDNA (I) or Calymna, an island (one of the Sporades) in the Aegean, between Cos and Lebynthus.

CAMIRUS (Ep XXII) A town of Rhodes, named after the son of Heracles.

CARIA (XVII) A country of Asia Minor, bounded by Lydia and Lycia.

CASTALIA (VII) A spring on Mount Parnassus, sacred to the Muses.

CASTOR (XXII, XXIV) Son of Zeus and Leda, wife of Tyndareus. Twin-brother of Polydeuces, q.v., half-brother of Helen, q.v., and Clytemnestra. Some legends said that Polydeuces and Helen were the children of Zeus, Castor and Clytemnestra of Tyndareus. But it is more generally accepted that the brothers were the sons of Zeus, and the sisters the daughters of Tyndareus. For XXIV, see n. 70.

CEOS (XVI) An island in the west of the Aegean, birthplace of Simonides, the lyric and elegiac poet.

CERBERUS (XXIX) The dog who guarded the gates of Hades.

CEYX (MIII) A king of Trachis, son of Lucifer. On his way to consult the oracle of Clarus, he was drowned; his wife Alcyone found his body on the shore and drowned herself. Both were turned into birds – the Halcyons, q.v., or kingfishers.

CHALCON (VII) Chalcodon, son of Eurypylus and grandson of Poseidon. King of Cos, he wounded Heracles when he attacked the island.

CHARITES (XVI, XXVIII, BI, MII) The Graces, daughters and attendants of Aphrodite; the embodiment of Charity, or kindness, on earth. They were three – Aglaia, Thalia and Euphrosyne – and were almost identified with the Muses, with whom they had much (including a temple) in common.

CHARON (XVI, XVII) The boatman who ferried the souls of the dead to the underworld.

CHIOS (VII, XXII) An island in the east Aegean, which claimed to be the birthplace of Homer.

CHIRON (VII) A centaur, who had turned himself into a horse to escape his wife. He was famous for his skill in music, medicine and shooting, which he taught various heroes at his cave on Mount Pelion.

CILICIA (XVII) A country of Asia Minor, on the coast to the north of Cyprus, west of the Euphrates.

CINYRAS (BI) King of Cyprus, son of Paphos. He was tricked into sleeping with his daughter Myrrha, who bore him Adonis.

CIRCE (II, IX) A mythical sorceress visited by Odysseus and his companions, whom she turned into pigs.

CLASHING ROCKS (XIII) The Symplegades, a pair of rocks at the entrance of the Euxine Sea, which clashed together to crush anything passing between them.

CLYTIA (VII) Wife of Chalcon, q.v.

COLCHIS (XIII) A country of Asia, at the east end of the Black Sea. Famous as the birthplace of Medea, and as the land where Jason sought the golden fleece.

COMATAS (VII) A mythical goatherd. His master locked him in a chest and opened it two months later to find him still alive and the chest filled with honeycomb. (Used in V as a functional name for a goatherd; see also nn. 17 and 54.)

COS (XVII) An island in the south-east of the Aegean.

CRANNON (XVI) A Thessalian town on the border of Macedonia, south of Tempe.

CRATHIS (V) A river in south Italy, flowing into the bay of Tarentum near Thurii. Its waters were supposed to turn yellow the hair of anyone who drank them.

CROESUS (VIII, X) A king of Lydia in the sixth century B.C., famous as the richest man of his day.

CRONOS (*passim*) Son of Heaven and Earth; married his sister, Rhea, who bore him Zeus.

CROTON (IV) A town at the south of the bay of Tarentum, known today as Crotone.

CYBELE (XX) A goddess usually identified with Rhea, or Demeter.

CYCLADES (XVII) A group of fifty-three islands in the south Aegean.

CYCLOPS (XI, XVI, MIII) A race of one-eyed giants who lived in Sicily, in the region of Syracuse. The most famous was Polyphemus, who ate some of Odysseus' companions and was in return blinded with a red-hot stake. Polyphemus was the unrequited lover of Galatea, q.v.

CYCNUS (XVI) Son of Poseidon, famous for his pure white skin. He was killed by Achilles, and turned into a swan when stripped of his armour.

CYDONIA (VII) A city in the north-west of Crete.

CYNTHUS (Vestinus *Altar*) A mountain on Delos, sacred to Apollo and Artemis, who were both born on its slopes.

CYPRIS (*passim*) Aphrodite, so called because of her famous shrine on Cyprus.

CYTHEREA (III, XXIII, BI) Aphrodite, long associated with the isle of Cythera.

CYTHERA (BI) An island on the coast of Laconia, famous for its temple of Aphrodite.

DAPHNIS (I, V, VI, VII, VIII, IX, XXVII, Ep II, III, IV, v) A Sicilian shepherd, son of Hermes by a nymph, taught music by Pan and cherished by the Muses. He is variously supposed to be the source of pastoral poetry, the mythical forerunner of Theocritus himself, and his death is one of its most characteristic themes.

DEIDAMEIA (BII) Daughter of Lycomedes, king of Scyros. She bore Achilles a son, Pyrrhus. (He had lived as a woman under the name of Pyrrha.)

DELOS (XVII) An island in the south Aegean, sacred to Apollo.

DEMETER (VII, X, MVII) Goddess of the Earth and thus of harvests and agriculture.

DEO (VII) Demeter.

DEUCALION (XV) Son of Prometheus, and ruler of Thessaly. He and his wife Pyrrha, daughter of Epimetheus, were the only survivors of a flood sent by Zeus to overwhelm mankind.

DIA (II) Another name for Naxos, an island in the south Aegean.

DIOCLES (XII) An Athenian who died saving the life of a boy he loved.

DIOMEDES (I, XVII) Son of Tydeus and Deiphyle, he was king of Argos, and one of the Greek heroes at the siege of Troy, where he wounded Aphrodite in the arm. His wife Aegiale gave herself to one of their servants in jealous anger.

DIONE (VII, XV, XVII) Mother of Aphrodite. Used as another name for Aphrodite herself.

DIONYSUS (II, XVII, XX, XXVI, Ep XII) Son of Zeus and Semele, daughter of Cadmus. God of wine and festivals, worshipped on earth particularly by women (v. Agave). Later known as Bacchus.

DORIAN (*passim*) Doris was an area of Greece bounded by Phocis, Thessaly and Acarnania. A migrant people, the Dorians took their name from Dorus, son of Deucalion, q.v. Their language and dialect are a central part of the tradition inherited by Theocritus.

DRACANUS (XXVI) A mountain, never geographically identified, on which Zeus is said to have taken Dionysus from his thigh, where he had hidden him from the jealous anger of Hera.

EARTHSHAKER (MII) Poseidon, q.v.

ECHO (MIII, MV, *Syrinx*) A nymph loved by Zeus, who was deprived of the power of speech by Hera, so that she could only answer those who spoke to her. See also pp. 222–3.

ELIS (XXII, BII) An area of the north-west Peloponnese, to the west of Arcadia and the north of Messenia.

ENDYMION (III, XX) A shepherd, son of Aethlius and Calyce, loved by the Moon (Artemis). She sent him into a perpetual sleep, so that his beauty might remain constant.

EPEIANS (XXV) Mythical inhabitants of a northern district of the Peloponnese.

EPEIUS (*Axe*) Builder of the Wooden Horse with which the Greeks entered Troy.

EPHYRA (XVI, XXVIII) Corinth.

EPICHARMUS (Ep XVIII) Doria's great comic poet and Pythagorean philosopher, also author of treatises on medicine. *Floruit c.* 470 B.C.

ERYX (XV) A mountain, now called Giuliano, in the west of Sicily; named after the man who was buried there. Sacred to Aphrodite.

ETEOCLES (XVI) A king of Orchomenus, in Boeotia, son of Andreus. Said to have been the first to worship the Graces or Charites, q.v.

EUMAEUS (XVI) Swineherd to Odysseus.

EUMOLPUS (XXIV) An ancient Thracian poet. Sometimes identified with a famous king of Thrace of the same name, son of Poseidon.

EUROPA (MII, MVI) Daughter of Agenor, king of Phoenicia, and Telephassa. (But see Phoenix.) Famous for the story told by Moschus; the children she bore Zeus were Minos, Sarpedon and Rhadamanthus. She later married Asterius, king of Crete, who adopted the children.

EUROTAS (XVIII) A river in Sparta, named after the son of Lelex, the country's founder.

EURYDICE (MIII) Wife of Orpheus, the musician. He won her back from Hades by the beauty of his playing, but failed to keep the condition of her return – that he would not look over his shoulder at her until they were on earth. He could not resist a glance back, and so lost her again.

EURYSTHEUS (XXV) A King of Argos, who – by a right of birth resulting from a divine squabble – had power over Heracles, which he exerted by imposing the twelve labours.

EURYTUS (XXIV) King of Oechalia, and a famous archer. He offered his daughter, Iole, to anyone who could shoot a better arrow; Heracles beat him, but was denied his prize, and so killed him.

GALATEA (VI, XI, BII, BXII, MIII) A sea nymph, daughter of Nereus and Doris. She was loved by Polyphemus, q.v., whom she treated with contempt; and by Acis, q.v., whom she loved in return. Polyphemus killed Acis in jealousy.

GANYMEDE (XII) A beautiful youth of Phrygia, loved by Zeus, whose cupbearer he became.

GLAUCE (IV) A poetess, apparently a contemporary of Theocritus. Not, of course, the Glauce of Ep XXIII.

GOLGI (XV) A town in Cyprus, sacred to Aphrodite and to Eros.

GORGONS (Vestinus *Altar*) Female monsters with serpents instead of hair. All that looked on them were turned to stone. One Gorgon, Mednsa, was killed by Perseus. Pegasus, q.v., emerged from her blood.

GRACES (XVI, XXVIII, BI, MII) See Charites.

HADES (*passim*) The underworld, land of the dead, named after the god who ruled it.

HAEMUS (VII) A mountain in a range of the same name separating Thrace from Thessaly. Named after the son of Boreas and Orithyia, who married Rhodope, and was changed to a mountain for emulating the gods.

HALCYON (VII, MIII) Alcyone was daughter of Aeolus, and wife of Ceyx, king of Thrace, q.v. Both were changed into king-fishers, known as the Halcyons.

HALEIS (V) A river of Sybaris in southern Italy. (In VII it is a river of Cos.)

HARPALYCUS (XXIV) A tutor of Heracles otherwise unidentified under this name. Thought by some to be Autolycus, son of Hermes, one of the Argonauts.

HEBE (XVII) Goddess of youth, daughter of Zeus and Hera. Heracles, when made a god, married her; their children were Alexiares and Anicetus.

HEBRUS (VII) A Thracian river.

HECATE (II) An earth-Goddess, associated with underworld spirits, and often – as here – with Artemis and the Moon.

HECTOR (XV) Son of Priam, hero of the Trojans at the siege of Troy. Killed by Achilles, q.v.

HECUBA (XV) Wife of Priam, king of Troy.

HELEN (XV, XVIII, XXII, XXVII, BII) Daughter of Zeus and Leda, q.v. She married Menelaus, king of Argos, but was carried off to Troy by Paris. The expedition of Menelaus and Agamemnon to get her back resulted in the Trojan War.

HELICE (I) Callisto, daughter of Lycaon, a mythical king of Arcadia. Loved by Zeus, and so changed by the jealous Hera into a star (Ursa Major).

HELICE (XXV) The capital city of Achaea.

HELICON (XXV, Ep I) A Boeotian mountain sacred to the Muses.

HELISOS (XXV) A river flowing through Arcadia and Elis.

HEPHAISTUS (MII) God of fire.

HERA (IV, XV, XVII, XXIV, MII) Wife of Zeus, and so queen of Heaven.

HERACLES (II, IV, VII, XIII, XVII, XXIV, XXV) Son of Zeus and Alcmena; the widely-worshipped Greek hero, most famous for performing the twelve labours imposed by Eurystheus, q.v.

HERMES (I, XXIV, XXV, BV, MII, *Egg*) Messenger of the gods, and patron of shepherds. Also patron of travellers and thieves.

HESIOD (MIII) Epic poet, born at Ascra, author of *Works and Days*. He lived at or around the time of Homer, to whom he is ranked second among the ancient poets.

HESPERUS (BIX) The evening star.

HIERO (XVI) King of Syracuse, 270–226 B.C.

HIMERA (V) A spring at Sybaris, in southern Italy.

HIMERAS (VII) A river in north Sicily.

HIPPOMENES (III) Son of Macareus and Merope. See Atalanta.

HIPPONAX (Ep XIX) An iambic poet of Ephesus, born 540 B.C., famous for his satires, which eventually obliged him to flee Ephesus. It is said that his literary attacks on Buphalos and Anthermus of Chios, two brothers who raised a statue mimicking his physical deformity, drove them to hang themselves.

HOMER (XVI, MIII, *Axe*) The most celebrated of ancient poets, reputed author of the *Iliad* and the *Odyssey*. Probably *floruit c.* 800 B.C.

HOMOLE (VII) A Thessalian mountain, sacred to Pan.

HYETIS (VII) A spring near Miletus, q.v.

HYLAS (XIII) Son of Theodamas, king of Mysia, and Menodice. Loved by Heracles.

HYMEN (XVIII, BI) Son of Dionysus and Aphrodite; god of marriages.

HYMETTUS (Vestinus *Altar*) A mountain two miles south-east of Athens, 22 miles in circumference, famous now as then for honey and marble.

IASION (III) Son of Zeus and Electra; he married Demeter, who bore him three sons – Philomelus, Plutus and Corybas.

ICARIA (IX) A small island in the eastern Aegean.

IDA (I, XVII, BII) A mountain in Troas, a rich source of springs. It was here that Paris judged the beauty contest between Hera, Athena and Aphrodite.

IDALIUM (XV) A town in Cyprus sacred to Aphrodite.

IDAS (XXII) Son of Aphareus, king of Messenia. One of the Argonauts, he married the daughter of King Evenus of Aetolia, Marpessa, who was then carried off by Apollo.

ILUS (XVI, Dosiadas *Altar*) The fourth king of Troy, grandfather of Priam. He was the son of Tros by Calirhoe, and married Eurydice, daughter of Adrastus, q.v.

ILITHYIA (XVII, XXVII) Goddess of childbirth. One of Artemis' various identities.

INACHUS (MII) Son of Oceanus and Tethys; father of Io, q.v. He was the first king of Argos.

IO (MII) An Argive princess, and priestess of Hera, who was loved by Zeus. He changed her into a heifer to protect her from Hera, who then discovered the trick and set Argus, q.v., to guard her. Zeus sent Hermes to lull Argus to sleep and release the cow; but Hera sent a gadfly to pursue and torment it. Zeus then returned Io to her natural shape; in time she married Osiris of Egypt, and eventually was deified as Isis. The child she bore Zeus was Epaphus, later king of Egypt.

IOLCUS (XIII) A town of Magnesia, in Thessaly, where Jason, q.v. was born, and whence he set out in search of the golden fleece.

IONIA (XXVIII) A confederacy of twelve states on the coast of Asia Minor, and thus a country known by that name.

IPHICLES (XXIV) Son of Alcmena, q.v., by Amphitryon; half-brother of Heracles.

IRIS (XVII) Daughter of Thaumas and Electra; messenger of the gods, handmaid of Hera.

JASON (XIII) Son of Aeson and Alcimede; king of Iolcus. He was sent by his rival, Pelias, to fetch the golden fleece from

Colchis, thought to be a journey from which he would never return.

LACINIUM (IV) A promontory of Magna Graecia, or southern Italy, sacred to Hera. Now Cape Colonna, at the entrance to the Tarentine Gulf.

LAERTES (XVI) King of Ithaca; husband of Anticlea, daughter of Autolycus; their son was Odysseus.

LAGUS (XVII) A Macedonian of humble origins, who married Arsinoë, daughter of Meleager. She was at the time pregnant by Philip of Macedon; the child, which Lagus adopted as his own, was Ptolemy.

LAMPRIADAS (IV) See n. 9. An unidentified person.

LAOCOOSA (XXII) Wife of Aphareus, according to Theocritus. In fact she is nowhere else mentioned as such; Aphareus' wife is more commonly accepted to have been Arane.

LAPITHS (XV) A Thessalian tribe famous for its feud with, and eventual conquest of, the centaurs.

LARISSA (XIV) A Thessalian town.

LATMUS (XX) A mountain of Caria, near Miletus; home of Endymion, q.v.

LATYMNUM (IV) A mountain of Croton.

LEDA (XXII) Wife of Tyndareus, loved by Zeus; mother of Castor, q.v., and Polydeuces. Also mother of Helen, q.v., and Clytemnestra. For the legends concerning paternity, see Castor.

LESBOS (MIII) A large island in the eastern Aegean; birthplace of Alcaeus and Sappho.

LETHE (MIII) A river of the underworld. To drink its waters was to forget one's life.

LETO (XVIII) Mother of Apollo and Artemis.

LEUCIPPUS (XXII) Brother of Aphareus, q.v.

LIBYA (I, III, XVII, MII) The Greek name for the continent of Africa.

LINUS (XXIV) Son of Apollo by Psammathe, daughter of Crotopus, king of Argos. A famous singer; mentioned by Martial in Epigram 78. (See also Introduction, pp. 9-10.)

LITYERSES (X) An illegitimate son of the renowned King Midas of Phrygia. He had an appetite for food as notorious as his father's for gold; it is said he made strangers reap his crops till evening, when he would behead them and hide their bodies in the sheaves.

LYCAEUS (I) A mountain in Arcadia, sacred to both Pan and Zeus.

LYCIA (XVI, XVII) The southernmost country of Asia Minor,

bounded by the Mediterranean on the south, Caria on the west, Pamphylia on the east, and Phrygia on the north.

LYCIDAS (VII, XXVII, BII, BVI) Simply a name traditionally used for shepherds; there is no evidence of any relevant prototype. Thus these four poems clearly refer to different people.

LYCOMEDES (BII) Son of Apollo and Parthenope; king of Sycros. Notorious as the murderer of Theseus.

LYDA (MV) A nymph.

LYDIA (XII) A country in western Asia Minor, of great power during Croesus' rule. (560–546 B.C.)

LYNCEUS (XXII) Son of Aphareus, king of Messenia. One of the Argonauts, famous for his remarkable eyesight.

LYSIMELEIA (XVI) A marsh in Sicily, near Syracuse. Now called Pantanella.

MAENALUS (I) A mountain in Arcadia, sacred to Pan. A favourite haunt of shepherds.

MAGNESIA (XXII) A district of eastern Thessaly.

MEDEA (II) A famous sorceress and musician, daughter of king Aetes of Colchis. She married Jason and helped him to win the golden fleece. The story of how she murdered their children when he later betrayed her is told in Euripides' play.

MEGARA (XII, XIV) A renowned city founded in 1131 B.C. at the eastern end of the Corinthian Gulf, equidistant from Corinth and Athens.

MELAMPUS (III) A seer; brother of Bias, who was in love with Pero, daughter of Neleus of Pylus. Neleus had offered her in marriage to the man who could retrieve his mother's flocks from Iphiclus. Melampus undertook the task on his brother's behalf, but was caught and imprisoned; but he later cured Iphiclus' childlessness, took the herds as his reward, and so won his brother his bride.

MELES (MIII) A river in Ionia, near Smyrna. Birthplace of Bion and reputed to be the birthplace of Homer.

MEMNON (MIII) Son of Tithonus and Aurora (Dawn); king of Ethiopia. He fought Achilles on behalf of Nestor, and was killed. Zeus, to comfort Aurora, turned his ashes into birds which thereafter visited his tomb each year.

MENALCAS (VIII, IX, XXVII) Traditional name for a shepherd.

MENELAUS (XVIII, XXII, MIII) Son of Atreus; king of Sparta. Brother of Agamemnon, q.v.; husband of Helen, q.v.

MENIUS (XXV) A river in Elis, flowing into the Ionian Sea.

MESSENE (XXII) A city in the Peloponnese, capital of Messenia.

MIDEA (XIII, XXIV) A town of Argolis in the Peloponnese.

MILETUS (XV, XXVIII, Ep VIII) A famous town of Asia Minor, the capital of Ionia. Now Milete.

MINYAN (XVI) See Orchomenus.

MYCENAE (XXV, BII) A famous and ancient city of Argolis, in the Peloponnese.

MYGDONY (MII) Mygdonia was a small province of Macedonia and Mygdony has come to be a synonym for Phrygia, where its inhabitants finally settled.

MYNDUS (II) A coastal town of Caria near Halicarnassus.

MYRINE (Vestinus *Altar*) Capital of Lemnos, an island in the north Aegean; now called Kastron.

MITYLENE (VII, MIII) Capital city of Lesbos, an island in the Aegean. Birthplace of Sappho and Alcaeus.

NAXOS (Vestinus *Altar*) An Aegean island, the largest of the Cyclades.

NEAE (Vestinus *Altar*) A small island near Lemnos.

NEAETHUS (IV) A river which flows into the Ionian Sea north of Croton; now the Neto.

NEILEUS (XXVIII) Son of Codrus, king of Athens. Founder of Miletus.

NEMEA (XXV) A town of Argolis, between Cleonae and Phlius, which gives its name to the wood where Heracles killed the lion.

NEREIDS (VII, MII) Nymphs of the sea, the fifty daughters of Nereus and Doris.

NICIAS (XI, XIII, XXVIII, Ep VIII) A doctor of Miletus, and a close friend of Theocritus.

NISAEANS (XII) Descendants of Nisus, son of Ares, a mythical king of Megara.

NYSA (Vestinus *Altar*) A mountain in Ethiopia; birthplace of Dionysus. Its adjective is 'Nysian'.

ODYSSEUS (XVI, MIII) King of Ithaca; one of the Greek heroes at the siege of Troy. His adventures on the way back to Greece are the subject of Homer's *Odyssey*.

OEAGRIAN (MIII) Daughters of Oeagrus, king of Thrace, by Calliope. They were the sisters of Orpheus, q.v.

OECUS (VII) A city in Caria, sacred to Aphrodite.

OENONE (BII) Wife of Paris, q.v., before he abducted Helen, q.v.

ORCHOMENUS (XVI) A Boeotian town, formerly called Minyeia; its inhabitants were thus referred to as Minyans, and the town itself often applied the epithet Minyan. Minyas, one of its ancient heroes, was the origin of the name.

ORESTES (BVIII) Son of Clytemnestra and Agamemnon, q.v. He killed his mother and her lover Aegisthus in revenge for their murder of Agamemnon. He was then pursued by the Furies; the story, from Agamemnon's return to Orestes' acquittal by the court of Heaven, is the subject of Aeschylus' trilogy, the *Oresteia*.

ORION (VII, XXIV) An ancient giant, born from the urine of Zeus, Poseidon and Hermes. After his death he became the constellation of stars referred to in both these poems; its rising was associated with storms and rain.

OROMEDON (VII) The highest mountain on the island of Cos.

ORPHEUS (MIII) Mythical poet and musician. Son of Oeagrus and Calliope; husband of Eurydice, q.v.

OTHRYS (III) A mountain in Thessaly.

PAMPHYLIA (XVII) A district of south Asia Minor, on the Mediterranean coast, bounded by Lycia on the west, Pisidia on the north and Cilicia on the east.

PAN (*passim*) God of shepherds, flocks, pastures and countrymen.

PARIS (XXVII, *Syrinx*) Son of Priam, king of Troy. Carried off Helen, q.v., from the court of Menelaus, thus causing the Trojan War.

PARNASSUS (VII) A mountain in Phocis sacred to the Muses, to Apollo and Dionysus.

PAROS (VI, MIII) An island in the south Aegean, one of the Cyclades, the birthplace of Archilochus, q.v. Famous for its marble; hence the epithet Parian.

PATROCLUS (XV) One of the Greek heroes at Troy; loved by Achilles, q.v., killed by Hector, q.v.

PEGASUS (MIII) The winged horse born from the blood of one of the Gorgons, q.v., and ridden by Bellerophon, q.v., in his conquest of the Chimaera. The fountain of Pegasus is Hippocrene, on the slopes of Mount Helicon, which he brought forth with a stroke of his hoof. It became sacred to the Muses.

PEIRITHOUS (BVIII) King of the Lapiths; he went to Hades with Theseus to aid his attempt to bring back Persephone.

PEISANDER (Ep XXII) An epic poet of Camirus, in Rhodes. *Floruit* sixth century B.C.

PELASGIANS (XV) A tribe of Greece, variously identified. The name is sometimes used to imply the whole of Greece itself.

PELEUS (XVII) Son of Aeacus and Endeis; king of Thessaly; husband of Thetis; father of Achilles, q.v.

PELOPS (VIII, XV) Son of Tantalus, king of Phrygia. King of Pisa, in Elis; father of Atreus, q.v. The Peloponnese took its name from him.

PENEIUS (I) A Thessalian river.

PENTHEUS (XXVI) King of Thebes; son of Agave, q.v. Murdered by his mother, while she was distracted, for opposing the cult of Dionysus and intruding into the women's ritual of worship.

PERIMEDE (II) An enchantress, otherwise unknown.

PERSEPHONE (XV, BI, MIII) Daughter of Zeus and Demeter; abducted by Hades as she played in the fields of Sicily, and taken to the underworld to be his wife.

PERSEUS (XXIV, XXV) Son of Zeus and Danae; grandfather of Alcmena. One of the great heroes; he married Andromeda.

PHILAMMON (XXIV) A celebrated pre-Homeric musician and poet; son of Apollo.

PHILINUS (II, VII) Son of Hegepolis; a famous runner of Cos.

PHILITAS (VII) Son of Telephus; a poet and scholar of Cos; tutor to Ptolemy Philadelphus, and to Theocritus himself. Also spelt Philetas.

PHILOETIUS (XVI) Oxherd to Odysseus.

PHOCIS (*Axe*) A country of central Greece, bordering on the east with Boeotia and on the west with Locris.

PHOEBUS (VII, XVII, BXI, BXVI) Apollo, q.v.

PHOENICIA (XVI, XVII, XXIV) A coastal area of Syria, at the east of the Mediterranean.

PHOENIX (MII) Father of Europa, according to the myth followed by Theocritus. But it is more commonly accepted that Phoenix was a brother of Europa, q.v., and that both were children of Agenor, king of Phoenicia.

PHOLUS (VII) Friend of Heracles; one of the centaurs, the rest of whom burst in on them at dinner. Heracles killed most of them, but Pholus was accidentally wounded by a poisoned dart, died, and was buried by Heracles.

PHORONEUS (XXV) A mythical king of Argos, grandfather of the Argos after whom the country was named. The sons of Phoroneus, in this instance, are therefore the Argives.

PHRYGIA (XV, XVI, XX) Central district of Asia Minor. Slaves were often named after their country of origin (XV).

PHYSCUS (IV) A mountain of Magna Graecia, near Croton.

PIERIAN (X, *Egg*) An epithet of the Muses, derived from Pieria, a small tract of country in Thrace, sacred to them.

PINDAR (MIII) The great lyric poet of Thebes, who lived from 518 to 435 B.C.

PINDUS (I) A mountain in Thessaly, sacred to the Muses and Apollo.

PISA (IV, MVI) A town of Elis, on the Alpheus; founded by Pisus, son of Perieres and grandson of Aeolus. Its people presided at the Olympic Games, which were held near by.

PLEIADS (XIII) A constellation named after the daughters of Atlas, who were placed in the sky after their death. It was traditionally favourable to sailors.

POLYDEUCES (IV, XXII) Son of Zeus and Leda; see Castor.

POLYPHEMUS (VI, VII, XI, BII) Son of Poseidon and Thoosa; see Cyclops.

POSEIDON (XXI, XXII) God of the Sea; brother of Zeus; father of Amycus.

PRAXITELES (V) The famous Athenian sculptor is probably the Praxiteles implied by Comatas; but as a boastful paragon, not as the true maker of the bowl.

PRIAM (XVI, XVII, XXII) Mythical king of Troy, among whose children were Paris, q.v., and Hector.

PRIAPUS (I, Ep III, Ep IV, MIII) Son of Aphrodite; god of fertility.

PROPONTIS (XIII) A gulf between the Pontus Euxinus and the Aegean; now the Sea of Marmara.

PROTEUS (VIII) A sea god, son of Poseidon, of whose seals he had charge.

PTERELAÜS (XXIV) Son of Taphius, granted immortality by Poseidon in the form of a yellow lock of hair; eternal life would be his as long as it stayed on his head. But his daughter, Cometho, fell in love with Amphitryon, who was besieging Pterelaus' city; and, Delilah-like, she lopped his hair. Amphitryon killed Pterelaüs; and rewarded Cometho by putting her to death.

PTOLEMY PHILADELPHUS (XIV, XV, XVII) Ptolemy II, king of Egypt 285–47 B.C. Patron of Theocritus, Euclid, Callimachus and Lycophron. See Appendix, pp. 228–9.

PYLADES (BVIII) Son of Strophius, king of Phocis, by one of Agamemnon's sisters. Brought up with Orestes, q.v., he formed a lasting friendship with his cousin, and accompanied him to the Tauric Cheronese. For this, and his part in the murder of

Clytemnestra and Aegisthus, Orestes rewarded him with Electra's hand in marriage.

PYLUS (III) A port in the western Peloponnese. See Melampus.

PYRRHUS (IV) A lyric poet, not clearly identified.

PYRRHUS (XV) Son of Achilles and Deidameia; also called Neoptolemus, because he arrived to fight with the Greeks at Troy during the closing years of the siege.

PYXA (VII) A town of Cos.

RHEA (XVII, XX) Wife of Cronos; their children included Zeus, Hera, Poseidon, Hades, Demeter and many other gods.

RHENAEA (XVII) A small Aegean island, one of the Cyclades, only 200 yards from Delos.

RHODOPE (VII) A high mountain in Thrace.

SAMOS (VII, XV) An island with a city of the same name in the east Aegean, near the coast of Asia Minor.

SAPPHO (MIII) The great poetess of Lesbos, renowned also for her beauty. *Floruit c.* 570 B.C.

SATYRS (IV, XXVII, MIII, MV) Country demigods, attendants of Dionysus. They were half man, with the feet and legs of goats, horns on their heads, and thick hair over their whole body.

SCOPAS (XVI) The ancestor of a noble Thessalian family.

SCYROS (BII) An island in the mid-Aegean, 28 miles north-east of Euboea.

SEMELE (XXVI) Daughter of Cadmus, king of Thebes, by Hermione, daughter of Zeus and Aphrodite; mother by Zeus of Dionysus, q.v.

SEMIRAMIS (XVI) Queen of Assyria; married first to Menones, who hanged himself when she was taken from him, and then to Ninus, whom she killed to make her throne more secure. She lived *circa* 1965 to 1903 B.C., it is suggested; others deny her any life outside myth.

SICELIDAS (VII) Used here as a pseudonym for the epigrammatist Asclepiades.

SIMICHIDAS (VII, *Syrinx*) Generally assumed to be a name used by Theocritus for himself.

SIMOIS (XVI) A river near Troy, which rises on Mount Ida.

SIRENS (MIII) Sea-nymphs who traditionally lured passing sailors to their death; they were also known as tomb-spirits who sang dirges over the graves of the dead.

SISYPHUS (XXII) Son of Aeolus and Enaretta; founder of Corinth, to whose coastline this is a reference. He was renowned for his cunning and infidelity; and is perhaps most famous for his punishment in Hades: perpetually rolling a heavy stone to the top of a hill.

SPARTA (XVIII, XXII, BII) A famous Peloponnesian city, capital of its country, otherwise known as Lacedaemon. Situated about thirty miles from the mouth of the Eurotas.

STRYMON (MIII) A river separating Thrace from Macedonia, which flows into the Aegean. Now the Struma.

SYBARIS (V) A Greek city on a river of the same name in Southern Italy.

SYRACUSE (XV, XVI, Ep IX, Ep XVIII, MIII) Ancient capital and chief city of Sicily, founded in 732 B.C. by Archias, a Corinthian.

SYRIA (X, XV, XVII, BI) Recognized by the ancients as a country bounded on the north by Mount Taurus, on the east by the Euphrates, on the west by the Mediterranean and on the south by Arabia. The name Syria is virtually interchangeable with Assyria.

TARTARUS (MIII) Hades; the underworld. (In fact a region of Hades, where the most impious of men were subjected to the most fiendish punishments; but the name is used as an alternative for the entire underworld.)

TEIRESIAS (XXIV) A blind prophet of Thebes.

TELAMON (XIII) Son of Aeacus and Endeis; king of Salamis. Brother of Peleus; father of Teucer and Ajax. He was one of the Argonauts, and Heracles' armour-bearer when he captured Laomedon.

TELEMACHUS (*Syrinx*) Son of Odysseus and Penelope. See p. 223.

TELEMUS (VI) A Cyclops; son of Eurymus. He was endowed with the gift of prophecy, and foretold much of Polyphemus' future.

TELEPHASSA (MII) Mother of Europa by Agenor (but see Phoenix). Also mother of Cadmus. She died searching for Europa, after her abduction, in Thrace.

TEOS (Ep XVII, MIII) A coastal town of Ionia, opposite Samos. Birthplace of Anacreon.

TEUCER (Dosiadas *Altar*) First king of Troy.

THEBES (XVI, XXVI) Capital city of Boeotia. Founded by Cadmus, q.v.

THEOCRITUS (MIII, Dosiadas *Altar*)

THESEUS (II, BVIII) Son of Aegeus and Aethra. King of Athens; one of the most celebrated Greek heroes.

THESSALY (XII, XIV, XVIII) A district of northern Greece; east of Epirus.

THESTIUS (XXII) Son of Parthaon; king of Pleuron. Father of Leda, q.v.; his sons, the Thestiadae, were killed by Meleager during the chase of the Calydonian boar.

THETIS (XVII, MIII) A sea-nymph, daughter of Nereus and Doris. Mother by Peleus, q.v., of Achilles, q.v.

THRACE (II, XIV, Ep XX, Vestinus *Altar*) A country in the north of the Greek peninsula; at the south of Scythia, bounded by Mount Haemus. Its people had a reputation for barbarous cruelty and a love of war.

THURII (V) A Greek city of Lucania, in Italy; built near the ruins of Sybaris in 444 B.C. Later Copia.

THYBRIS (I) A river in Sicily.

TIRYNS (XXV) A celebrated city near Argos, dating from the Mycenaean era.

TITYUS (XXII) A famous giant, son of Zeus by Elara, daughter of Orchomenus. For interfering in Zeus' amours with Latona (at the request of Hera) he was thrown into Hades; and finally condemned to having vultures forever feed on his entrails. Not to be confused with the Tityrus of Idylls III and VII; a country name used for convenience, on both occasions.

TRACHIS (XXIV) A Thessalian town, where Heracles was received in his retirement by Ceyx.

TRIOPIAN HILL (XVII) A promontory in Caria, now Cape Crio. On its headland, at the extreme south-west of Asia Minor, stood the temple of Triopian Apollo, the centre of the Dorian Pentapolis (comprising Cos, Lindus, Ialysus, Camirus and Cnidus).

TRITONS (MII) Sea deities, sons of Poseidon.

TROY (XV) A city near Mount Ida; the capital of Troas. Besieged by the Greeks after the abduction of Helen, q.v., by Paris, q.v.

TYDEUS (XVII, XXIV) Son of Oeneus, king of Calydon, by Periboea. Married Deiphyle, daughter of Adrastus, q.v. Thus became one of the Seven Against Thebes. Mortally wounded by Melanippus; before he died, however, he dealt Melanippus a fatal blow, had his head cut off, and tore out his brains with his teeth.

TYNDAREUS (XVIII, XXII, MIII) Son of Oebalus and Gorgophone. Married Leda; for their children, see Castor.

TYRE (*Syrinx*) An important port in Phoenicia; Europa was daughter of Agenor, king of Phoenicia.

XENEA (VII) A nymph loved by Daphnis. He had vowed celibacy, and so died of desire for her.

ZACYNTHUS (IV) Island in the Ionian Sea, off the coast of Elis.

ZEUS (*passim*) King of the gods; father of mankind; source of all life. Son of Cronos and Rhea; husband of Hera.

ZOPYRION (XV) Possibly an affectionate diminutive for Zopyros, a more common forename.

MORE ABOUT PENGUINS
AND PELICANS

Penguinews, which appears every month, contains details of all the new books issued by Penguins as they are published. From time to time it is supplemented by *Penguins in Print*, which is a complete list of all available books published by Penguins. (There are well over four thousand of these.)

A specimen copy of *Penguinews* will be sent to you free on request. For a year's issues (including the complete lists) please send 30p if you live in the United Kingdom, or 60p if you live elsewhere. Just write to Dept EP, Penguin Books Ltd, Harmondsworth, Middlesex, enclosing a cheque or postal order, and your name will be added to the mailing list.

Note: *Penguinews* and *Penguins in Print* are not available in the U.S.A. or Canada

A PELICAN ORIGINAL

GREEK LITERATURE IN TRANSLATION

Edited by Michael Grant

Greek literature provides powerful evidence in support of Sophocles' statement that language is what raises mankind above the animals. Not only did Greek provide the earliest literature in the western world, but it maintained a flow of masterpieces for a thousand years, well into Roman imperial times; and today (because of the Greek writer's faculty for reaching to the heart of his subject) this literature still possesses significance.

In this companion volume to his *Roman Readings* Michael Grant displays, as far as possible, the whole range of Greek poetry and prose, from Homer and Hesiod to the Hellenistic poets and the works of Ptolemy, Galen and Plotinus. His selection vividly demonstrates the extraordinary extent of Greek achievement in every literary field – in epics, lyrics and drama, in history, biography and oratory, in philosophy, criticism and satire, and in works of fundamental scientific thought.

Moreover Michael Grant's choice of English versions serves to show how the mounting wave of modern translations now challenges the splendid output of the Elizabethans.

THE ODYSSEY

HOMER

Translated by E. V. Rieu

Homer's *Odyssey*, composed some three thousand years ago, is still among the very pinnacles of all literature. The story of Odysseus' epic voyage home from Troy to his kingdom of Ithaca brims, like some splendid novel, with a fathomless humanity.

In his introduction to this famous edition Dr Rieu states: 'I have done my best to make Homer easy reading for those who are unfamiliar with the Greek world.' This is too modest. His inspired translations of *The Odyssey* and *The Iliad* have made Homer a modern best-seller.

AESCHYLUS

PROMETHEUS BOUND
THE SUPPLIANTS
SEVEN AGAINST THEBES
THE PERSIANS

Translated by Philip Vellacott

Aeschylus (525–*c*.456 B.C.) was the first of the great
Greek tragedians. The four plays presented in this volume –
together with the Oresteian Trilogy – are all that survive of
his work. *The Persians* is set against the Athenian victory at
Salamis, which took place only eight years before the play
was written. In *Seven Against Thebes* the two sons of Oedipus
are relentlessly pursued to their death by a family curse. But
in *The Suppliants* and *Prometheus* conflict of principle is
resolved by rational compromise.

THE PENGUIN CLASSICS

Some Recent Volumes